MW00619525

HAIR OF THE DOG

HAIR OF THE DOG

John Norman Harris

With an Introduction by Howard Engel

FELONY & MAYHEM PRESS • NEW YORK

All the characters and events portrayed in this work are fictitious

HAIR OF THE DOG

A Felony & Mayhem mystery

PRINTING HISTORY
First Canadian edition (Seal): 1990
Felony & Mayhem edition: 2018

ISBN: 978-1-63194-120-7

Manufactured in the United States of America

Library of Congress Cataloging-in-Publication Data

Names: Harris, John Norman, 1915-1964, author. | Engel, Howard, 1931- writer of introduction.
Title: Hair of the dog / John Norman Harris ; with an introduction by Howard Engel.
Description: New York : Felony & Mayhem Press, 2018. | "A Felony & Mayhem mystery."
Identifiers: LCCN 2017060954| ISBN 9781631941207 (pbk.) | ISBN 9781631941238 (ebook)
Subjects: LCSH: Mystery fiction. | Humorous fiction.
Classification: LCC PR9199.3.H345965 H35 2018 | DDC 813/.54--dc23
LC record available at https://lccn.loc.gov/2017060954

John Norman Harris is widely credited with having written the first genuinely Canadian mystery novel; in *The Weird World of Wes Beattie* and *Hair of the Dog* he not only set his story in Toronto, but also crafted plots that relied specifically on various Canadian preoccupations and concerns.

"First true Canadian mystery writer" would be sufficient accolade for most people, but Harris was also a gold-plated war hero: After graduating from university, and with Europe on the brink of war, he traveled to England to train as a pilot, eventually joining the RAF. In 1942 his plane was shot down over Germany, and he spent the rest of the war in a POW camp known as Stalag Luft III. While there, he was instrumental in planning the largest prison-break in the history of WWII. The story of the breakout was eventually turned into several novels and films, including "The Great Escape," starring Steve McQueen.

After the war, Harris returned to Canada, and built a thriving career in public relations and as a short-story writer. He died suddenly, in his late 40s, on a family vacation to Vermont. *The Weird World of West Beattie* was the only mystery he published during his lifetime.

The icon above says you're holding a copy of a book in the Felony & Mayhem "Traditional" category. We think of these books as classy cozies, with little gunplay or gore but often a fair amount of humor and, usually, an intrepid amateur sleuth. If you enjoy this book, you may well like other "Traditional" titles from Felony & Mayhem Press.

For more about these books, and other Felony & Mayhem titles, or to place an order, please visit our website at

www.FelonyAndMayhem.com

Other "Traditional" titles from

FELONY & MAYHEM

NATHAN ALDYNE

Vermilion

Cobalt

Slate

Canary

JOHN NORMAN HARRIS

The Weird World of Wes Beattie

MARISSA PIESMAN

Unorthodox Practices

Personal Effects

Heading Uptown

ANNA PORTER

Hidden Agenda

Mortal Sins

DANIEL STASHOWER

Elephants in the Distance

HAIR OF THE DOG

Introduction

In mid-November 1988, I was preparing an article about John Norman Harris, the author of *The Weird World of Wes Beattie* for the *Kingston Whig-Standard*. I knew next to nothing about my subject, so I went to see his widow in her east-Toronto home, so that I would get my facts right. After a pleasant conversation and when I was on the point of leaving, Aileen Harris handed me a typewriter-paper box containing 141 closely typed pages. It was the manuscript of a novel that had been in that box for nearly a quarter of a century. "Have a look at it," she said, "and let me know if there's anything salvageable inside." Back home, I read through the manuscript at once and in a state of some excitement called an editor friend, John Pearce, who promised to have a look at it. John got back to me with enthusiasm early in 1989. We both loved *Wes Beattie*, and now we were both delighted with its sequel, *Hair of the Dog*.

I first read *The Weird World of Wes Beattie* when I was a producer of radio programs at the Canadian Broadcasting Corporation. It was years before I wrote my first "Benny Cooperman" mystery. At the time, I thought Wes Beattie was great entertainment, but I didn't realize that it represented a major step forward in Canadian crime writing. Harris had written about a Canadian lawyer who solves a crime, working the way a private eye works in the novels of Hammett and Chandler. But Jack Harris's mean streets weren't in San Francisco or Los Angeles: Harris wrote about Yonge and Bloor and Bay. He didn't talk about Malibu or Pasadena or Brentwood, but about Forest Hill and Rosedale.

Not since the earliest work of Margaret Millar, the well-honoured writer now living in Santa Barbara, had a Canadian —Harris was born in Fort Francis, Millar in Kitchener— published a crime novel flying its own native colours. In *Wes Beattie* a Canadian sleuth solved a Canadian crime and sold the proof of it in the American market. Why so much emphasis on nationality? We didn't start it. Before Millar and Harris, editors (both Canadian and foreign) were convinced that the reading public began to yawn visibly when the action moved north of the US/Canadian border. Writers and readers alike knew better, but it took a lot of convincing.

Before Millar and Harris, Canadian crime writers had to pretend to be British (like Grant Allen and Robert Barr) or American (like Arthur Stringer and Frank L. Packard) so that their books would be accepted. Margaret Millar and Jack Harris and certainly Hugh Garner made the present boom in crime writing possible.

According to people who knew him well, Jack Harris was a genial but choleric companion, who enjoyed completing the *Times* crossword puzzle before his subway stop came up. He used to give biting descriptions of his friends and acquaintances, characterizing one harassed editor as having "all the affability of a wounded grizzly bear." To many he looked like a man about to explode. When the bomb went off, it took the form of the energetic and winning story of the hard-done-by Wes Beattie. When the the smoke cleared and the public began to ask for another Harris whodunit, the author was dead, felled by a sudden heart attack while he was holidaying with his family on Lake Champlain. For years we have had to deal with the sad fact that there would never be a second case for Harris's sleuth, Sidney Grant.

If you are among the readers who discovered Harris back in the 1960s, I don't have to tell you what a treat lies in store. I envy you your discovery of the sequel. If you are on the point of making Harris's acquaintance for the first time, may I say how lucky you are.

HOWARD ENGEL, 1990

One

THERE HAD BEEN LARGE-SCALE thefts of furs during the winter and spring, and the loot had vanished without trace. Inspector Frank Young of the Metropolitan Toronto Police, whose chosen field was Stolen Goods, made a close study of what he called "the Fur Trade" and made long-range plans to put an end to it, or at least to reduce its volume. He was aware that the fences who buy stolen furs are expert at making very slight alterations to the collar and styling of an expensive coat, putting in a new lining, sewing on new buttons and then peddling it (with the heat off it) in some showroom in Dallas or New York or Montreal. After such an expert has dealt with a coat, even its true owner would not recognize it.

Young did a tremendous amount of work for seemingly small results. He lent an ear to underworld gossip, he talked to furriers and insurance men, and he read up the whole history of fur thefts contained in the police files. From it all he came up with the name Martin. There were two Martin brothers, both trained fur cutters, who were almost certainly involved in the fur traffic. He also learned (by getting Traffic to drop an impaired-driving charge) that the Martins had the key to an ostensibly vacant loft above a row of dingy shops. Actually the loft contained cutting tables, and it had a live telephone.

Frank Young determined to set a trap. First he made an unobtrusive survey of the loft—from outside. He drew a plan showing the field of vision from all the windows. Behind the row of shops was a rough-paved lane. The small, grassless yards behind the shops were separated by high board fences, but the back fences that had once bordered the lane had almost all been removed, so that the yards could be used for parking or deliveries.

Working quietly, Young made arrangements that he should be informed whenever anybody entered the loft, and he drew up a plan for covering all possible exits quickly when it came time to make a raid. Bearing down remorselessly on the wretched man who had been let off the impaired-driving charge, he found out a great deal about the Martin security methods. When it came time to process a batch of stolen furs, a Martin would go to the loft and wait for a while. He would look from all windows for signs of police activity. When satisfied, he would telephone—possibly to the other Martin—and then a pick-up truck carrying the furs, bolts of material for linings, buttons, thread and tools would set out from some secret hideaway and would approach the loft. It would circle the district, watching for suspicious signs and—when the driver was satisfied—it would head up the one-way lane behind the shops, back in to the rear entrance to the loft, and discharge its cargo. That was the moment when Young planned to act. The pick-up truck was to be stopped at the exit to the lane, and hidden detectives were to step forth and approach both entrances to the loft. It was only one of a dozen operations Young had in his head, awaiting the right moment for action.

But before the summer was very old, Young gave up hope of trapping the Martins. Underworld gossip said that the brothers had quarreled with the go-between, the man generally supposed to be behind the organization of the thefts. They had held out, or double-crossed, according to the police informer.

But then, early on the morning of an August Saturday that promised to be a scorcher before it was finished, Young received a telephone call. Not one, but both Martins had entered the loft via the street door at intervals of five minutes. Young set things in motion at once. By prearranged routes, plainclothesmen were conveyed to their stations, and Young went to the spot he had chosen as his field headquarters. But he had scarcely arrived when he saw a sight that sent his blood pressure soaring. A yellow police cruiser of the accident squad was parked opposite to the entrance of the all-important lane, and a motorcycle policeman had stopped to talk to the driver of the cruiser. It was quite enough to queer the entire plan.

Muttering something about coordination, Young left his place of concealment and strode down the street, meaning to tell the cruiser and the motorcycle to clear off, although clear was not the precise word that had formed in his mind. However, whatever the word was, it never got spoken. Just before he reached the cruiser, Young saw a Volkswagen approaching from the opposite direction with its turning indicator flashing for a right turn—into the lane. But the driver, as he slowed down, was eyeing the men in the cruiser somewhat dubiously. The driver was a man well known to Frank Young. He was a man who had been released from Kingston Penitentiary some months before, after a long stretch for bank robbery. And the man who had captured Lamberti with a football tackle and sent him to Kingston had been Frank Young, at the time a sergeant of detectives. Lamberti turned his eyes from the cruiser, spotted Young, and made a quick decision. He turned into the lane and accelerated violently.

Young ran to the lane to take down the Volks's license number, but he was just in time to see it turn into one of the yards and hear it shriek to a sudden stop. Young ran after it and found it parked, empty, by the rear entrance to the Martins' loft. He pounded on the door, assuming that Lamberti had gone in to warn the Martins. After a long delay there was the sound of bolts being drawn back, and Jack Martin's pasty face peered out cautiously.

Young pushed the door fully open and barged in, explaining that he had a search warrant. He hustled Martin, protesting piteously, up the stairs ahead of him, then through the loft where the other Martin stood with a nervous grin on his face. Down the front stairs they went, and Young opened the front door, from which point he signaled his watchers to join him. Nobody, they said, had come out the front way.

They searched the place thoroughly, yet found no tools, materials, furs or even buttons, and not a trace of Vince Lamberti. Both Martins, now talking volubly about their legal rights, were herded out to the backyard.

It then took Young about twenty seconds to figure out what had happened. Vince Lamberti had seen the police trap, or what he thought was a police trap. He had decided not to be captured with a load of stolen furs at the end of the lane. So he had turned into the yard, parked, scrambled over a few fences and then, at leisure, crossed the lane farther down and made his way through some alleyway to the street. It would be typical of Vince's quick thinking.

So Young, working with great care, opened the trunk of the Volks—and found it empty, as was the inside of the car. He was now completely lost. The trap had failed utterly. The Martins, sensing it, began to talk placatingly. They had come to look at this loft with a view to renting it. There must have been some mistake…

But they were still nervous.

Young's eye roved about the yard, and lit on a large wooden box, a sort of lean-to built against the building. It had a sloping lid and was evidently designed to hold half a dozen large garbage cans. A spasm that crossed Jack Martin's fat face told Young, as he strode to the box, that he was in pay dirt.

Sure enough, in the big garbage box Young found a huge brown-paper parcel. The trap had not, after all, been entirely unproductive. Young opened a tiny slit in the parcel with his penknife and inserted a finger. The parcel contained furs.

Young smiled, and the Martins began once more to wail. The inspector gave crisp orders. The Volks was to be towed carefully to the police garage and examined for fingerprints. Steering wheel, cigarette lighter, glove compartment, door handles and truck catch were to get particular attention. The registration of the Volks was to be checked at once, in case it was stolen. The alarm was to go out at once for the apprehension of Vince Lamberti. And the Martin brothers, as well as the parcel of furs, were to be taken to Police Headquarters.

❀❀❀

At the outset Inspector Young was under the impression that the furs in the parcel were furs that had been stolen during the big robberies of the previous winter, and that they had been lying ever since in some safe hiding place.

But the fact rapidly emerged that they were not on any list of stolen goods, and Young was somewhat puzzled because there had been no report of a fur storage warehouse having been robbed.

The furs themselves were magnificent. A full-length wild mink, a shorter mink, a blue fox, a chinchilla, several mink stoles. The fur department manager of a large department store was invited to come and look at them, but even before he arrived the owner's name was found in a pocket.

The man from the store confirmed it. All of the furs, he believed, were the property of a Mrs. Thurston, who lived in Rosedale. Where, Young wanted to know, had she stored them?

"The way I get it," the store man said, "she didn't store them this year. She's gone a bit queer in the head. Her arteries are bad, and she had a fall in the spring and broke her hip. She is now bedridden, and quite a handful for her family. She insists on keeping all her valuables where she can see them."

Young promptly phoned the Thurston house, and got a busy signal. He checked with the exchange and found that the receiver had been left off the hook, so he took an assistant and raced by car to the address to investigate.

He found that Mrs. Thurston lived in a large, old red-brick house with a conservatory on one side and a porte cochère—the main entrance—in the driveway on the other side. He rang the bell, and not long afterward the door was opened and a man's tousled head protruded.

"Police," Young said, exhibiting a badge.

The man looked startled and apprehensive. His eyes were bloodshot, he was still in slippers and dressing gown, and he was trying to manage a cigarette and a cup of black coffee while manipulating door catches. He was visibly hung over.

Young suppressed a smile. He had often encountered men who were nervous when meeting the police in the morning. As a rule they were worried about their drive home the night before. Had they hit something, or gone through a traffic light?

"We understand you've had a burglary," Young said. "Mind if we come in?"

They entered, and presently a slender woman of about fifty joined them. Her hair, too, was untidy, and she was dressed in a long housecoat.

As they talked, two more women joined them from different doorways. They were all standing in a large entrance hall in the middle of the house. Ahead of them was a staircase. At the foot of it, on their left, was the entrance to the large drawing room that stretched right across the front of the house. On their right was a tall double door. Young opened it to reveal a paneled dining room, and he could see another door leading from it to what he presumed was the kitchen.

"Are you Mrs. Thurston?" Young asked the woman in the housecoat.

"No, I'm Martha Thurston, her daughter. This is my brother Gerald. What did you say about a burglary?"

Denton, the assistant, had walked into the dining room, and now he called from the window that let out onto the driveway.

"Here's where they got in," he said. "The screen is slit down both sides and across the bottom, and the window catch was forced."

"Really?" Martha Thurston said. "Surely not..."

"We've recovered some furs," Young said. "Where did your mother keep her furs?"

"Heavens—in her bedroom closet! You don't think...?"

"Is she there now?" Young asked.

"Yes—she sleeps late," Miss Thurston said. "We leave the telephone off."

There was a general stampede up the stairs. The large front bedroom was dark. While Young fumbled for a switch, Miss Thurston strode across and drew the long curtains that covered one of the tall windows flanking the bed.

The room was suddenly flooded with light, and everyone simultaneously saw the figure of an elderly woman lying back on the pillow in the big four-poster bed, with her toothless mouth wide open. Her pallor and her stillness told the story at once. She was dead.

"Strangled, it looks like," Young said.

Gerald Thurston said, "Christ!" and dropped his coffee cup. Martha screamed and put her hands over her face to hide the sight. The other two women—one a youngish woman in a nurse's uniform—advanced a few steps into the room. Then the other, who appeared to be in her early sixties, turned, reeled and would have fallen if Denton had not caught her.

"Great heavens! And all of us asleep in our beds!" the nurse said.

Martha, who recovered her self-possession fairly rapidly, stayed with Young while Denton herded the others downstairs. They quickly discovered the plastic zipper-bags in the big clothes closet that had contained the furs. They had been ripped open with a knife, by someone too impatient to fool with zippers. Young examined the door of the clothes closet. It had a spring lock—but the key was in the lock!

"Can you think of anything else that might be missing?" Young said.

Martha thought a moment, then told the inspector that her mother had kept a number of valuable rings and brooches in her bedside table. She walked across and opened a drawer. The jewelry was gone.

Young called Headquarters and made a brief report. He requested with much emphasis that no mention should be made on the radio and that nothing should be told to the press. Then, until the first two carloads of police arrived eight minutes later, he examined the scene of the crime and asked a few questions of the people in the house.

When he had briefed the new arrivals, he made his escape with Denton as quickly as he could. On the way back to Headquarters he outlined the position of the people in the house.

"Vince Lamberti," he said, "might bash somebody in temper, but he isn't a killer. Furthermore, he wouldn't fool with stolen goods while carrying a murder rap. So it's a cinch that Lamberti knows nothing about the murder. Now here's what I figure happened. Spider Webb's outfit heard about these furs being at home. They planned a job. Vince needed dough. He took it on. But Webb's outfit always fixes it that the old hands don't go into the house on jobs like this. The old hand drives the car. He sends in a young punk to get the stuff. If anything happens, it's understood that the old hand drives off and leaves the punk holding the bag. Okay, Vince has got hold of one of those nervy young punks from the pool halls—some of those kids would strangle their own mother for fifty bucks—and he's sent him in. While the kid was pinching the jewelry out of the bedside table, the old lady woke up and grabbed him. The kid strangled her to shut her up.

"But he was scared! He was scared he would lose the dough he'd been promised. So he came out and never said a word to Vince. He got his fifty or a hundred bucks and lit out. He never told Vince how hot those furs were, so Vince walked smack into a murder rap.

"Okay. If word of that murder gets out before we get Vince—and the kid—we'll never get the kid alive. Webb's outfit will rub him out tonight to protect Vince. We'll find a kid in some lane tomorrow morning, killed in a fight. No witnesses. So I figure we've got till dark to find the kid."

"How do we go about that?" Denton asked.

"Pull out all the stops," Young said. "Back-track on Vince. Find out where he's been, who he's been talking to. Find out if any kid has disappeared today, like left town, or if any kid has acted funny. Check that Volks—see if we can find any prints. If so, do a quick check against the cards of likely young punks that might be used on a job like that. But we've got to move fast."

And the police did move fast. Shirts and collars wilted in the scorching heat, but all the stops were pulled out. The Volks proved to be registered in the name of a professor, though it wasn't listed as stolen. The professor was holidaying in Muskoka. A provincial police officer drove to his cottage to talk with him. The professor said he had sold the car for cash, ten days before, to a young fellow, whom he could describe only vaguely. The professor was about to leave for Europe on a sabbatical year and was buying a new car in England. Therefore he had advertised his Volks for sale in one of the evening papers.

Vince Lamberti was rounded up, early in the afternoon, drinking cold lager in an air-conditioned bar. He offered no resistance, but flatly refused to answer any questions at all.

Research on the Volks proved fruitful. Some good prints were lifted from the area of the trunk catch (some of them belonging to Inspector Young, and some to a person unknown), and a triangular piece of brown paper was found in the trunk, which fitted exactly a corner missing from the paper that had encased the furs.

Then reports came in that a wretched youth called Marvin Easting—usually known as Stoopid Easting—had been behaving strangely, flashing rolls of bills and buying clothes and liquor. Easting had been convicted of shoplifting and other petty offenses, so there was a card for him on file. His prints were compared with those on the trunk catch of the Volkswagen—and they fitted.

So the alarm went out: get Stoopid Easting before the underworld does.

Getting him proved to be relatively simple. He had left a broad trail. He had gone to a very drab downtown hotel shortly after noon and had bought rounds of drinks in the bar. Then he had picked up a woman and disappeared. He hadn't gone far though. Only upstairs. The desk clerk was surly, but under pressure admitted that he had rented a room to Easting, cash in advance. The police found Easting on the bed in Room 28, and at first they thought they had come too late. He was completely inert. But he was not dead, only hog drunk, and he was removed by stretcher to Headquarters. There was an empty whiskey bottle in the room, and another half empty, and there were two glasses, one of which bore traces of lipstick. There were also many lipstick-smeared cigarette butts. Reluctantly the desk clerk admitted that he knew the woman who had been with Easting. She was Red Maggie, well known to the police and old enough to be the object of Marvin Easting's Oedipus complex.

Her trail, too, was broad. She was drunk. She resisted arrest. She called the police evil names. But she was hauled in, and in her large handbag were discovered a bottle of whiskey—removed from Easting's room—and a handful of jewels wrapped in Kleenex. She insisted that the jewelry had been given to her by admirers, but it was quickly identified as the property of the late Mrs. Thurston.

Easting recovered consciousness shortly before midnight, and was questioned. Modern practice frowns on the use of torture in questioning. However, Easting was equipped with built-in torture during his interrogation. His eyeballs ached, his head was splitting, his stomach was churning in agony. The cards were stacked against him. The police were able to tell him that his accomplice, Lamberti, was in custody and had confessed. They were able to produce the furs and the jewels and to tell him that the jewels had been found in his pocket. They were able to get him talking—lying and dodging, but talking. They were able to take him step by step, keeping his mind off the larger issue while they got him to talk bit by bit about the burglary, and every moment was physical agony for him. Precisely what went on in the room would never come out. What did come out was a statement, signed no doubt in desperation, but a statement, and the police were able to announce, early on Sunday morning, that two men were under arrest for the murder of Mrs. Thurston and that one of them had "made a statement," which everybody knew meant a confession.

It had been a swift, intelligent and successful piece of police work, and the main credit for it went, quite rightly, to Inspector Frank Young, of Stolen Goods.

Two

IT HAD HAPPENED IN AUGUST, sometimes called the silly season, when there is usually a dearth of real news and the daily papers are filled with hot-weather stories and other nonsense. The Thurston murder was therefore a godsend, even though the story broke at the worst possible time. Radio and television had it all their own way through Sunday, and the morning paper was able to monopolize the known facts on Monday morning.

But such disadvantages meant nothing to the Toronto evening papers. All through the scorching Sunday their reporters and photographers combed Cabbagetown and Rosedale, looking for angles and digging into the pasts of the two accused men.

Vince Lamberti was something of a celebrity. He had disappointed a great many people when he went off the rails. He had been a promising athlete, and a colorful one. Yet dames, and a hot temper, and lack of discipline had ruled him off the course after playing football, hockey and baseball. He had fought some pro bouts as a middleweight, but when he outgrew the weight limit he was a little slower and never caught on as a light-heavy. Then he had drifted, until the day he was apprehended as a bank robber.

Easting was something else again. He came from a chronically poor family. He was a third-generation welfare case. His parents were professional spongers. Students of social work had written theses about them to gain their degrees. The boy had a very dull brain, but suffered horribly from a delusion that he was smart. The cynical outlook is generally associated with clever people. Marvin Easting was a dull-normal cynic, a lad who believed that every race is fixed, that every cop is bought. He had stolen from schoolmates and from shops. He had served short jail terms. Nice ladies had taken an interest in him and had tried to bribe and wheedle him into going straight. He had accepted their gifts, bragged to his pals about how he had taken them in, and then he had got into trouble again.

"Objective news reporting," as everyone knows, received its death blow when Henry Luce discovered interpretive journalism. The Thurston story illustrated in almost classic fashion the need for an interpretive approach, lest the bare facts, objectively reported, peter away to nothing after the first day. The particular approach chosen by one publisher (and taken up, perforce, by everybody else) was set forth in an editorial that appeared in a Monday evening edition.

The editorial was written as a series of questions, but the answers were pretty easy to guess.

Whom should society hold responsible, the writer wanted to know, when a professional criminal, about whom there is an aura of glamour, and furthermore a man notoriously able to look after himself in a roughhouse, uses as his dupe an impressionable boy with a low I.Q.? An older man, an experienced man, uses the glamour of his name and notoriety to dazzle a feckless youth; though social agencies are spending much time and effort to salvage that youth, their chances of success are nil against the temptations and inducements held forth by the world of organized crime. An inexperienced youth might well be flattered by the attention of an experienced criminal; he might well be tempted by promises of big rewards if he "played along with the guys." He might also be terrified by veiled threats of what would happen to him if he *didn't* play along or, worse still, if he talked.

Against such threats and inducements, the editorial writer said, social agencies were helpless in trying to salvage young offenders. However, there was another aspect worthy of close public attention. The experienced criminal habitually arranged things so that if anything went wrong, he himself would escape and leave his young accomplice to face the consequences. And his young accomplice always knew very well what penalty would be exacted if he didn't keep his mouth shut.

Partly by chance, the writer said, and partly through brilliant police work, an experienced criminal, making use of a youthful accomplice, had been laid by the heels. Let the public examine its conscience and ask itself where the chief responsibility should lie: with the dazzled and frightened junior, or with the coward who sat in the car and protected himself while the younger man took all the chances?

To drive home the point of this social message, the editor had had a cartoon drawn showing a leering and simpering thug handing a wicked-looking cosh to a simple youth and saying, "Go on in, son. *I'll* be quite safe."

Judges and lawyers tore their hair when they read the papers, but most of them were far away at their summer cottages, and although they strongly disapproved of the prejudicial handling of the case in the press, there was nothing much they could do about it.

The actual news reporting of the case followed the line taken in the editorial. Vince Lamberti came through as a thorough blackguard. But day by day, the public image of Stoopid Easting grew into a strange, exotic thing, totally unlike the real Easting according to those who knew him. He became a puzzled, well-meaning youth struggling against a world of evil that he did not understand. He was a boy who had been led to steal from shops because he wanted to help his mother feed the younger children.

It was known that Easting had taken jewelry from the Thurston house, but it was not generally known that Red Maggie had in turn taken it from him. So the hypothesis appeared—as a quotation from some anonymous authority—that Easting had kept the jewelry, had in fact held out on Lamberti because he wanted to give the rings and bracelets to his dear old mum.

The most powerful single piece of propaganda that appeared was a photograph, taken by a burly, crewcut photographer called Stan.

It showed Mrs. Easting, the mother of Marvin, kneeling before the statue of a saint, her face turned up pleadingly and anxiously and a holy light pouring down on her countenance.

It appeared under the overline "Mum Prays for Boy in Death Row."

"Look at that face! I ask you!" Stan said at the Press Club bar. "See, she was worrying whether we were really going to give her the twenty clams we'd promised her, me and Dulcie Dale. The dame is terrific. Honestly, at her house she sat there smiling and happy with all the neighbors around and reporters asking her questions, but just raise a camera and she'd pull out her handkerchief and turn it on. I hadda take that church picture at f 5.4 at a goddam tenth, because I hadda use the Roly—I didn't dare lug the Speed Graphic into the church. But by god, she sat still enough we got a dream of a shot."

Dulcie Dale—she had chosen the name herself, as an effective byline—was a young reporter who was to build a big reputation on the Easting story. She was indefatigable. She looked up old Sunday school teachers who had taught young Marvin, she sought out ancient group photographs, she talked to friends and neighbors. She took reams of notes back to the office and turned them into inspired copy.

She was a girl with a certain ingenuity. One lad who lived near the Eastings told her that Marvin was a "real mean guy, always twistin' little kids' arms." She asked him if Easting had also tortured animals—had he been the kind of boy who tied cans to dogs' tails? No, the boy said, he was just mean to kids. That interview had been obtained before the interpretive approach to the story had been chosen, which is why the interview appeared under the subhead "Was Kind to Animals": "'You never saw Marvy tying cans to dogs' tails,' Billy Cashman, 14, said. 'It was like all animals were Marvin's friends.'"

Dulcie felt that a little imagination could do a lot for a news story. In the Rosedale area, imagination was nearly all the press had to go on. The press had had no inkling that a murder had taken place until midafternoon on the Saturday, and by the time reporters reached the Thurston house, the place was locked up and under police guard. The family had ostensibly gone to their cottage in Muskoka and were incommunicado. Most of the neighbors were away, and the ones that weren't were not inclined to talk to reporters.

The family had not, in fact, left for the cottage, it was later learned. They were hiding out with friends, and would leave for the cottage in the evening. They were waiting in the city to pick up the late Mrs. Thurston's youngest son, Mr. Crawford Thurston, Canadian ambassador at a European capital, who was due to arrive on a direct jet flight from Paris early in the evening. The family kept very quiet because they did not want the embarrassment of photographers at Malton Airport at the moment when the awful news was broken to Crawford.

The conspiracy of silence failed, however, through a sheer fluke. One newspaper's Ottawa correspondent had wired in a rumor a day or so before that Crawford Thurston had been recalled to Ottawa to be briefed for an even bigger ambassadorial post but would be going direct to Toronto to visit his family for a few days before the briefing. A bright assistant city editor remembered the wire and checked back, late on the Saturday afternoon. In fact, he had to call Paris in order to get the confirmation, but it enabled him to have photographers at the airport when Gerald Thurston met his brother and broke the news.

But from that moment on, the press was unable to get in touch with the Thurstons, who were holed up in their island retreat.

Which was why the newspaper emphasis was entirely on the villainous Lamberti and his dupe Easting. It was a highly successful propaganda job, and it happened in August. People in their scorching kitchens read the stories and forgot their own troubles. "Such a shame!" they said. "That poor young boy!" And others said, "I surely hope they hang that fella, the way he used that poor kid."

And suddenly there appeared, of all things, a Save Marvin agitation, a spontaneous and unorganized public reaction, which didn't remain unorganized. Several Save Marvin funds were started, mostly fraudulent, and lots of sympathetic people handed a quarter to the collectors.

Like many of the follies of August, the thing was getting out of hand.

Three

SIDNEY GRANT, WHOSE OLD classmates—and a wide section of the public—knew him as the "Gargoyle," had found a secret retreat on a high rock, where he could lie in the sun and peer down through some blueberry bushes at the water-skiers on the lake below.

It was a place of security. Behind him, to the left, on the edge of the bay stood the large frame summer cottage that belonged to his wife's grandmother.

In it and around it people were working, because old Mrs. Beattie believed that a busy guest was a happy guest, and she showed great ingenuity in inventing chores for her family and friends. She herself, being the executive type, spent the morning either writing letters or sitting in a wicker chair under a broad straw hat and directing all the activities.

Around her people collected brushwood for the dual purpose of reducing the risk of a forest fire and increasing the risk of a bonfire, which she threatened to hold on the first fine evening; or sawing and splitting logs and kindling for the fireplace—such wonderful backwoodsy exercise for the sedentary worker; or dislodging a wasps' nest from under the eaves, a job with the spice of danger about it; or collecting rocks for a rockery, or ferns for a fernery, or weeds from the croquet lawn, because Mrs. Beattie believed that these modern weedkillers interfered with the balance of nature; or repairing the wharf where a board was broken; or shelling peas for dinner, because people today seldom get the chance to shell genuine garden peas.

The only safety lay in concealment. Sidney Grant, who had told his grandmother-in-law with some dignity that he had come north solely to help with the drinking, looked more than usually like a gargoyle as he leered in triumph at the scene of forced labor below. The tattered paperback had been tossed aside; he mused sleepily. "A king sate on the rocky brow," he murmured, "that looks on sea-born Salamis; and ships by thousands lay below...ships and Salamis...two salamis on rye and a dill on the side...ah, Heaven!"

His eyes were just closing in sleep when a new development below focused his attention. Three small craft, driven by outboard motors in the eight to twelve-horsepower range, were approaching Mrs. Beattie's wharf in loose formation.

They contained, in all, nine passengers, eight of them women and one an elderly man. The women appeared to be of an age with his wife's Aunt Claudia, a large and earnest woman with all the organizing urge of her mother—old Mrs. Beattie—but little of the old girl's executive ability.

"Invasion!" Sidney murmured. "Ring the church bells and take cover!"

He glanced about nervously, but was happy to see that he was completely concealed. He drowsed. He slept.

He was awakened by the voice of his wife, repeating his name in various keys and pitches. "Sid…NEE…SID…Nee!" Presently the pitch took a turn for the worse, the voice grew sharper, and June Grant mentioned another name, not Sidney's. She meant business.

"Yes, what is it, darling?" he called.

"Oh, there you are, you cunning wretch," she said, scrambling up the path. "Oh good God…put something on. You've got visitors. A flock of female fans."

"Tell them, 'Autographs later, fans,'" he said. "Tell them their idol wishes to remain idle—Ouch, damn it woman, have you neither decency nor mercy?"

"No," she said. "Get your clothes on and get down there. The only person who can get rid of these dames is you."

A few minutes later Sidney entered the huge, beamed living room of the cottage and met a group of women dressed variously in shorts and halters, slacks, pedal pushers and sunsuits, and an old man with skinny legs who wore a flowered shirt and Bermudas. They had already been furnished with iced tea and were showing impatience. They proved to be a sort of delegation, and presently their spokeswoman spoke.

"Mr. Grant," she said. "I am sure you have read in the papers the terrible story of the murder of poor Mrs. Thurston, and you have seen the course that events are taking. We are a group—some of us are professional social workers, others are women interested in welfare agencies in a voluntary way. Naturally we deplore the maudlin sentiment that has been lavished on Marvin Easting. He is a wretched youth. Yet this whole case, in a way, symbolizes a struggle that is taking place all the time, unknown to the general public. We, of the social agencies, toil ceaselessly to rescue boys like Marvin, who hardly have a chance, coming as they do from hopeless backgrounds. Our efforts are continually hampered because of the specious glamour that attaches to the 'big time,' the professional criminals.

"The professionals can recruit with the greatest of ease. They can offer money and a sort of evil celebrity. So the Fagins and Sykeses get these boys in their clutches, and after that the boys are frightened to death of falling foul of the professionals. And time and again we see the apprentice get caught and sent to jail—very proud of himself because he did not talk—and the old, hardened criminals who used him go scot free. If only the public knew the odds that we face! If only some light could be thrown into these dark places!"

She paused and looked about her, then resumed on a lower, more confidential note.

"Mr. Grant," she said. "We have decided to take advantage of this momentary public interest and to strike a blow at the criminals who systematically mislead youths. We want to harness this public sentiment to some useful purpose. Therefore, we have come to ask you to undertake the defense of Marvin Easting. He has already confessed. We want you to urge him to go further. We want you, as his lawyer, to urge him to come completely clean. To reveal everything. To tell how the job was planned, how he was dragged into it, what threats and promises were made to him, to focus a searchlight into the dark places of the underworld. And then, we feel sure, you can make a strong appeal to the jury not to convict him, because you can demonstrate that he was working under the almost hypnotic influence of that terrible man, Lamberti."

"An interesting line of defense," Sidney said.

"We thought so," the lady said. "So you will accept?"

"No," Sidney said gently. "I'm afraid not."

The little group sat back as if stunned, and then exchanged puzzled glances.

"If Easting, in the course of a burglary, strangled a woman," Sidney said, "and if this can be proved beyond all reasonable doubt to a jury, then he ought to be convicted of capital murder, which carries an automatic death sentence. I'm afraid this hypnotic cat won't fight. Your only hope would be to work up sympathy to pave the way for a commutation. And, frankly, I want no part of it."

"Mr. Grant," the lady said. "Are you refusing to defend this boy because you think he's guilty? Is that it?"

"No," he said. "If you had Judas Iscariot or Heinrich Himmler on trial, it would be impossible to convict them if they couldn't find a defense counsel. The defense is an integral part of our system of justice. I would defend anybody, on my own terms."

"And what, may I ask, are those?" the lady said.

"A free hand," Sidney told her. "In this case, Easting is alleged to have made a statement. He didn't *have* to make a statement. He could have refused to answer questions until they let him see his lawyer. Now I will bet that there was just the tiniest bit of duress used in getting that statement. I will bet that he sat for several hours being shouted at, until he was sick and confused. My first effort on his behalf would be to try to have that statement excluded from evidence. Then we would see what we could do with the rest of the evidence."

"In other words, *knowing* that he has confessed, you would simply try to get him off."

"Yes, except that I don't *know* that he's confessed."

"You are quibbling, Mr. Grant," the lady said. "But I quite agree with you that you are not the lawyer we are looking for. We don't want to see this case handled by the normal, pettifogging methods. We want it to be tried on the larger social issues involved, namely, on where society is to place the blame for this systematic corruption of underprivileged boys."

"Splendid," Sidney said. "However, the specific charge is murder. The Crown cannot offer immunity to Easting for turning Queen's Evidence and implicating his accomplices. Now I will contend that Easting's lawyer will best discharge his duty to society by looking after Easting's narrow, immediate, personal interests and seeing that he has a fair trial."

"Ah!" the spokeswoman said. "Now then. Suppose *you* were defending him, and suppose you *couldn't* have his statement excluded, and suppose they convicted and hanged him. What then? That would be a splendid way to protect his interests. Suppose that you realized that the sentence *might* have been commuted if he had spoken forth frankly and told all he knew, had, in short, offered full cooperation to society. What then, Mr. Grant? How would you feel then?"

"Just awful," Sidney said. "Except for one thing. Pursue your line of reasoning and you would make our courts just like the late Comrade Stalin's. All accused persons trying to curry favor by denouncing themselves. No ma'am. My feeling is that if Easting killed Mrs. Thurston, he ought to be convicted, provided the Crown can prove it to a jury. After his conviction there will be time to start propaganda for commutation of the sentence. But to return to the main point, if I defend a man, I won't permit anybody to tell me what line of defense I am to take, and that is the reason why I'm forced to decline your kind offer."

A few minutes later the delegation left, looking somewhat disconsolate.

And then the fat was in the fire. Aunt Claudia set about Sidney for being arrogant and getting on his high horse. June, his beloved wife, set about him for destroying his public image.

"You could be the young, dynamic crusader for justice," she said. "Instead of which you want to be Mr. Pettifog."

He might have got off lightly but for the unexpected help of old Mrs. Beattie, who located misguided enthusiasm and insisted that the informal committee, no matter what they might say, had been swept up in the mass hysteria generated by the newspapers. Which inspired June to accuse Sidney of first-degree finking and currying favor with her grandmother in the hope of getting the best slice of roast beef at dinner. But in time the whole thing blew over, and Sidney put the Thurston case out of his mind.

In due course he read in the paper that Mr. Lionel Raines, Q.C., was going to defend Marvin Easting, and he grinned as he showed the story to June.

"There, that's the man they were really looking for," he said.

Lionel Raines, Q.C., had, to use the current idiom, a fine public image. He was tall and slender and had a fine shock of white hair. He wore a pince-nez, which he carried on a long black ribbon attached to his lapel. It was the last of its kind seen in Southern Ontario. He was a leftishly inclined politician, who often accepted large fees from rightishly inclined corporations. More frequently he represented the little man in actions against large corporations, which gave him a splendid chance to build his image as the friend of humanity and the defender of the little man.

He was an eloquent and emotional pleader, and a tremendous orator, always in the public eye.

But, strictly among lawyers, his reputation was less glowing. It was said that Mr. Raines didn't always do his homework. He had lost out on points of law that any good lawyer's clerk would have caught. Brilliant but unsound was the professional verdict. He cared more about appearances than realities.

"I'm sure the plans of those earnest females will suit old Silvertongue perfectly," Sidney told June.

On that very same day, early in the afternoon, the Thurston murder case brushed close to Sidney once more. He and June were lying at anchor in a cumbersome punt, powered, if that is the right word, by an ancient three-horsepower outboard. They had anchored on a reef, where June was fishing while Sidney lay back and read.

Presently their peace was disturbed by a powerful Fiberglass boat that hove to alongside and hailed them. The boat was driven by a surly youth wearing swimming trunks and a yachting cap—obviously a water-cabby from Port Carling. His two passengers were dressed in city clothes, a large man with a close crew-cut, surrounded by cameras and strobe lights, and a pretty but petulant young woman of about twenty.

"Hi," the girl said. "Can you tell us where the Thurstons' cottage is?"

June said she could, but it was a little complicated. It would be much easier to demonstrate on the chart. But nobody had a chart, so June suggested that they should land and consult one. The people looked hot and angry, so she also suggested a cold gin and tonic. The crew-cut man grinned happily and said it was the best idea he'd heard for weeks.

So they all came ashore in a small cove on the back side of Mrs. Beattie's island. The crew-cut man, somewhat brusquely, ordered the water-cabby to stay with the boat.

The foursome followed the path over the hog's-back ridge to the sleeping-cabin occupied by June and Sidney, happily equipped with a small fridge and a secret supply of ingredients.

The man introduced himself as Stan, a press photographer, and his companion as Dulcinea Dale, a reporter. Dulcie had a beef. She hated what she called Society People. In her days on the Women's Page these people had called up constantly to make sure that their dinner parties and dances got reported and to talk all about their hospital and ballet committees and all that jazz. And they wanted to make sure that what they were wearing was reported accurately and that their names got spelled right and don't forget their husband's C.B.E., and when they were entertaining some English lord they were terribly concerned about getting the style and title right.

But just let those people get involved in a *real* news story, Dulcie said, and they start phoning the publisher to keep their names out of the paper and putting pressure on the business department if they happened to be big advertisers. Like these Thurstons, she explained. The police had acted, she said, like they were interested only in preserving the privacy of these snobs.

The news given out concerning the Rosedale end of the deal had been scanty. The police said that at the time of the murder, there were four women living in the house: Mrs. Thurston; her daughter, Martha; Miss Viola Lang, a relation who acted as a sort of secretary-housekeeper; and Mrs. Edna Foster, a practical nurse. The nurse had given sedatives to Mrs. Thurston and Miss Lang, as was her custom, shortly after nine o'clock, and Miss Lang, an early riser, had gone to bed at once. Martha Thurston had gone to her own room earlier in the evening to write letters and said she had turned in about ten and slept soundly. None of them had heard any disturbance.

The nurse had a sort of apartment in the attic, to which she had retired shortly after ten.

Medical and other evidence indicated that the burglary and murder had taken place at about half past eleven, a well-chosen time. Some of the large houses nearby had been turned into rooming houses, occupied by a largely bohemian crowd—TV people, artists and musicians, who habitually had parties on a Friday night. So there were usually strange cars arriving or leaving all evening, and at half past eleven some parties were starting and others finishing. Some time after the burglary, Mrs. Thurston's son Gerald had arrived. He was a Sarnia businessman. He had come up for the weekend in order to welcome his brother, Crawford, the ambassador, on his arrival from Europe. But Gerald, knowing the early-to-bed habits of the womenfolk, had stayed downtown drinking at a club until a late hour. Since he had a key to the family house, he was able to let himself in without disturbing any of the sleepers, and he had noticed nothing wrong.

On the following day, after the police had finished questioning them, the members of the household had scattered to various friends' houses—obviously for the purpose of dodging the press. Later they had met at a rendezvous, after Gerald had fetched Crawford from Malton in an airport limousine. All except the nurse, who had been paid off and had gone away for a holiday.

The family group left the city after dark, drove north in Martha Thurston's car, stayed at a motel overnight and opened up the family cottage on its secluded island on Sunday. So much Dulcie had pieced together from police and other reports. Because they had been able to take only light luggage, Gerald had returned to the city on Monday, to settle certain business details and collect other articles for the north, removing them from the Thurston house to some other hideaway, and on Tuesday the rest of the family had come down for the funeral and had stayed over until the inquest on Thursday morning. They hadn't gone near the house, and so were able again to dodge the press.

"They won't give you much of a welcome at the cottage," June said.

"That won't hurt our feelings, just so we get on shore," Stan said. "Lessee this chart now, so we can figure out a plan."

June showed him where the Thurstons' island lay and pointed out a suitable landing spot, which, she said, was out of sight of the cottage. The news contingent finished their drinks, thanked their hosts and departed, much refreshed, on their odyssey among the islands.

And on that same evening Sidney and June met the bereaved Thurstons, Crawford, Gerald and Martha, on the veranda of somebody else's cottage, where they had been invited for drinks. The Thurstons were correctly subdued, but not desolate. They discussed the case briefly, to show that they were rational people, mentioning that after all Mother had been old and was in constant pain, and at least the thing had been quickly over, and they stopped just short of saying that in a way it had been a blessing.

"I hear a rumor," Martha said to Sidney, "that *you* refused to defend Easting."

Sidney punctiliously stated that he had never been asked by Easting or his family, that something or other had been said by some other people, but that there had never been any serious question of it.

"A damn good thing," Gerald said. "The sooner they hang those clods the better."

His brother, Crawford, gently reproved him, pointing out that every accused person is entitled to a defense, and then Sidney, changing the topic slightly, asked if the Thurstons had been much troubled by the press.

"No, thank God," Crawford said. "Gerald and Mart handled it very adroitly. We kept under cover in the city and came up here whenever possible."

"Haven't the papers tried to follow you up here?" Sidney asked.

"No, thank heaven," Crawford said. "We haven't seen hide nor hair of 'em!"

Which set Sidney to wondering about the fate of the adventurers who had asked for directions that afternoon.

"Should we send out search parties?" he asked June.

But June thought that the newspaper people could look after themselves.

The Thurstons appeared to have recovered pretty well from their ordeal, though June, who knew them, expressed some surprise at the fact that Martha had chain-smoked through the evening and had, as she inelegantly put it, had her nose in the booze pretty steadily.

"Nerves," she said. "Martha was always the high-principled do-gooder. She used to leave the drinking to Gerald, who has professional status."

But at that moment Sidney wasn't interested in gossip about the Thurstons. He was on holiday, trying, as he put it, to get in some serious loafing.

Four

ON THE FOLLOWING MORNING mail arrived at about ten and included a letter from Sidney's office. After reading it he sat for half an hour in furious concentration, wearing the scowl that had given him his nickname, and then he announced that he was going at once to the city, heat or no heat.

He didn't say why, and June, though dying with curiosity, decided to be too proud to ask. But she nobly gave him the keys to her beloved Citroën ID 19 and drove him to the mainland in her grandmother's big mahogany launch.

So that Sidney, after a hamburger lunch on the highway, reached his office early in the afternoon and said: "All right, Miss Semple, where is this fellow?"

Miss Semple was his secretary. She had come to his employ after being pensioned off by an old, established firm of corporation solicitors. She wore a gorgeous bouffant of improbable red hair, and was in her late forties or early seventies. She was wearing a starched white outfit, and managed to look cool in spite of the frightful heat.

"At the Prince George hotel, Mr. Grant," she said without looking up. "Shall I ask him to come over?"

Sidney told her yes, and busied himself with throwing away mail for twenty minutes until Miss Semple ushered into the office a very fierce old man with terrifying handlebar mustaches. The man was perfectly bald and had a noble aquiline nose that hooked over his mustache and made him look like an eagle carrying a fish in its beak. He fixed Sidney with a dark and flashing eye and said, "Mr. Grant, I want you to defend my grandson, Vince Lamberti."

"Yes," Sidney said. "So Miss Semple told me, Mr. Ducatti. Now, since you came from Montreal to see me, I thought I ought at least to come down to the city and talk to you. But right away let me warn you: there's not much point in retaining me."

"No?"

"No. Unless your grandson has a pretty good story, or alibi, nobody can do very much for him."

"Yes, so I hear," the man said.

"You see, the law is this way: if two or three or ten men go out on a hold-up or a burglary, and someone gets killed as a result of it, all of the men are equally guilty of murder. Now, if the Crown can prove to a jury that Vince was mixed up in that burglary—I believe they allege that he waited outside in the car while Easting went into the house—then he is equally guilty with Easting of any murder that Easting committed. We are told that Easting has confessed to the murder, which more or less cooks Vince's goose."

"Yeah, I know," the visitor said, piercing Sidney with an eye designed to quell Sicilian bandits. "So how much do you charge?"

The simplest way was to price himself out of the market.

"I might have to spend fifteen days in court," Sidney said. "I would have to ask for a retaining fee of ten thousand dollars. So under the cir—"

He stopped. The old man had yanked out a fine leather wallet and was shuffling out thousand-dollar bills.

"What I figured," he said. "Vince should have been a lawyer—you get it without a gun."

He threw ten nice new thousands on the desk.

"Look after Vince," he said.

Sidney tried to protest, but the man rose and turned. Miss Semple, who was right on top of the game, had the receipt all made out by the time he reached her desk, and she handed it to him as he went past.

"How do you like that?" Sidney called to her.

"I just love it," she said. "It's a splendid start for the season."

"He's right. It's robbery," Sidney said. "I can't possibly do anything to earn it. Under that proud and leathery old hide he must have a great love for his grandson."

It was nearly three, so he got Miss Semple to make out a deposit slip, and he put the ten thousand dollars in the bank on his way to the Don Jail, for the purpose of meeting his new client.

There was no doubt about it, Vince Lamberti was a tough hombre. His beard showed blue-black against a strangely fine skin of pale ivory, and his jaw was a rugged promontory. He had the same hooked beak as his grandfather, except that Vince's had been broken. He walked gracefully, almost like a dancer, and there was a litheness about him that suggested a relaxed tiger. His features were composed, and he had an air of dignity.

"Nice to meetcha, Mr. Grant," he said when they were introduced by a jail official. "I'm real glad I'm gonna have you in my corner for this one."

"You'll need more than a lawyer for this one," Sidney said. "You'll need a good story. Suppose we get right down to it now. Let's hear your version of what happened. I want to know everything."

"You want the whole works, start to finish?" Vince asked.

"Yes."

"You got lotsa time?"

"My time," Sidney said, "is your time. It's been bought and paid for."

"All right," Lamberti said, shaking his head dubiously. "You asked for it, so here goes. I was in this joint, see? A real nice air-conditioned bar, and it was hot as hell, so I was drinking cold beer. Jeeze, could I go for one now! Anyways, in comes this cop, a plainclothes guy, see? He says, 'Vince, we wanna ask you a few questions. Will you come along quiet to Headquarters?' I tell him sure, and next thing I know they got me booked for murder. And that's my story, complete and unabridged like they say on those paperbacks."

"But what," Sidney said, "were you doing on the night of the murder? Have you got an alibi?"

"Well I have, but I don't think it will do much good," Lamberti said. "I was with a woman."

"Yes?"

"And this dame is..."

"Married and has a jealous husband, and you are too much of a gentleman to compromise her honor, even though you may be hanged for it."

"That's just the way it is, Mr. Grant. But the way things are, I wouldn't try to use that alibi."

"Very wise of you," Sidney said. "But you're not giving me much help."

"Gee, I'm sorry," Lamberti said. "But that's the way it is. I knew a guy useta always say, 'Never talk till they let you see your lawyer, and after that, shut up.' The guy had something. Listen, Mr. Grant, I wouldn't blame you if you walked offa the case, but I'm tellin' ya, this is how it's gotta be."

"Well, at least I don't have to contend with a foolish statement made to the police," Sidney said. "But frankly, at this moment, I can't see too much hope."

"I got only one hope, Mr. Grant, there's only one chance," Lamberti said solemnly.

"And what is that?" Sidney asked.

"That they won't have no size nineteen noose," Lamberti said.

In spite of himself, Sidney smiled at the bit of *Galgenhumor.* "Your grandfather must be pretty worried," he said, "He thinks a lot of you."

"Me?" Lamberti said. "Oh, the old guy is all right. Listen, between you and I, he don't win no medals from the Pope when he's a young guy. He was pretty goddam mad at me when I got into trouble last time, and he wouldn't have nothin' to do with me. I guess maybe his conscience got him. But anyway, the old guy is loaded with dough, even though he don't go around advertising it."

Sidney scrutinized his new client searchingly, and finally shrugged. "All right, Vince," he said. "We'll see what we can do for you."

He went back to his office, shaking his head sadly.

"Well, what do you think about it all?" Miss Semple asked.

"I think," Sidney said, "that ten thousand dollars is a lot of money."

She looked at him sharply. "Yes indeed, quite a bundle," she said.

"Ah well," Sidney said. "Our client tells me his grampa is really loaded, though not a conspicuous consumer. Now then, as to earning this fat retainer, you will please commence, Georgia, your customary research, and please make use of our student as much as possible."

The office staff had recently been enlarged, by the addition of a typist and an articled law student, a serious-minded young woman called Edith Moon, who had taken a degree in Sociology before entering Osgoode Hall to study law. Miss Moon was a hard worker, but unfortunately lacked any semblance of a sense of humor.

Having given some specific instructions about the routine investigation, Sidney went out, bought the evening papers, tossed them into the back seat of the Citroën and headed back north to resume his holiday.

❀❀❀

In the morning June had resolved to be proud and not ask her husband what business it was that dragged him away from Muskoka into the inferno of Toronto. If he didn't wish to confide in her, she had decided, then she would ignore the whole thing.

But curiosity had eaten at her during the day, and when Sidney arrived in a water taxi just before eight o'clock she had worked up a good head of steam.

"You're back early," she said. "I didn't expect to see you for a couple of days."

"Ah! But I escaped," he said. "Back to loafing."

They were in their sleeping-cabin, getting ready for dinner.

"I thought you'd gone off to have an affair," she said. "I thought you'd fixed a date with that Dulcie."

"Gad!" he said. "That flawless intuition! I thought by coming back in the evening I'd fool you."

"Sidney darling," she said, "I'm terribly relieved! So it *was* an affair. In all that *heat*, too. Air-conditioned apartment, one hopes?"

"Aye, and lots of nice cold beer," he said.

"I'm so glad, Sidney dear. When she's left alone, a wife gets to *wondering*. Your imagination plays tricks. I kept getting horrible visions of you taking on the defense of that man Lamberti. But then I kept reassuring myself. I said, 'June, you've got to stop this. Sidney has gone to see some nice girl, there's not a thing to worry about.' And I was right!"

"Light of my life," he said. "I have a teensy confession to make. Uh—er—I have, in fact, taken on the defense of Lamberti."

There was an ugly silence, but it didn't last long.

"Sidney Grant," she said, "you are a clot. You are stupid. You are sly, low and cunning. You sneaked away this morning, not daring to tell me what you were planning. So you've done it! You refuse to defend the ignorant dupe on the large, important issues. Then you blithely agree to defend the hardened old lag. And why, answer me that, why?"

"Why? Well, Lamberti's grandfather came and asked me to take the case on. He retained me."

"You refused the Easting case. May I ask how much you were paid to take the Lamberti case?"

"Certainly you may ask. What's more, I'll tell you. I was paid a retainer of ten thousand dollars."

"God's teeth!" she said. "You did it for *money!*"

"All my work, except some legal assistance stuff, is done for money," he said.

"And whose money? Answer me that!"

"Lamberti's grandfather's..."

"Lamberti's grandmother's Aunt Fanny!" she said. "You know damn well his family never put up that money. You know that's underworld money. Lamberti is one of the boys—so they plan along. Oh, Lamberti will be a good guy, he won't sing, he'll protect all the fences and the go-betweens, and the boys will pay the shot for some tricky lawyer to try to get him off the hook. You clot! You fool! Do you know what you've done to your public image? You've ruined it. There you were, a dynamic, rising, sensational young barrister who had made a brilliant marriage with a rich and beautiful heiress. You were a crusader for justice. The world was at your feet. Ottawa beckoned. You'd have gone to Parliament, then into the Cabinet. But now, now, you've kicked it all away. People will say you're nothing but an underworld mouthpiece. They'll say you turned down Easting because the underworld said nix. Then you took on Lamberti because Mr. Big said, 'Okay, Gargoyle, spring dis monkey offa da murder rap! You *half*-wit."

They were late for dinner, but she followed him about the room, upbraiding him, nagging him, her voice rising higher and higher and her text becoming less reasoned and more abusive at every step. He was a goat, a peasant, a booby. Sidney remained calm, but pale. His eye lighted on an old hand-wound gramophone with a cabinet full of ancient 78 rpm records, and he had a happy thought. He pulled out a record and shoved it on the turntable, turned the crank and set the needle in the groove. Then he walked away and was on the other side of the room when the gramophone burst into the "Ride of the Valkyries." When the message got through to her, June's personal *Walkürenritt* reached new heights, culminating in a scream of "Why, why, WHY did you DO it?"

"Because." Sidney replied primly, "I considered it the proper thing to do."

"Well then, why didn't you *say* so, for heaven's sake?" she said, and flung her arms about him.

Aunt Claudia was going to be a bit harder to win over.

After dinner Mrs. Beattie conscripted her daughter Claudia and two innocent guests into a rubber of bridge, which June dodged on behalf of her husband and herself by repeating brightly, "No, no, I wouldn't *think* of it—you two go ahead."

So Sidney finally got at the evening papers, in which he found a story that both fascinated and amused him.

It was the sort of story that could only get played big in August. There was a huge head-and-shoulders portrait, five columns wide, of a Kerry blue terrier with its head cocked on one side in an engaging manner, under a line that read: "What Have They Done to My Mistress?" Inside the paper there were other pictures of the dog, showing him barking, growling, snarling and tearing a man's trouser leg. The accompanying story explained that the dog's name was Chippy, short for Chippewa, and that Chippy had been the pet and watchdog of the late Mrs. Thurston. The story was written by Chippy himself, in the first person singular, but under his byline appeared the explanatory words, "As told to Dulcie Dale."

> They wouldn't have got away with it if I'd been home [Chippy wrote]. For eight years I've guarded my mistress and if anyone came near the house at night I woke up the whole neighborhood.
>
> But see, Mr. Crawf was coming home—that's my mistress's son, the Ambassador—and I had to get all shampooed and prettied up to welcome him.
>
> So when those guys came, I was away at a dog-gone beauty parlor that they call Dr. Prince's Animal Clinic, although usually I'm a reg'lar he-dog that likes to chase...

A sample of Chippy's prose style is sufficient. He had written several paragraphs more, ending up with the words: "Gee, I'd like to sink my teeth in those guys!"

The mysterious mission of Stan and Dulcie Dale was explained. They had made a secret landing, they had been challenged by Chippy, whom they promptly corrupted with gifts of beefsteak, and then they had led him to some secluded spot where they could take photographs at will. Sidney felt certain that Stan had charged a new suit on his expense account.

There were explosions from the Thurston cottage, where, it was reported, the story was regarded as yellow journalism in the poorest possible taste, and there was even talk (but just talk) of an action for trespass. Coming on top of everything else, the story so upset Martha Thurston that she was said to be on the brink of a full-scale breakdown. Dulcie Dale had larned 'em to snub the press!

Five

SIDNEY'S ATTEMPT TO resume serious loafing was a failure. He was restive. He was miserable, and June finally suggested that he ought to go back to the city. He accepted the suggestion with obvious relief. She told him frankly that she couldn't see the sense of it. There was nothing to be done for Lamberti. His fate was tied to that of Easting.

Sidney explained to her patiently that there were things to be done. On the face of it, the main evidence against Lamberti was the statement of his alleged accomplice. The uncorroborated evidence of an accomplice could not convict.

No doubt there would be bits of corroborative evidence, but take away Easting's statement and it would probably be flimsy. So the first line of defense was to talk really pretty to Lionel Raines and get him to cooperate in an effort to have the Easting statement excluded.

So Sidney returned to the city, and was pleased to find that Lionel Raines was also in town. He made an appointment, after which he rehearsed in his mind the pitch he was going to make. *See here, Raines, nobody goes into court asking for an automatic verdict of Guilty. Plenty of time to come clean after the trial. Let's see if we can't get this confession excluded on the grounds of duress or...*

"Suppose Mr. Raines won't play. What then?" Miss Semple asked.

"Then we try to get a separate trial. We won't succeed, of course. But I'll bet if the statement *was* excluded, the Crown Attorney would wish he had Lamberti up for separate trial—and perhaps get Easting as a Crown witness. I'd love to cross-examine Easting. He's a shifty little beast."

❀❀❀

Lionel Raines rose to meet his visitor and did things with his pince-nez. "To what, precisely, do I owe this honor, Mr. Grant?" he asked.

There were to be no preliminaries.

"I wanted to explore possible areas of cooperation between us," Sidney said.

"Ah! Cooperation! You had something in mind?"

"Yes," Sidney said. "I believe that Easting made a statement not long after his arrest. Now, as I get it, he was dead drunk when arrested. I feel certain he was confused and fuzzy and hardly knew what he was saying or signing. It could just be that the police, with a fresh murder on their hands, overstepped the line in their enthusiasm. If so, might we not exclude the statement?"

Lionel Raines gestured to a chair, then walked with long, swooping strides around his desk and sat down on another. He swept back his silvery locks and stared at the ceiling.

"You are entirely right, Mr. Grant," he said. "Easting was drunk—virtually incoherent, I believe, when he was interrogated. And I understand that one young detective laid hands on him and, in excess of zeal, threatened to knock him about if he didn't talk. I believe also that somebody said they would see that he got a better shake if he spoke up. And so: duress, threats, inducements. The statement—anything he said that night—would be, strictly speaking, inadmissible. Yes, yes. You are quite right, Mr. Grant."

"So we can bar the statement, then?" Sidney said, scarcely able to believe his luck.

"Bar? Statement?" Raines said. "The question doesn't even arise. It is absolutely agreed that, within the meaning of the laws of evidence, Easting made no statement whatever at Police Headquarters."

"Well that's splendid," Sidney said. "You mean the police agree with this?"

"Of course. The only statement that Easting has made, the only one that will be heard in court, is one that he made in my presence, and after full consultation with me—and I can assure you that he was quite sober when he made it. I can also assure you that there were no threats and inducements, because I was present."

Sidney's heart sank, and he tried to keep his face from showing it.

"This statement," he said. "I suppose it was prepared in advance and that it was read to Easting in the presence of the police, and then he signed it?"

Raines smiled. "You wish to cross-examine me, Mr. Grant? I'm terribly sorry. But just so there shall be no misunderstanding between us—on this 'areas of cooperation' business—Easting's statement, which will be read into the evidence with my blessing, is full and frank. He has—not without a certain understandable reluctance at first—decided to cooperate fully with the forces of law and order, rather than with the accomplice who got him into this mess. In short, he told all: the planning of the crime, the flattery, bribes and threats that Lamberti used to get him into it, everything."

"Including the strangling?"

Raines lowered his eyes from the ceiling and his voice from the upper register. "There are limits, of course, Mr. Grant," he said. "Remember that it was dark. That Easting was working with a pen light. Vaguely he remembers something clutching at him in the dark. He didn't know whether it was an old lady or Whipper Billy Watson. Vaguely he can remember being frightened and pushing this assailant away...but I need not burden you with all this."

"There's a sort of funny thing about this crime," Sidney said. "According to what I read in the papers, these fellows were lucky or unlucky enough to pick the one night in three thousand when the watchdog was away from the house being shampooed. I ask myself, was this sheer coincidence?"

"You have a client," Raines said. "Ask him."

"My dear sir," Sidney rejoined. "You have the good fortune to have a client who will talk to every Tom, Dick and Harry, but particularly to the dicks. My client won't even talk to me. I am genuinely mystified by the dog angle."

Raines looked at him sharply, then laughed soundlessly. "Well, it's simple enough," he said. "Lamberti sent poor Easting up every afternoon to look around for houses to burglarize. He had to look for places that appeared deserted—you know, the usual things, uncut grass, handbills on the porch, curtains drawn, the hall light burning in the daytime. *Inter alia,* he reported the Thurston house, and Lamberti took due note of it. Later, no doubt after consultation with underworld sources, he told Easting that this was a great find, that there were valuable furs there, and plans were made to rob the house. But, on a further reconnaissance, Easting found that there were people in the house, and also a dog. The plan was therefore canceled.

However, Lamberti had found a ready market for the furs. He lent Easting his Volkswagen to keep an eye on the place and—I regret to say—suggested that he should run over the dog if he got the chance. You may have noticed in the papers that kindness to animals is one of Easting's redeeming features. He says he simply couldn't do it.

"However, on that fatal Friday evening, while he was sitting parked in the Volkswagen, watching the house, he saw a woman, obviously Martha Thurston, come out of the house leading the dog. She got into a car—a Pontiac, he thinks, which in fact is the make of vehicle driven by Miss Thurston—and drove off. On impulse he followed and saw her take the dog into Dr. Dorothy Price's Animal Clinic on Yonge Street. In considerable excitement he raced back to report to Lamberti—he had waited, by the way, to see Miss Thurston emerge *without* the dog—and Lamberti at once gave orders that the burglary should take place that very night. He warned Easting that there would be people in the house, that he would have to move with great care, but the loot was worth it. He was able to give detailed instructions about the location of the loot—the underworld knows these things—and so poor young Easting, after being given two 'reefers' to smoke—went with Lamberti to the scene of the crime. Actually, he didn't know he had killed. He was frightened and confused. He didn't intend to 'hold out' on Lamberti by keeping the jewelry—he was so confused he actually forgot he had it!"

"Remarkable," Sidney said.

"Yes, but even more remarkable is the almost hypnotic influence that Lamberti, the glamorous bigtime crook, exercised over Easting. Now I shall contend, more or less under the law of agency—*qui facit per alium facit per se*—that it was really Lamberti who killed Mrs. Thurston. Lamberti, the ruthless one. Easting wouldn't hurt a dog, even when ordered by Lamberti. Now then, Lamberti drummed it into him: be tough. Attack. In the darkness there, when the old lady clutched Easting's arm, and he was frightened, it was the words of his master that caused him to do what he did."

"Perhaps you could have him marked as Exhibit A, and produce him as the murder weapon used by Lamberti," Sidney suggested.

"That, in effect, is what I plan to do," Raines said triumphantly. "And now that I have made the position crystal clear...?"

"I will slink away," Sidney said humbly, and did.

❀❀❀

"And so, Georgie dear," Sidney said to Miss Semple, "we find ourselves in a comic situation straight out of Gilbert and Sullivan. When the case comes to trial, the police will try to read a statement made by Easting. I will object to it. I will be overruled. The judge may even say something fatuous like 'This statement can be considered as evidence against the accused Easting, but not against the accused Lamberti.' One fat-headed judge in England actually did that—as if the jury could blot the statement out of their minds when pondering Lamberti's case.

"But *then*, Georgie dear, we get to the real comedy. In cross-examining the police inspector, *I* will be demanding to know if Easting made and signed any *other* statement, and when I have forced them to admit it, I will demand that it be produced. Then *Raines* will object; he will say that the other statement was obtained by means of duress, et cetera. So a handy young policeman will be called (with the jury excluded) and he will admit that in all the heat and excitement he forgot himself and threatened to punch Easting in the nose if he didn't sign the first statement, and the judge will then exclude it.

"I will then rant and rave about that first statement when I address the jury; I will suggest that it would virtually clear my man if introduced. By golly, I might even goad them into producing it, to shut me up."

"What do you think it would show?" Miss Semple asked.

"A vast difference in style," Sidney said. "You know about statements, of course. The interrogation is all question and answer, sort of 'All right, Muggsy, we know you burned down the orphanage. Quit stallin'. You done it, huh?' And Muggsy murmurs, 'Sure, I guess so.' Well, these answers and questions are switched around and put in a statement that is a piece of continuous prose, like 'Using my new Calibri lighter, I set fire to the southwest corner of the orphanage at 10.23 P.M.' Now that first statement of Easting's would be crude and incomplete, and Easting might have been unsure about certain things that he became certain of in his *next* statement. The next statement, written by old Silvertongue Raines, will be in limpid and exquisite prose, and is sure to be ninety percent fiction."

"But what's the idea of it?" Miss Semple asked. "What does Raines hope to achieve?"

"A splash," Sidney said. "He wants to take this line. Easting will hand over his accomplice, Lamberti, on a silver platter. He will give full cooperation to the police. He will express anguish and contrition. Then Raines will hope for a recommendation for mercy from the jury. This will be the springboard from which Raines will leap into a campaign for public sympathy and an executive commutation of the sentence. Now to achieve this, Raines finds out all the odds and ends that the police or the prosecution are puzzled about, and gets Easting to explain them.

"Now Georgie, I will bet ten thousand dollars, which I happen to have, that Easting never had any part in planning or organizing that burglary. I will further bet that he never was sent to spy out the land beforehand. I know how these things are done. Easting is what is technically known as 'the punk,' a guy who knows nothing and does what he's told. But now we have Easting telling improbable tales about snooping around the Thurston house and reporting back to Lamberti.

"What has happened is simply this: Raines has bullied and bulldozed his client. He's told him that he'll be hanged for sure if he doesn't cooperate. He signed a statement, so they've got him. Easting wouldn't recognize the truth if he met it walking naked down the street. He agrees to everything. Raines says: 'Now you must have known the dog was going to be out that night. Maybe you saw Miss Thurston taking it away to the animal clinic.' 'Sure, that's right,' the submissive Easting says. 'You didn't follow her Pontiac in your Volkswagen, did you, and see her leave the animal?' 'Sure I did,' says Easting. 'See, I had this Volks of Vince's...' That's the way it's done, and Raines convinces himself that it's all true. But Georgie, my pet, I think, I hope, he may have gone too far."

Mr. Raines was more noted for zeal than discretion.

Sidney wiped the sweat off his brow with a limp handkerchief and prepared to go out. When Miss Semple asked him where he was going, he said, "I'm goin' fishin'. Among our stalwarts in blue."

❀❀❀

Sidney found Inspector Frank Young sitting at his desk in a shirt that was wringing wet. The inspector was, at the moment, inspecting a collection of cameras, telescopes and binoculars.

"Hi Sid," he said. "What can we do you for, as if I don't know what you're after, you cunning devil. Well listen, old man, I'll tell you something. If I could honestly do anything to help you spring the Big Guy, I would, and that's no kidding."

It was certainly a promising start. Sidney enquired delicately as to why the inspector felt such sympathy.

"Well, I'll tell you, Sid," he said, continuing his job of removing the lens from a Zeiss Ikon, "back there a few years we sprung a trap on this bad bank gang, and I was run in on the job. Well it ends up with me chasing one big guy up alleyways and over fences, and I get a look and see it's Vince Lamberti. Sure, I knew him to see him. Everybody interested in sports did. I shouted after him, called him by name. Then I cornered him in a backyard with a high fence. Okay, the guy knew he'd been recognized. Getting away was no use if he left me alive. Furthermore, I was close behind. If he went up the fence I could either grab him and haul him down or shoot him in the back. He had a gun. He knew what he had to do. He turned and aimed at me.

"Well, you know, Sid, you can laugh all you like, but I had a feeling about this guy. I knew he was a safe man with a gun, and I kept right on going for him. He fired twice—and missed. Vince! So I hit him with a tackle and knocked him down. Okay, I got a medal, I was promoted, and I was called a bloody fool. Okay, I acted on this hunch, and I was right. *Vince is no killer.* So if I can give Big Vince a break, all kosher like, I will."

"Maybe you wouldn't mind talking unofficial like to Vince's lawyer," Sidney said. "You know Vince. He won't even talk to *me.* Well, I'm kind of intrigued by this burglary. It doesn't exactly fit the patterns. What is Vince doing as a housebreaker? How come he tied in with a clot like Easting? How come they sent such a clot into a house full of people? I'd expect to hear that the burglar carried at least a toy pistol, so if anyone woke up he could cover them and tell them to keep quiet. Another thing: if the burglars are going into a house with people in it, do they really expect the fences to take the furs and start processing them while the alarm is out for them? What I mean is, the minute the theft of those furs is reported, you'd be looking around at all the fences. They wouldn't touch the stuff till the heat was off. The thing is wacky."

"Sidney old boy, you are a bad bastard and a thorn in the flesh of Stolen Goods," Young said. "But I like you. You don't believe in any goddam fairy tales. You know how things are. Okay, you bashed the nail on the noggin. It's screwy. I get a tipoff that the Martins were up to something, so I set up a trap. What I figured, of course, was that the boys were bringing stuff out of hiding, stuff stolen last winter, to get it processed and moved along the line.

"Now this was kind of funny in itself, because I'd also picked up a story that the Martins were on the outs with Spider Webb and the guys that organize these things. Like the Martins had been doing a little double-dealing and cheating. And there's one thing you can say for Webb: he just won't put up with dishonesty. A dishonest thief or a dishonest fence doesn't stand a chance with him.

"Well naturally it never occurred to me that the Martins were there waiting for furs stolen the night before, or I would have arranged things differently. As it was, there was a kind of louse-up, because a lot of traffic guys started buzzing around the district, and when I came out to tell 'em to buzz off, Vince saw me. Well Vince is smart. I mean, he thinks quick. He went up the lane, parked his Volks, tossed the bundle of furs into a big garbage box and lit out—over the fences again! Now then, if Stoopid Easting hadn't left some prints on that Volks, we'd be halfway to nowhere. Those prints connect Stoopid with the Volks. The jewelry connects Stoopid with the burglary and the murder. A torn corner of brown paper connects the bundle of furs with the Volks. And I saw Vince driving it. We still haven't found the owner of it. It's thin, but it just ties in. Now, do you want to know how I figure it?"

"I sure do," Sidney said.

"I figure the Martins organized the whole deal. Webb had nothing to do with it. They got the dope on where the furs were, and where the jewels were—and that's a funny thing too—how come they're interested in jewels? They tried to sell the scheme to Webb, and he gave them the brush. They shopped around and they found Vince hungry for dough. Dame trouble, no doubt. Jack Martin—knowing Vince is safe, like he never talks—sold the scheme to Vince. Maybe he told him he'd throw the jewels in as part of Vince's cut. Vince looks for a punk. The kids all hero-worshipped the guy, and Vince picked the wrong one."

"Now *that*," Sidney said, "begins to add up, except for one thing. *If* the Martins dealt direct with the burglar, and sent Vince up there, they must have thought the house was empty. They wouldn't have stood by to accept the furs unless they'd thought they had a day or two to work. And *if* they thought that, then there wasn't any talk of jewels, because the jewels would have followed the old lady. So to make the thing work, you've got to figure it like this. Easting is getting the coats, the old lady wakes up and starts to gurgle. Easting rushes over, scared stiff, and strangles her. Then he stands there. He sees the drawer where the jewels are, and with his sneak-thief instincts he opens it, sees the stuff and pockets it. He's frightened to tell his accomplice that he had killed somebody, so he just hangs onto the jewels as *his* private cut."

"Okay, Sidney, okay," Young said. "Hang on while I call Personnel. You can start work immediately. We can use a guy like you."

"But it means," Sidney pointed out, "that somebody gave the Martins a bum steer. Somebody gave the burglars a bum steer. Damn it, they *must* have thought the house was empty."

"I—could—not—agree—with you more," Young said. "And I'll tell you another thing. The guy that gave that bum steer was lucky if he was dealing with the Martins. Webb wouldn't have let it go. The guy's life wouldn't be worth a nickel if he stayed in town. And I'll tell you something else. Maybe it isn't anyway."

"How come?" Sidney said.

"How come? Listen, no matter what he did on this job, Vince stood in with the Webb mob. Listen. Try this for size. Martin offers the job to Webb. He gets the brush. Vince is bugging Webb to find him something, Webb says he wants no part of it himself, but if Vince wants to talk to Martin, he'll find the guy has a proposition. And if *that's* right, Webb right now will be pretty mad at the Martins and whoever gave them the bum steer, for the way they loused everything up."

"This now begins to make some sense," Sidney said. "Look, Frank. I've talked to Raines, and there's one thing Raines can't resist: an audience. It seems as if Easting has made a big confession, claiming he went up and cased the joint for his alleged accomplice. This is strictly fiction, I will bet. But the one bit that fits is this: he talked about finding the place with the grass long and handbills on the porch, which made the place look *empty*. What do you think of that?"

"I went to the house on the Saturday morning, just after eleven," Young said. "The place looked okay then. I mean, the grass was all right, the hedge was clipped. It looked all right to me."

"Okay," Sidney said. "But there's one other thing. This damn dog. If this gal reporter hadn't kept at it, we might never have heard about the dog. Easting claims he saw Miss Thurston taking the dog to the vet's. I suppose this all fits—it was Miss Thurston who took him?"

"Oh sure," Young said. "You know how these things work, so I'm not giving away any state secrets. Some smart youth in the Crown Attorney's office looks at the evidence and sends a memo to the police, asking for more evidence on this and that. Like we found the cellar window in the driveway kicked in. How come? Well, with Easting playing the dummy for Raines's ventriloquist act, we put it to Raines. So Easting tells us sure, he tried to get in that way first. He bust the window, but the bolt was too rusted to shift, so he went to the dining room window. Which gets our boys off the hook with the Crown Attorney's office."

"And the same thing, I suppose, with the dog. I mean funny-funny-funny the burglars pick the night the dog's away."

"Oh sure," Young said. "I wasn't at the house when they checked up on the dog stuff. It was Al Borak who questioned them. But you can bet your shirt that if Easting said he saw Miss Thurston take the dog out, then it was Miss Thurston. Like to ask Borak?"

"Sure," Sidney said, and Young made a brief phone call.

"Al Borak, you old horse," Sidney said as the detective entered, and there was an effusive exchange of greetings in spite of the heat.

"Al," Young said, "Mr. Grant here is representing a poor boy who was led astray by evil companions, and he's smelling about looking for information. I told him the police have nothing to hide, so why should we worry? He wants to know who took the dog to the vet's hospital from the Thurston house—the night before the murder."

"It was the daughter," Borak said. "Martha. They wanted to have it all fixed up for the son coming home. The old lady did. She'd been bugging them all week about it."

"Oh. How did you happen to find out about the dog?" Sidney asked.

"Well," Borak said. "I was nosing around, and out in the back room—sort of a room behind the kitchen, filled with old newspapers and empty bottles—out in this room I found a basket with a green cushion in it and a rubber bone lying beside it. So I figured they had a dog."

"God!" Sidney said. "What chance does a criminal have against police work of that caliber?"

Borak reached over and seized the top of Sidney's hair with his left hand, and raised his right in a position for a judo chop.

"No, it's too hot to kill you," he said, releasing him. "Anyway, I took the basket in to this big front room and asked them where the dog was. The daughter tells me he's at this clinic. So I phoned the clinic to check the arrival time, and they tell me seven-thirty the night before. So I go back and tell them it checks and ask them who takes the dog in. The daughter tells me she does. Okay?"

"Very thorough," Sidney said. "So then someone gives this information to Raines, so that Easting can decide he saw her taking the dog."

Borak shrugged and smiled, and after that the three men went out in search of cold beer. As he drank and chatted with the detectives, Sidney thought with pity of Vince Lamberti, longing for a cold beer in the sultry and un-air-conditioned jail.

Dimly, vaguely, a plan was forming in his mind. It might not be so impossible, after all, to defend Vince Lamberti.

Six

SIDNEY EXPLAINED HIS plan to Miss Semple on the following morning.

"Our hands are tied in this case," he said. "We can't talk to Easting, we can't talk to the Crown witnesses, and Lamberti won't talk to us. But luckily we *can* talk to the police, and even more luckily Raines opened his big mouth in order to show off his silver tongue. Under the circumstances there isn't much we can do, except hope for a lucky break. But at least we have to be ready to recognize the lucky break when it appears."

"You mean it may be wearing a disguise?" Miss Semple said.

"Could be. But here's what we want: we want some way of blowing that statement of Easting's to smithereens. I think it was mainly invented by Raines and piped into Easting's mouth. I'd love to read the whole thing, but I'll bet that when I ask the Crown for particulars of the charge, they won't let me see the statement. My only knowledge of it is what Raines told me, and a bit that Frank Young gave me. We'll hear the whole thing in court—and then we've got to be ready to light on any provable falsehood in it. If we can really discredit the thing, prove that it's made out of whole cloth, then I've got a great talking point to bear down on. That statement is almost the whole case against Lamberti."

"How can you discredit the statement, do you suppose?" Miss Semple asked.

"I don't know yet. But for example, the police found a cellar window broken. I guess someone at the Crown office queried the point, so the police asked Easting—through his lawyer. Easting obligingly said, no doubt at Raines's suggestion, that he had tried to get in that way, but the bolt was too rusted.

"Now I ask you: is it likely that Easting would try to go in that way? I mean, so often the door at the top of the cellar stairs is locked; it would be silly to go in that way. Now suppose I found that some kid bust that window with a baseball on Friday afternoon or Thursday. Wouldn't that go a long way to weaken Easting's credibility? Or if I could show that the dog went to the animal clinic a lot earlier or a lot later than Easting says. Two or three provable discrepancies and the statement blows sky high. Jurors would be very reluctant to convict Lamberti on the strength of it."

"I hope you're right," Miss Semple said. "How do we go about our hunt for discrepancies?"

"How indeed? A good question." Sidney frowned in concentration for several minutes, while Miss Semple sat with pad and pencil watching him. At last a slow grin spread over his face.

"Go, Georgie," he said. "And get me an animal."

"Yes sir. Right away," she said primly, and left the office.

Sidney nearly called her back, but pride prevented him. He shuddered at the possibilities. In her more skittish moments, Miss Semple sometimes displayed an odd brand of deadpan humor. The curt order to fetch an animal might well produce dreadful results. He could well imagine a van pulling up with a crate from which strange jungle cries escaped.

The reality, however, proved to be less exotic than Sidney's imaginings. Miss Semple returned to his office in less than ten minutes carrying a large cardboard carton, well tied up and Scotch-taped. Strange noises emerged, but they were recognizable as the battle cry of the common or alley cat.

"I captured Cedric, with the help of the janitor," she said. "I presume you wish to take him to Dr. Dorothy Price's Animal Clinic. You could have his eye seen to, and I believe animals are supposed to have rabies shots."

"Cedric! Good God!" Sidney said.

Cedric was an ugly, evil-tempered beast who held *de jure* prowling rights in the group of ancient buildings where Sidney had his office. It was believed by many that at night Cedric turned into a broker-dealer.

"A taxi," Sidney said. "You're quite sure this carton is safe?"

The cab driver turned and shook his head ruefully several times during the journey at the fearsome noises coming from the carton, and he cautioned Sidney to make sure that goddam ocelot didn't get loose in his cab.

So it was with some relief that Sidney entered the clinic and put the cartoned Cedric on the counter.

A pretty young woman in a pink smock was arranging gladioli in a vase at the counter. She didn't hurry. She continued to work dreamily until the effect was what she wanted, and then she turned to Sidney and smiled ravishingly.

"Rabies shots," Sidney said. "And maybe you could put something on his eye. He's been in a fight."

"On his eye? Does he need glasses?" she said and drew a book from a drawer behind the counter.

It was a school exercise book, and Sidney noted that the pages were ruled off into columns by hand for such information as type of animal, name, age, sex, name and address of owner, type of treatment required and the time of the transaction. At the end of the previous day's transactions a line had been drawn across the page in ball-point pen, and below it was written the new day and date.

Sidney answered questions and the girl made the necessary entries and collected a ten-dollar deposit from him.

"I'll give you a receipt in a minute," she said. "Now how about yourself, sir? Are you quite well? Nose a bit dry?"

He heard her giggling as she toted Cedric in his carton to some location at the rear. He seized the counter journal and leafed through it. He was disappointed to discover that it had been opened only ten days before, or about a week after the Thurston murder. He studied it with some care until the girl returned and started to make out his receipt. He asked her if Dr. Price always used school exercise books for counter journals, but she said she was new and couldn't say.

When he had his receipt, he asked to see Dr. Price.

"She's in surgery," the girl said. "But she won't be long. Would you like to sit down and read till she's out?"

Sidney would. He read an Audubon Society journal for about ten minutes and was becoming an authority on the Ussuri raccoon dogs of Siberia when he heard sounds in an inner office, and the girl motioned him to go in.

He found Dr. Price at her desk. She was a formidable woman, large, with a high, outdoor complexion and powerful hands.

"Mr. Sidney Grant?" she said, reading his card. "Aren't you the lawyer who married Claudia Beattie's niece?"

"I am," he said.

"And you are a remarkably kind-hearted man," she said. "I mean, it isn't everybody who would wish to provide medical treatment and rabies shots for a stray tomcat. Now what do you *really* want?"

A tremor of excitement ran through Sidney. The woman was on her guard.

"I want to pin down the exact time that Mrs. Thurston's dog came here on the evening of the murder," he said.

"I have already furnished that information to the police," she said. "As I recall it, Martha Thurston brought the dog in at seven-thirty on the Friday evening."

"And were you here when she brought it?" Sidney asked.

"No. I was playing golf at Ancaster," she said.

"I believe the police called at about noon on Saturday and asked about the dog. Who talked to them?"

"I did," she said.

"So you had to ask your staff what time the dog was admitted?"

"No. I was in a hurry to get away for a tournament at London Hunt. The police called—I had no idea what it was about. The man asked if the dog was here and what time it had come in, so I went out and consulted the counter journal. But I knew all about the arrangement, you see, because I was only doing the job as a special favor to Mart Thurston."

"Oh," Sidney said. "It had been arranged in advance?"

"Yes. Mart called me early in the week. She said her mother insisted that the dog should be clipped and shampooed. Well heavens, we were short-staffed and it was really impossible, but Mart is a very old friend. So I said all right, I would be in early on Saturday to look after some other things, and I would personally clip and shampoo the damn dog if she could get it here before eight A.M. And believe me, I don't do much clipping and shampooing. So I told her that if she wanted to sleep late on Saturday morning, she could bring the dog in on Friday evening and we'd put it in a kennel."

"Who was on duty to receive the dog?" Sidney asked.

"Really, I don't see the point in these questions, Mr. Grant," she said. "In the summer I take on high school girls who think they would like to become vets. A few weeks usually cures them. I usually leave two of them on weekend duty. There's a small apartment upstairs with two beds, a kitchenette and a television. The girls keep each other company, they feed the animals and so on. Mostly they watch TV and chew gum, and there is a strict rule against male visitors. If anything goes wrong, they have a list of numbers to call. Normally they wouldn't admit any cases, but I told them to expect this dog."

"Are the girls here now? Could I talk to them?"

"No," she said. "They've both left. They wanted to have a holiday before school started, and frankly they weren't much good. Very careless and sloppy."

"Then perhaps I could see the counter journal in which they entered the admittance or admission or whatever you call it."

"Really, Mr. Grant, I have more to do than answer silly questions," she said. "However, if you want it..."

She got up a little angrily and stalked out, returning a moment later with the journal that Sidney had already seen. She handed it to him. He leafed through it and shook his head.

"Not here," he said. "This book only goes back ten days. Do you always use school exercise books on your counter?"

"Yes," she said. "I suppose I ought to ask the stationers for something ruled off the way I want it. I guess the old one was full."

"Where would it be?" Sidney asked. "Did the police impound it as evidence?"

She hesitated. She started to speak and stopped, and again Sidney felt a strange excitement. He knew that Dr. Price was toying with the idea of saying yes, the book was in the hands of the police. But he saw her reject the idea.

"I have no idea," she said. "It isn't in the drawer. It may have been thrown out. What on earth would you expect to learn from it, anyway?"

Sidney pondered the question for half a minute, and then the answer came to him in a flash. Her eyes were on his face, and he struggled to control his features.

"Nothing, I guess," he said. "I just wanted to be sure about the exact time."

But he could see that she could see that he had the answer, and as he rose to go she apologized for her abruptness, and he for his troublesomeness, and each was attempting to convince the other that the whole matter was satisfactorily closed, although each knew perfectly well that it was far from closed.

Dr. Price got up and shook hands, and Sidney went away with exciting new vistas floating before his eyes.

"We have found our discrepancy, Georgie," he told his secretary. "And it is a great big beautiful one. In fact it is so delightfully discrepant that I can't figure out all the implications."

"Do tell," she said.

"Dr. Price," he said, "gave the game away by being cautious. She was on her guard from the very start. She must have met Cedric, valuable animal, when he was being put in his cage. She recognized him for a stray. She was wondering before we met. She had something to conceal. But what? And why? I vectored in on the answer. Dr. Price has 'lost' the journal that gives the time when Chippy was admitted to the clinic. She is worried about it. Then, by golly, she asked me what on earth I would expect to find in the journal—and immediately I knew."

"What?" Miss Semple said. "For heaven's sake, don't keep me in suspense."

"The journal," he said, "would show that Chippy didn't go to the clinic until Saturday morning. A careless girl admitted the dog. She wrote down all the answers, like name, sex and so on in this journal, without bothering to rule a line across and write in the new day and date. She wrote in the time—seven-thirty. Later the line would be ruled, and Chippy would appear as the last transaction on Friday evening instead of the first on Saturday morning. When the police called and asked Dr. Price for the time the dog came in, she read the journal and was fooled, or else she lied. But I am prepared to bet that some other animal was admitted or discharged *after* seven-thirty on Friday, so Chippy's entry would be an anachronism. It would appear *after* a nine-thirty entry on the same evening. Now then, someone found it convenient to let that mistake stand. Possibly someone tried to alter the figures in the book, made a mess of it and so destroyed it.

"Now *who* was interested in letting that mistake stand? I find that Martha Thurston was trying to make an appointment to have the dog shampooed early in the week. She was the one who set the deal up. Dr. Price took the dog as a special favor to Martha. Can you see the possibilities? What was formerly a simple burglary and murder becomes something quite different."

"But heavens," Miss Semple said. "What are you trying to suggest? Isn't the heat affecting your head a little?"

"That is possible," Sidney said. "But look you here. Martha arranges for the dog to be out of the house on Friday evening. But the dog doesn't go out. Why?"

"You tell me," she said.

"All right, I will. Go back to Chippy's byline story in the paper. As I recall it, somewhere in the story Chippy revealed the fact that Mrs. Thurston would never let him be away from the house when she was there. She had great faith in him as a watchdog. Martha has arranged for the dog to be away on Friday night. But Mrs. Thurston raises hell and says they're not going to take her Chippy away, so he stays. How about that? Then Martha and Dr. Price, her old pal, decide that the dog *did* spend the night there after all. Dr. Price fires the girls who admitted Chippy, loses the journal, and everybody is happy.

"But heavenly days," Miss Semple said. "You can't suspect..."

"I can so," Sidney said. "Suspecting is a tool of my trade. The question is, did Martha expect burglars that night? Did she have a motive, perhaps, for murdering her mother?"

"Oh, don't *say* it—it's too frightful," Miss Semple said.

"I *will* say it. Was there a motive...emotional...financial?"

"Oh, good lord!" Miss Semple said. "Just one minute, please." She went out to her desk and returned with a manila folder, from which she drew a document. "Read that," she said, laying the document on Sidney's desk. "There's your motive, if you really want one."

Sidney read the document carefully, and Miss Semple watched him closely.

"Good God," he said. "Martha became a millionairess the minute her mother stopped breathing."

"Yes," Georgie said. "She did. But I don't see how she could possibly have been implicated."

"Neither can I," Sidney said. "But that's not my concern. My defense is now complete. I'm going to play a pat hand. I'm going to go into court and cross-examine everybody in that household. I daren't move before the trial otherwise I'll tip my hand. There may be some perfectly innocent answer to this flimflam about the dog. In that case, Martha Thurston or Dr. Price might, if they knew what I was up to, go to the police and put the record straight. Then the police would talk to Raines, and Easting's statement would be quietly altered.

"So what I have to do is hope that, by excluding witnesses, I can bring out in court the fact that the dog didn't go to the clinic until Saturday morning. That will, once and for all, discredit Easting's statement about seeing the animal go in on Friday so that the *judge* will warn the jury about believing the things that Easting says about Lamberti. Georgie dear, we're in pay dirt."

"Unless you've simply built a house of cards on this faint suspicion," she said.

"Faint suspicion, my foot," he said. "I'm nine-tenths certain. And Georgie, if the dog wasn't at the clinic that night, where was he? Why didn't he bark? That's another good question. The curious incident of the dog in the night."

Seven

IT WAS A TENSE AND delicate situation. Lamberti was in a spot where, according to the law, a man with the most peaceable intentions can become guilty of murder without even knowing it. And, as Sidney explained to Miss Semple, it was the one situation in which he had no ethical qualms whatever about getting his man off on a technicality. But it was necessary to tread lightly. If it was true that Martha and the vet had cooked the time of the dog's entry, Lamberti had a fighting chance, but only if Martha and the vet remained ignorant of Sidney's intention.

"Suppose," Sidney said, "we proved some sort of inside help to the burglars. Just to stretch it to the limit, let's suppose we could show that Martha collaborated with them. That wouldn't alter Lamberti's guilt or innocence in the slightest degree. The only earthly use we have for this bit of information is to blow up Easting's statement. I don't even dare to go back to Dr. Price and ask who *removed* the dog from the clinic, and when."

But there were still things to be done. In the routine way, Miss Semple always opened a file on every person connected with a case. From credit bureaus, vehicle registration offices, land registry offices and other sources she collected items and put them together. The morgues, or libraries, in newspaper offices were other useful sources, as well as the surrogate court. This type of routine enquiry took on a new importance in the Thurston case after Sidney's visit to the animal clinic.

For a couple of days he tried to plan some innocent way of asking Dr. Price about Chippy's departure from the clinic, with a view to using it when he went to collect Cedric. However, the occasion never arose, because on the Friday morning, Cedric reappeared in his usual haunts, his eye nicely healed, and a girl called from the clinic to apologize for having let the cat escape.

Sidney went off for the Labour Day weekend, the official end of summer, and he found that he was chain-smoking and had a bad case of the fidgets. He decided, with much reluctance, not to tell June about the new development, in case she might unconsciously betray some suspicion if she ran into the Thurston tribe.

But June had matters to report. When the news had reached the Thurstons that Sidney had taken on the defense of Lamberti, a strain had been placed on social relations. Martha Thurston, who was in a bad state of nerves, said to somebody who said to somebody who repeated it to Aunt Claudia that she regarded it as a personal affront that one of the Beatties (Sidney was regarded as an honorary member of the Beattie tribe) would defend the killer of her mother.

But the sensational news broke on Labour Day, the first Monday in September. Gerald and Crawford Thurston had quietly wheeled Martha away to a private mental hospital the day before. She had been found walking naked through the woods early Sunday morning, carrying a bulls-eye lantern and looking for Truth. Gossip said that her brother Crawford, having discovered that Martha was drinking in secret, had tried to cut her off the booze, and this had caused the final blow-up.

Sidney would have paid a good sum (chargeable to the Lamberti account) to know if a letter from Dr. Dorothy Price had arrived to upset Martha's applecart.

But summer was over. Cottages were being closed. The Thurston household was breaking up. Crawford went to Ottawa for several conferences and later headed back for a new appointment in Europe. Gerald sold up his Sarnia interests and moved to Toronto, where he camped in the old house for a time before shutting it up. Miss Lang moved out to a little place of her own. Mrs. Foster, the nurse, took on the care of a rich old man in Forest Hill Village. Martha had disappeared from view, to her idyllic country retreat.

There was also much activity in the Beattie clan. June Grant's brother Wes, who had been acquitted on a murder charge some months before, returned from a summer of hard work on the DEW line in the far north, twenty pounds heavier and much more self-assured than he had been for years. There was a big family party for him before his departure for the University of British Columbia. June and Sidney moved into a new apartment in the southern extremities of Rosedale, far enough from June's grandmother's house to preclude casual visiting.

The move was part of a larger strategic scheme to get rid of an old family retainer. Betty Martin, a Barnardo orphan who had labored for old Mrs. Beattie for more than half a century, had insisted on coming to keep house for "Miss June" after her marriage. The Beattie clan were heavily in debt to Betty, for once having served Wes Beattie when he was faced with a murder charge.

The arrangement had not been happy. Betty had nearly driven June up the wall by constant attention and by frequent gnomic references to the arrival of a Little Stranger, an event she coyly hoped for at the earliest moment consistent with propriety. June was in terror lest Betty, through prayer or some other unfair method, put the hex on her and ruin the coming skiing season. "Either she goes or I do," she told Sidney many times. A happy solution was found whereby Sidney and June moved into a smaller apartment, and Betty returned to the old Beattie house with the rank of housekeeper, a large bedroom and her own TV. Like the prisoner of Chillon, she had come to love her chains and was really pleased to return to the tyranny of Mrs. Beattie.

Solving the Betty problem nerved Sidney to deal firmly with another problem, namely Edith Moon, his articled law student. Miss Moon had chosen to take on the routine investigation of Easting and his family and of Lamberti and his family. For each of these tribes she produced a fat typescript bound in a red cover, complete with appendices listing source material, and richly studded with footnotes.

"I'm sorry I'm not able to do a proper sociological job in *my* little researches," Miss Semple said a little sourly. "Perhaps you would like her to start on the Thurstons now?"

"A-a-a-a, shaddap," Sidney said. He was in no mood for office politics. "Good God, she's got everything from sibling rivalries to calcium shortage in early diet. What good is all this stuff? Listen to this: 'Ample instances of a violent aggression pattern are observable in Marvin's early sibling relationships.' I suppose that means 'Gimme my goddam teddy bear or I'll punch you in the nose.' And how about this: 'Acquisitiveness, bordering on kleptomania, albeit with no hint of the substitute-crime aspects of kleptomania, were encountered in early school years when thefts from pockets in the school cloakroom were traced to

Marvin, often involving objects of little value.' How much prose do you have to wade through to get the meat of that?"

The report on the Lamberti and Ducatti families was even heavier going. Miss Moon, mounted on her hobby horse, traced the gradual integration of poor immigrant families into the Canadian way of life. Ducatti, the grandfather, for instance, had been driven by desperate poverty into certain sinister activities in youth, following (Miss Moon thought) an ancestral pattern. He had, in short, been a bootlegger during the twenties. He had worked in the U.S.A. and had been deported to Canada as an undesirable alien. Luckily he had acquired Canadian citizenship before that (or the status of a British subject, as it was then called). But having got a start in legitimate business, he had become an exemplary citizen, and all his children had become "contributing members of society" except one. An uncle of Vince Lamberti's had shown delinquent tendencies but had been successfully rehabilitated. In the next generation, however, the Ducatti and Lamberti families had produced musicians, teachers, dentists, a surgeon and other "contributing citizens," and even Vincenzo, the throwback, had shown undoubted talents before his relapse into crime.

"Dammit, I didn't ask for an M.A. thesis on citizenship," Sidney complained, and sent for Miss Moon.

Miss Moon was aloof and superior. She was very proud of her reports. Sidney showed her a report prepared by Miss Semple on Crawford Thurston, and suggested that this was the sort of thing he wanted. The information was brief and easy to absorb. Date of birth, education, whereabouts at time of crime (Paris—absolutely proved), financial position and so forth. Miss Moon curled her lip and said that any finance company snoop could do that sort of thing.

The upshot was that, after some violent words, Miss Moon not only left Sidney's office but also abandoned the study of law, and enrolled in the School of Social Work to study for her M.A. Her place was rapidly taken by a youth who had majored in snooker and beer-drinking at college but who appeared to know how many beans make five.

There was plenty of work in the office, and the Lamberti case tended to be pushed into the background, partly because of the need for discretion in the matter of the dog.

But in mid-September a development shattered the calm. It came on a golden Sunday morning, when June and Sidney were packing a picnic basket and planning an escape to the Caledon Hills. Sidney was looking out of the front window, sipping a cup of black coffee, when he saw a bright red Sunbeam Talbot sports car pull up in front. He watched a youngish man with untidy brown hair get out, but he thought nothing of it until the buzzer sounded.

"Take cover," he shouted. "We have a visitor."

But June had already pushed the answering buzzer, releasing the inner door of the apartment building. A minute later the youngish man appeared. He apologized for the Sunday morning intrusion, accepted a cup of coffee and said his name was Norris, Dr. Norris. He was he said, a psychiatrist. He had come up the day before from Sunnydene, for a party with some pals, and he was about to return.

"But I wondered, old man, if you'd mind coming with me," he said. "You see, I have a patient, a Miss Thurston, who puzzles me. Very much locked up. You, it seems, are one of her *bêtes noires*. Your name keeps cropping up. You are plotting against her. Dreadful plots. Now I know the situation, of course. No doubt she has some guilty feelings with regard to the late lamented parent. But what I want, old man, is to lead you in and say 'Here's your Gargoyle Grant' and leave you to it. In other words, I would like to precipitate the thing."

"Maybe I *am* plotting against her," Sidney said. "Maybe you'll precipitate more than you bargained for."

"I'll chance that," Dr. Norris said. "Actually, I don't think this woman is in terribly bad shape. I think we can bring her out of it. There's an element of hysteria in it. At any rate, old man, would you mind?"

It was agreed that the picnic should be transferred to the charming grounds of Sunnydene, so June, driving her Citroën, had a race with the Sunbeam Talbot, and when they arrived Sidney said he was ready to be admitted as a patient. But instead, Dr. Norris led him to a small sitting room, where Martha Thurston was smoking and twisting a handkerchief, and left him there without a word.

Eight

SIDNEY ENTERED THE little sitting room with a real sense of guilt. He had, in a half-hearted way, protested to Dr. Norris that his visit might do more harm than good to the patient. But in addition, he felt that it might do more harm than good to his client. He had nothing to gain, and everything to lose. It was probably mere curiosity that was driving him on. He felt that he was at one with poor Miss Thurston, walking naked through the woods with a bulls-eye lantern, searching for Truth.

Miss Thurston's appearance shocked him. She had lost weight. She was haggard. She was smoking her cigarettes almost inside out. As soon as she recognized her visitor, she got up and walked to the window, where she stood looking out into a garden where phlox and cosmos struggled for supremacy. At intervals she stole a furtive glance at Sidney, as if to see whether he had gone. Sidney sat down and lighted a cigarette.

"So it's me you're after now!" she said suddenly and whirled to face him. "Good. Maybe now you can leave *her* alone."

"Maybe I can," he said.

"If you've got a shred of decency you will," she said. "What did Dorothy ever do to you? Why do you snoop around her and have people following her and open her letters? Why do you do it? What do you expect to find out?"

"What *could* I find out?" Sidney said.

"Oh, *you* know very well. Dorothy lost a book, a school scribbler! *You* think that gives you a chance to help that guttersnipe you're defending, *don't* you? My brother Gerald knows what you're up to! He says you'll go into court and you'll *scream* at Dorothy and at the judge and at the jury, 'Where's the scribbler? Where's the scribbler?' And you'll make out that Dorothy's trying to conceal something and throw mud over her and us, and all to help some guttersnipe from the *Ward*."

Sidney noted the word "Ward," which was an outmoded term for an old slum area in Toronto. He hadn't heard the word for years.

"Leave Dorothy alone!" she screamed. "Dorothy's all wool, she's straight and decent and honest. You've got no right to persecute her."

"All right," Sidney said. "You can stop worrying about Dorothy. We'll see that she's absolutely protected."

"We will? *You* will? How can you do that?"

"Look, Miss Thurston," he said. "Dorothy has done nothing wrong at all. I don't think she ever said a word to the police that she didn't believe was the truth. So I don't for a minute think that she will come to any harm."

"You don't think so? Of course she told the truth. Why *shouldn't* she tell the truth?"

"Everybody should tell the truth," Sidney said righteously. "If they tell lies they get caught up in them. Now when Dorothy told the police that the dog went to her clinic on Friday night, she really believed it. That's all she ever told the police. I think it was later that she found out the dog went in on Saturday morning. Dorothy decided not to say anything about it, because if she did it might embarrass *you*. But if the police ask her again and she tells the truth, she won't have any trouble. Now *you* might have told a lie, I don't know, and if you have it will be hard for you to come forward and speak the truth. It always is."

"Yes, it always is," she said. "That's what Brown Owl said."

"Eh?"

Her statement came as a terrible shock. His wife, who had a vein of irreverence, had frequently stated that Miss Thurston was "with the birds." For a moment it struck him that she had actually been talking with them.

"When I was a girl," she said, "I stole a box of Many Flowers powder from another little girl—from her sample collection. I didn't really steal it—I didn't mean to steal it. I took it as a joke. I meant to hide it and when she missed it I'd tease her a little and then give it back. But she didn't miss it for so long that I forgot. Then there was an awful inquisition. It was in school. We used to collect samples in those days. You clipped a coupon from a magazine and sent it in with ten cents and got samples of perfume and powder and cold cream. Anyway, first thing I knew all the girls that sat near this girl were called in one by one before the principal and asked if they had taken the sample. The atmosphere was ghastly, all loaded with guilt and shame. I said no, I hadn't taken it. I lied. I sneaked the powder home and hid it. I wanted to put it in the furnace, or return it secretly. I lost weight, it was awful. They took me to the doctor. Finally I broke down at Brownies and told Brown Owl the way it had happened, and she went and told the principal, and she told me never, never again to get caught in a skein of lies. She said always to face the music right away."

"Ah!" Sidney said. "Brown Owl was indeed a wise owl"—he praised heaven that his wife wasn't present to hear him—"and if she were here right now she'd tell you to face the music again and tell me why you fooled the police about the dog."

"But I can't," she said. "Oh dear, what a horrible bloody mess! Why was I ever born?"

"You mean you can't tell," Sidney said. "Because it involves somebody else?"

She stared at him wildly and twisted her handkerchief until it ripped. "Christ!" she said. "Gerald was right! You're a weasel! You're a wretch! You came here to snoop, didn't you. You would stop at nothing."

"Look here, Miss Thurston," Sidney said. "Truth will out. Nothing you can do will prevent it. Now, you can stick with this story until the trial is in progress, and then the truth will out—perhaps after someone has committed perjury. But it *will* come out. Brown Owl was right. You may think you're in a mess, but it's nothing like the mess you'll be in if this comes out publicly in court. Now then, you've mentioned Gerald several times. It seems to me that Gerald is mixed up in this. Is it for Gerald that you and Dorothy are concealing evidence?"

She whirled about and walked back to the window, where she stood looking out at the glorious mass of color.

"Good-bye, Mr. Grant," she said. "I've said all I'm going to. You might as well go now."

"All right. Good-bye," he said. "Sorry to trouble you. You will be responsible, of course, if Dorothy Price finds herself in an awful mess. But it isn't going to help Gerald at all. Gerald will be in a worse mess."

"Go away," she said, calmly enough. "I have nothing more to say."

"Now obviously Gerald had some reason why he wanted to fool the police about the dog," Sidney continued. "Perhaps it was a perfectly innocent reason. If so, it's too bad there isn't some nice Brown Owl to tell him to face the music. Because if he doesn't, the time will come when the police will think he did it for some other reason. They will think he had a really guilty secret. So Gerald will be in a mess, and Dorothy will be in a mess, and it will be all your fault."

"It will be nothing of the kind!" she shouted, turning. "*You* can't prove anything at all. Now get out! Get out! Get OUT!" Her voice rose to a scream and her eyes were wild.

"All right, I'll go," he said. "Sorry. I just thought you might like to get everything straight and tidy. I feel quite sure that Gerald had some perfectly innocent reason…"

He let the sentence tail off as he walked slowly to the door. He had his hand on the knob when she spoke again.

"All right," she said, and he turned. She was twisting the shreds of the handkerchief. "Gerald was a fool," she said. "Just a fool. Gerald never learned about truth. He thought he could get away with a lie. But I *won't* let him drag Dorothy through the mud."

Sidney sat down and waited.

"You're right," she said. "It was perfectly innocent. You see, ever since he was a student, Gerald used to go for long walks at night. Often he couldn't sleep. And he liked to take a dog with him. All the dogs we ever had. It was a well-known habit of his. And that night, you see, he came home after we'd all gone to bed, and he took Chippy for a long walk. I heard them come in. Chippy must have smelled the burglars, because he barked and made an awful row, and Gerald had quite a job to shut him up."

"Oh, so that was it," Sidney said, and his heart sank. His defense had suddenly evaporated.

"Yes. And you see, in the morning, after we had found Mother, and the police were all over the house, we were standing in the drawing room: Viola Lang, the nurse, Gerald and I, and Gerald and I had brandy and coffee, and just then it suddenly occurred to him. He said, 'But what about Chippy? What was Chippy doing when the burglars were here?' I looked at him very severely and said, 'Gerald, you of all people ought to know what Chippy was doing.' He was in a state of nerves. He tried to play innocent, but he didn't fool me. He demanded to know what I meant.

"I said, 'Gerald, you know very well that you took Chippy for a walk. I heard you coming in.' He fumbled about and then said, 'Did I, Mart? Did I? I can't remember a thing.' Well, then he started to worry. I think I know what was on his mind. He's often done stupid things, like forgetting to lock the cottage, or not tying a boat up properly, and he hates looking like a fool. He was thinking what a fool he would look when it came out that his mother was murdered because he took the dog for a walk. People would talk.

"He came back at me. He said, 'Mart, are you sure? Do you have to tell the police? Couldn't we shut up about it?' I told him not to be a fool. I said the police would have to know why the dog didn't bark. Then he said, 'Where's Chippy now?'

"For a minute I wondered myself, and then I remembered about the clinic. I'd arranged for Chippy to go in and be shampooed. He'd been rolling in tar, and Mother insisted that he had to look his best for Crawford. She was inclined to be childish about Crawford. I had intended to take him in the night before, but Mother wouldn't hear of it. She said Viola could take him in the morning. So I called across to Viola and asked her if she'd taken the dog. She said yes, she'd got him in well before eight, as promised.

"Then Gerald said, 'Why don't we tell the police he was there all night? They'd never know the difference.' I told him not to be a fool. They'd be sure to check up, so he just stood there looking miserable and muttering. Then he tackled Viola. He asked Viola if *she* would back him up, and she laughed and said it was impossible.

"Well, that's the way things were when this detective came in carrying the dog's bed and asked us where the dog was. I told him. He never asked us *anything* about when the dog went in. He just said, 'I'll have to check that' and went out. We heard him telephoning in the hall, and then he came back and said, 'Okay, the dog went in seven-thirty last night. Who took him?' Well, I looked at Gerald's hang-dog face, and the way it suddenly lighted up with hope—he looked so pleading that I weakened. I said, 'I arranged it, Officer.' I didn't actually say I *took* the dog. I just said I arranged it. And that was all there was to it. Gerald was terribly grateful.

"Now if *I* had had my way, that would have been the end of it. Nobody would have done another thing. But Gerald just wouldn't let well enough alone. He insisted on tying up all the loose ends."

"Such as what?" Sidney asked.

"Well, the girls at Dorothy's place, for instance. They hadn't seen *me*. So he said that when he went out to get Crawford in an airport limousine, *I* should drive to Dorothy's clinic in the Pontiac and arrive at seven-thirty. I should ring the bell and go in and get Chippy. Of course the girls hadn't heard anything about the murder, and Gerald said I should act in a perfectly natural manner but drop in some harmless little remark like, 'Not quite so hot as *last* night.' The idea was to make sure the girls would recognize me again, but not to make too strong an impression. Well, fool that I am, I did it."

"It worked?"

"It must have. On Monday Dorothy got back, and believe it or not she hadn't heard a word about the murder. She had stayed at London Hunt, and she was playing golf all the time. She never looked at the papers. I was at the cottage, of course, but Gerald, the fool, came down and talked to Dorothy, taking my name very liberally in vain, telling Dorothy I was very anxious to let things stand. He looked in the journal and saw how Dorothy had made a mistake in talking to the police. You see, this book..."

"I know how the error arose," Sidney said.

"Oh, you do? Anyway, he persuaded Dorothy to cooperate. She kept the two girls on a few days, then paid them off and packed them off to one girl's cottage. And later in the week Gerald went in and stole the book, which was the stupidest thing he did. Dorothy was pretty angry about it. Well then the story came out in the papers about the dog, and Gerald was afraid the girls might get together and wreck things. So he made a journey to this lake where the girls were—colossally stupid and dangerous, if you ask me—just to check up. And he was lucky. There was a sort of jukebox dance-hall and hamburger place where all these kids hang around in Bala. Well, Gerald had got the girls' names from Dorothy, so he hung around there in a flowered shirt behaving like a silly old goat and met them. He just called himself Gerry. And so he found that the girls were telling everybody about this dog, the one that had been in the papers, and how they had admitted him and fed him, et cetera, at Dorothy's place. And he never told them who he was."

"Quite a thorough job he did," Sidney said. "Weren't you afraid of Viola Lang or the nurse spilling the beans?"

"Well, not Viola," Martha said. "She whines and complains a bit, but her heart is in the right place. Whatever the family wanted would be all right for her, and you see, she was never called on to say a word, true or otherwise."

"And the nurse?"

"*That* woman," she said, and her features worked violently. "No. *I* wasn't worried about her. I just let Gerald look after her. She'd do *anything* he said."

"Oh, *that's* the way it was," Sidney said.

She looked at him sharply and checked herself. "Well yes. She's the sort of woman that—well, men, you know. Anything that a *man* says. She sort of dropped her eyelids and exuded a sort of aura of sex whenever there was any man around the house."

"And this went down well with Gerald?" Sidney suggested.

She sat very still and looked at him for half a minute, then came to a decision. "Yes," she said. "It's too awful! His mother's *nurse*—the next thing to having an affair with his mother's *servants*. Oh, it was remarkable how much more frequent his visits were after *she* came to the house. Ostensibly he is visiting his poor sick mother—but then he sneaks off to the attic with *her*. Oh, he's just as bad, probably worse, if the truth were told. It was all very cozy, but *I* never said a word. I was simply disgusted."

"But I guess he didn't visit her on the fatal night?" Sidney said.

"Oh yes he *did*," she said, "That was why he was so guilty and hang-doggy. I think he was afraid that if the police got to investigating what went on in the house too closely, they would find out about this disgraceful clandestine affair."

"You mean, after he came back from walking the dog, he went prowling..."

"That is correct," she said. "It's rather horrible. You see, he was a bit drunk. I *suspect* he took the dog out so that he could sober up for—in order to..."

She stopped and blushed.

"Quite," Sidney said. "I know what you mean."

"Anyway, he came in the front door, that is really the side door, in the driveway, and then Chippy started barking and carrying on, and Gerald was trying to shush him. He took him into the kitchen to give him something to eat, and maybe to drink a glass of milk himself, which he used to do when he'd had too much. And then he went up to his room—he always kept his own room at home, you know—and took Chippy with him. Chippy quieted down, and a few minutes later I heard Gerald sort of drunkily groping his way up to the top floor. Heavens, I had slept right through the burglary and murder, but I heard every other sound in the house that night."

"You mean you heard him descending again?"

"Yes," she said. "And he needed *help*. *She* was helping him down the stairs and saying Shhh. I heard her help him into his room and then creep back upstairs. So now you know the whole horrible story. I don't mind, if only you'll see that poor Dorothy Price doesn't have any further embarrassment. And please, if you can, don't drag these nasty details out in court."

"I will do my very best not to," he promised. "Now then, I have some free advice for *you*. Write at once, today, to brother Gerald and tell him to go to the police and tell them frankly about the dog. Tell him to tell Dr. Price what he is doing. And don't give the matter another minute's worry."

❀ ❀ ❀

They had their picnic with Dr. Norris in the hospital grounds. June believed that the one essential for a good picnic was iced champagne, so it was a very happy little party. Sidney told Dr. Norris that Martha Thurston had got certain matters off her chest, but did not specify. He thought—but wisely did not say—that by helping her to unburden herself he might have improved her mental condition. When a report came through later in the week that she was much worse, he was glad he hadn't spoken.

As soon as he and June got away from the hospital, she set to work to interrogate him. He told her all that he had been concealing, about his visit to the animal clinic, his suspicions and their confirmation. In spite of himself, he was in a high state of excitement.

"I gambled," he said. "I tossed away a nifty little defense. And I thought I'd lost. There was a perfectly innocent explanation—Gerald, in accordance with long habit—had taken the dog for a walk. But NOW what have I got? June darling, this new thing is staggering! How come Gerald was so desperate to conceal the fact that he'd taken the dog for a walk? He behaved like an utter idiot. Martha was much smarter. She was all for letting it ride. But Gerald even sneaked around checking up on the girls. He went to this place in Bala..."

"Very simple for him," June said. "A short ride from his cottage by car or motor boat. And you could bet on finding a teenage girl in Dunn's Pavilion."

"Yes. But the point is, *why*? Now, when I knew that Martha was fiddling with the evidence about the dog, I wasn't too excited. I mean, I couldn't, by the wildest stretch of the imagination, figure how she could be in any way implicated in the crime. But Gerald is a different kettle of fish entirely. It would be possible to formulate a very coherent case with Gerald right in the middle of it. Head down by the lakeshore and we'll stop by the office. I'll get out Gerald's file and show you. He had motive, opportunity and everything."

"Motive for what?" June asked.

"Murder," Sidney said.

"Murder? You mean killing his own mother? Gerald?"

"Yes ma'am."

"But Easting killed her. He's confessed," she reminded him.

"I know. That poses a difficulty, but probably not an insuperable one. It seems to me a possibility that Gerald might have organized a burglary so that *he*, or an accomplice, could murder the old lady. But wait. We'll get the file."

June remained dubious, but when she looked at the contents of the file on Gerald Thurston she shook her head in amazement.

"Maybe he played wolf to Easting's Red Riding Hood," she suggested.

"How do you mean?" Sidney said.

"Well, he hired these burglars to rob the house," she said. "Then he rushed home, strangled his mother and shoved her under the bed. Then he jumped into bed, and when Easting arrived, he grabbed him by the arm. Easting seized his throat and said, 'Oh Granny, what a big Adam's apple you have.' 'All the better to tempt you with,' says Gerald..."

"Will you shut up, woman?" Sidney said. "The question now resolves itself thus. Martha writes to Gerald and tells him the game is up. Does Gerald go to the police and tell the truth like an innocent man who's behaved foolishly, or does he panic—draw a lot of money and run away to Mexico or Brazil, or murder Martha, or me? The next move is up to Gerald, and if Gerald decides to sit tight, then I am going to have some real fun in court. Now I have to watch closely for signs of Gerald having told all to the police."

But the week crept along and there was no sign of activity. Sidney began to wonder if Martha had actually written to her brother. He salved his conscience with the thought that he had, quite properly, advised Martha that the police should be told, but tended to cling to the hope that either she or Gerald would decide not to follow his advice. Friday came, and still no word, and on Friday evening Sidney and June went to a cocktail party. Cocktails, six till eight, the invitation said, but nobody took it very seriously.

Nine

THE GRANTS ARRIVED just before seven, when the party was getting into full swing. It was the first real wingding of the season, and people were excitedly telling each other about their summer adventures all over the world.

"What a blessing they're not allowed to bring their color transparencies," June said.

At eight o'clock the party was going well. A few guests left for dinners, but more arrived to replace them. At nine the hostess produced, as by magic, some *vol-au-vents*, which she had filled with some sort of cream chicken, small rolls and various other edibles that added up to a good dinner. And the party rolled on.

Other guests began to arrive, people who had been to other cocktail parties, and then people who had been out to dinner. It was that sort of affair. June, who was incurably convivial, loved it.

Shortly after ten o'clock Sidney looked up to see Gerald Thurston entering the room with a male companion. Gerald looked as though he had come from two other cocktail parties and hadn't had any dinner. He was in a heavily jocular mood. He went about kissing women and wringing men's hands, but at intervals he paused and looked sad and sober. Sidney deduced that these were moments when people had said, "Gerald, I was terribly sorry to hear about your mother," and Gerald had to demonstrate that beneath his great jocularity there lay a deep sadness—although he was too much of a gentleman to let his private sorrow spoil the party. In due course Gerald's orbit brought him face to face with Sidney. He stopped, straightened up to attention, and all but clicked his heels. He gave a stiff little bow, such as one might expect a belligerent ambassador to give to the ambassador of an enemy country at a party in some neutral capital.

"Ah! Mr. Grant," he said. "A pleasure, sir."

Sidney extended a hand, which Gerald Thurston ignored, and Sidney left his hand extended for some time, examining it, before he murmured, "Must remember to wash when I come out." Having said it, Sidney realized that he, as well as Gerald, had had a drink or two, and was on the borderline of juvenile behavior. Gerald moved on, but a moment later he remarked to somebody, in a voice with some carrying power, "Charming to meet the defender of one's mother's murderer at a cocktail party." He repeated the remark, or variations of it, at intervals, creating much consternation and embarrassment—but, if the truth were told, adding a new zest to the party.

June, who could be a happy hoyden on occasion, was no encourager of trouble at parties. As soon as she was aware of what was going on, she crossed the room, seized her husband's sleeve and said, "We're on our way, Bub." But Sidney planted his feet firmly and refused to budge.

Later she told Sidney that it all seemed like a scene from an adult western. The bad guy was parading the main drag in front of the saloon with his guns in his holsters. The good-guy sheriff's wife was clinging to his knees saying, "Don't go, Lemuel, what sense is there in all this killin'?" But the good-guy sheriff, though he agreed with his wife, was setting his jaw and strapping on his gun belt, because some deep inner male categorical imperative forced him to take up the challenge.

But in fact, it was something more than the male prejudice against being outfaced that kept Sidney where he was.

"Lookit, Gorgeous," he whispered. "These are the kind of troubled waters I like to fish in."

"Oh God," she said. "He'd eat you in one bite if it came to trouble."

"I bet I'd be delicious," Sidney said. "Look, sweetie, I'm agonna haid out to the kitchen, walkin' slow and stiff-laiged like, see? Five bucks says Gerald follows me. He's in the mood to light into me. I'm on his mind. When he follows me, you seal off the kitchen. Bar ingress to all. Got it?"

"Aye aye sir," she said. "But remember he's big and strong."

"I'll bet I can run faster," Sidney boasted, and strolled off a trifle ostentatiously.

The kitchen was empty. He looked about, then opened the fridge in order to inventory his hostess's larder. While he was at it he heard a heavy step behind, and Gerald Thurston's voice spoke up.

"Well well," Gerald said. "Mr. Grant, as usual, snooping."

"Good evening," Sidney said, turning and slamming the fridge door.

"Good evening," Gerald said meditatively. "Yes indeed, an excellent evening. And it so happens that I bump into the very man I've been wanting to see. There's a little something I want to say to you, Grant."

"There is? Well by all means say it."

"I certainly intend to. Nothing shall stop me," Gerald said, taking a gulp of his whiskey. "Grant, I'm no in a mood to mince words. I happen to know a little bit about the law. I know, for instance, that there's a rule, or a convention or something, that the counsel for an accused person can't go about questioning Crown witnesses. But leave that, for the moment. Among gentlemen there are certain rules of chivalry. I mean, for instance, that a gentleman doesn't go bullying women, especially women who, by reason of their nervous condition, have been placed in rest homes or mental hospitals. But it appears to me that neither the rules applicable to lawyers nor the rules of gentlemanly conduct mean anything at all to you. Isn't that right?"

"If you intend to employ the Socratic method during this conversation," Sidney said, "I shall have to demand you abstain from asking leading questions."

Gerald Thurston paused to figure that one out, and the pause was fatal. He was unable to regain the original impetus or the air of loftiness.

"Look here," he said. "You wangled your way into Sunnydene to see Martha. Now, we knew you'd been snooping around Dotty Price's dump looking for anything you could get hold of. In order to defend this thug, you thought you might throw some mud at *us*, because that's great stuff; smear a prominent family and make good newspaper copy. Oh great! So you get hold of a trifle and blow it way up big. Martha was in a depressed state. Her nerves are terrible. The thing preyed on her mind and she started imagining things.

"So that was bully for you. I don't know how you did it, but someone's going to have his tits in the wringers for helping you. Anyway, you got in to see poor old Mart, and you bullied her and badgered her and played on these morbid imaginings until she practically *believes* this yarn about the dog. Well don't worry, she won't be able to give evidence, so you won't have any way of making capital of it. You can just feel happy that you've helped to destroy my sister's mind. Now I'm telling you that since your visit her condition has deteriorated very, very considerably, and I hold you, personally, responsible. That is something that will be gone into thoroughly at the proper time, and in the proper place.

"But meanwhile there is this smear attempt of yours. It's going to bounce back on you in a way you never imagined. You want to pillory a fine old family—yes, I'll say it—a fine old family, to help a thug. Well, every decent person in this town who *is* anybody will turn away from you in disgust. That's going to hurt your wife, because *she* happens to come from a fine old family too. After this thing is over you'll be happy to creep away and live at Baby Point or even Balmy Beach.

"But that isn't all. I propose, without delay, to inform John Massingham about your activities and see just what action should be taken against a lawyer who flouts the rules and betrays his trust and takes advantage of his position the way you have done. And it just may happen that you'll find yourself selling encyclopedias for a living before Christmas."

He paused and finished his drink, then looked around himself owlishly. His face was red and he was sweating freely after his effort, which he had evidently enjoyed.

"There's a bottle of Scotch by the stove over there, if you're looking for a refill," Sidney said.

"Thank you so much for your consideration," Gerald said, striding to the bottle and pouring a large jolt into his glass.

"Ice?" Sidney asked and fished two loose cubes from the tray in the fridge. "Excuse my fingers," he added. Gerald held out his glass and allowed Sidney to drop the ice in. Then he paused, stared at Sidney and held his breath, as if trying to get up steam again.

He resumed his harangue, but in a lower, more reasonable voice. "Now," he said gently. "Let us examine the actual ploy you are trying to pull off. You are trying to suggest—and you've succeeded in the case of my sister—that there was some funny business connected with the dog. Chippy, Chippewa to give him his full name. And what have you got to go on? The fact that some record or other is missing. Now wouldn't you get a nasty shock if that record turned up? Stranger things have happened. But leave that for the moment. *You* are trying to insinuate that the dog did not go to the vet's until Saturday morning. Isn't that it? Well, there will be several witnesses who will put *that* one straight—including, Mr. Grant, the girls who admitted the dog to the clinic.

"But what is of vastly more importance is this: I happen to have connections, and it has come to my ears, never mind how, that Marvin Easting, the accomplice of your distinguished client, has formally stated to the police that *he* saw Mart taking the dog in on the Friday evening, which is the reason that your Mr. Lamberti was able to work up sufficient courage to send his stooge in to rob our house. Now, against *this* array of evidence, what chance do you think you've got?"

A tremor of excitement ran through Sidney. Gerald Thurston had completely missed the point. Sidney realized that he had him on toast.

"It looks a bit difficult, doesn't it?" he said.

"Im-bloody-possible," Gerald said emphatically. "Now then. I've very nearly said my say. Where's your glass? Grab that one, and we'll pour ourselves a little shot. Say when. Thanks, two lumps. Okay, cheers. Now you listen to me."

Gerald Thurston's manner was suddenly confidential, almost avuncular.

"Now then, Sid," he said. "There's no goddam reason whatsoever for any trouble between *us*. I've showed you how this deal of yours isn't going to work; it just won't come off. Furthermore, I've showed you how it would rebound on you and June if you tried it. Now what I suggest is this. That you and I, here and now, come to a gentleman's agreement and shake hands on it, as follows: You drop this dog nonsense, and I will forget about your improper conduct in wangling your way in to see my poor sister in her disturbed state. Now how's about that, boy? Is it a deal?"

"No," Sidney said sadly. "No deal. No dice. And if you like, we can go and phone the Crown Attorney right now at his house and you can give him the whole story."

"Very well, you have made your choice," Gerald said, drawing himself stiffly to attention. "You have made your bed, you can lie in it. Your blood be on your own head. I wash my hands of it. But I'm going to do nothing tonight. You've been drinking, Grant, you're not in a fit state to make a decision. Go home. Talk it over with June. Be honest with her. Tell her of the possible consequences to herself and her family. I will give you until noon on Monday to make your final decision. After that I shall be forced to act. It will be my plain duty to act."

"Good," Sidney said. "Well, you don't really need to wait. My decision will be the same on Monday as it is now."

"Nevertheless," Gerald said with heavy magnanimity, "I am allowing you those days of grace, for sober reflection, and in the hope that June will make you see sense."

He tried to turn smartly on his heel to perform his exit, but unhappily the kitchen tiles were slippery and he staggered badly, ruining the effect. Sidney followed him out and found June in conversation with the hostess in the kitchen doorway. He signaled her that it was time to go, thanked his hostess and made for the door. Gerald had returned to the bar in the living room and was kissing a new arrival at the party. The Grants left quietly. It was midnight, and the party was beginning to warm up.

❀❀❀

At home they made coffee and drank it at the kitchen table.

"Can he really make trouble for you?" June asked.

"It's possible. But I'm not going to worry about it. The fool doesn't know what he's doing. He's showing pretty convincing signs of guilt. He's panicky. Anything to cover up that business of the dog. He may run his head into the noose yet."

"You don't mean that he was involved in the crime?" June asked.

"Well—you've read the file. Plenty of motive, plenty of opportunity, a possible inside accomplice—and all this guilty behavior afterward. But you see, if he's guilty of anything, it's premeditated murder. There is simply no chance that he was interested in the proceeds of the burglary. Damn it, I'd love to have half an hour alone with Easting. Or get Lamberti to open up. Ah well, the one bright spot is that Gerald may haver along until the trial without taking any action. He may just hang on and hope that everything will right itself—and if he does, God help him when I get him in court. I'll disarticulate him at every joint."

"You damned sadist," she said.

"Call me a sadist again," he replied, "and I'll burn your other hand off."

They talked of other things, then went to bed. It was a glorious weekend, and they spent Saturday at a friend's house in the country. They hardly referred to the Thurston case until Sunday afternoon, when June looked out the window and said, "Heavens! Hide, Sidney! Here's Gerald Thurston arriving, trailing a big rawhide horsewhip."

"Aha!" Sidney said. "Put the kettle on, woman. I can foresee an interesting little tea party."

Gerald Thurston was completely sober, and on his best behavior. He was nicely spruced up and made a fine figure of a man.

"Ah, Juney!" he said, for it was June who opened the door for him. "I just dropped in for a little visit. I wondered if you might even find a cup of tea for me."

Friday evening was completely forgotten. He came into the living room, shook Sidney's hand, called him "Sid, old man" and sat down. June suggested that he might prefer something other than tea, but he said no thank you, he felt just like a good cup of tea.

They sat and talked of the usual things: Tobin Rote, Jackie Parker and other cultural topics. Sidney waited, perfectly composed, to hear the real reason for the visit.

It came as Gerald passed his cup for the third time.

"By the way," he said. "Sorry about the other night, old man. I had drink taken, you know, and I didn't mean all that. Actually I knew enough about you to know that it's useless to threaten you."

So now, Sidney said to himself, we'll see what a little bribery can achieve. He exchanged a glance with June, whose face showed that the same thought had occurred to her.

Gerald launched indirectly into the matter by talking about his business interests, He had owned two small companies in Sarnia, but since his mother's death he had sold them at a handsome profit. He was now interesting himself in a number of enterprises in Toronto. Companies were being formed. There was much legal work...

He paused and sipped at his tea.

"I was talking about you with my business associates, Sid. They say you are really one smart lawyer."

Much of this new legal work could be passed Sidney's way. There would be retainers, and lots of registration fees and such like. Sidney shook his head sadly. "Gerald, old man," he said. "Let's save some time. Does this handsome offer of yours entail, perchance, an agreement to let certain other matters drop? Because if it does, the answer is still no dice. As a matter of fact this type of commercial work isn't in my line anyway."

"Sid, I'm sorry to hear you say that," Gerald said.

Sidney sat thinking for a minute, while Gerald stared into his teacup, as if to read the future.

"Gerald," Sidney said at last. "I am going to take a big gamble. I don't quite know why I'm doing it. Perhaps I should just let you continue your Gadarene rush down the slope to destruction. But I ain't agonna do it. I am going to level with you. As you mentioned, I am not permitted by the rules to go about interrogating the prosecution witnesses. So I'm not going to ask you questions. I'm going to *tell* you the questions you will have to answer in court, and furthermore I'm going to tell you the answers you'll have to give. And when I finish, you will either be on your way to Brazil or on your way to common sense."

"My dear fellow, this is strange talk indeed," Gerald said, casting a smirking glance at June.

"You think so? Well you ain't heard nothin' yet," Sidney said. "Now in a few short weeks you're going to find yourself in the witness box, facing me. And straight off the reel I'm going to establish how the death of your mother affected your financial position."

"Favorably, naturally. Everyone knows that," Gerald said.

"But not everyone knows just *how* favorably. I will ask you about your financial position on the Friday afternoon, the day of the murder. I will ask you about the fourteen writs issued against your companies by various creditors. I will ask you whether your bank had called your loan. I will ask about your personal finances, your overdue department store and credit card accounts. I will ask you if you had not been warned that further use of certain credit cards would be regarded as fraud. I will demonstrate, old man, that you and your companies were bankrupt and that you were even strapped for cigarette money. You had even reached the stage where you were frightened to borrow ten bucks from an acquaintance, because word was racing round that you were in Queer Street. That can all be established very satisfactorily."

"I imagine it can," Gerald said nonchalantly, lighting a cigarette.

"In other words, nothing could have saved you from bankruptcy and disgrace on the Monday morning but the death of your mother during the weekend. I will, of course, be forced to ask you if, having a rich mother, you did not ask her for assistance to bail you out of your financial difficulties. You can, of course, say that you never asked her, that you were too proud to ask her, that you wanted to paddle your own canoe. But since your own canoe had been sinking for months, I don't think anyone will believe that you *didn't* try to bite your mother's ear."

"No, they won't. And as a matter of fact, I *did* try to bite her ear, fifty times. But she was old and crotchety and you couldn't even get her to listen. She used to make poor mouth. She'd tell me she couldn't even pay her doctor's bill—and—well, wait until her estate is probated. She had a couple of hundred thousand in a savings account, among other goodies."

"Well, having established that, we shall bring out the happy circumstance that you and Martha and Crawford were all millionaires on Monday morning."

"And now then, since I can see the direction you're heading in," Gerald said, "let me interrupt a minute. You say that I became a millionaire on Monday morning. That is true. That was money that was coming to *me*—my one-third interest in a trust. Mother had held a life interest. You ought to know that, if the worst came to the worst—oh, I was a bit tight for money, no question—but if the worst came to the worst, I could always borrow for accommodation against my expectancy on that estate. All I had to do on Monday morning was to go downtown and give my S.O.S. in the right quarter and everything would have been hunky dory. Actually, for sound reasons, I had postponed that step until the very last moment."

"And to all of that, sir, I say hogwash," Sidney said. "You couldn't borrow a nickel against that estate. Your father left the house, the summer cottage and a goodly sum of money in trust. All maintenance, heating, et cetera, for the house and cottage were to be paid by the trust. Your mother had a home for life in the house and cottage. The three children also retained a right to their rooms while they remained unmarried."

"Or became unmarried again, as I did twice," Gerald said. "And of course if Crawford had turned Arab and brought four wives home, he still would have owned the joint."

"Indeed? Well now. On the death of your mother, the trust automatically became the property of the surviving children—or on her remarriage, for that matter. But if one of the children, or more, predeceased her, then his share, if he had no issue, simply went to swell the kitty. But if he had issue, then his children automatically inherited. Now you have three children by your first marriage. If you had died before your mother—or even within forty-eight hours of her death—then no money whatsoever would have passed to your estate. It would have gone direct to your kids. And I don't think their mamma would have countenanced the paying of your debts out of their money, any more than the courts would have. So anybody who lent you money against that inheritance was simply gambling on you outliving your mother. There was no way you could secure them. So having dealt with that aspect, let's get on with it. Bankrupt Friday, millionaire Monday. Motive? Plenty.

"Next point. We ask you if you knew of your brother's impending visit. You say yes, of course. In fact, your aim in coming to Toronto that weekend was almost certainly to see Crawford. You wanted to beg Crawford to use his influence on your mother. You wanted to urge on him the fact that your bankruptcy would reflect on the family and wouldn't help his career. I believe he's ambitious."

"You're damn right he is, and he's a cold fish too," Gerald said. "And you're absolutely right. I came down to try to talk Crawford into helping."

"Good. Now we ask you if you knew, early in the week—through a phone conversation with Martha—that the dog was going into the clinic on Friday evening. You can take your chance on denying that, if you like, as Martha won't be in court."

"Since it is true, I shall certainly not deny it," Gerald said.

"Good. Now then, Crawford was to arrive Saturday evening, but *you* came to Toronto on Friday evening. Why, I wonder. To visit your mother? But you didn't go home until the wee small hours. Furthermore, you took desperate measures to get to Toronto on Friday evening. You didn't even have enough cash in your pocket to buy a bus ticket—so you drove up in your own car."

"Now how do you happen to know that, and what of it, anyway? What is more natural than that I should drive up in my own car?"

"It was a grave risk," Sidney said, "seeing that your driver's license was under suspension. If you'd been stopped, you'd have gone to jail, very likely."

"That's true. But who told you I drove up?" Gerald asked. "I never even told Martha."

"I ought to leave you mystified, but I won't," Sidney said. "You drove up and left your car in some garage over the weekend. On Monday morning, just to get some cash in your pocket, you took the car out to the Danforth and sold it for what you could get. I guess the man didn't believe that a seven-year-old Buick really only had twenty-seven thousand miles on it, or he might have given you more. I went out and had a look at the car, and it was a real bargain. But you couldn't have sold it on the Danforth on Monday morning if you hadn't brought it up Friday."

"By God sir," Gerald said, "you're a pretty deadly operator. It's true enough. When my license was suspended, I just hung on to the old heap for emergencies and never traded it. Sometimes I'd get an employee to drive me to Chatham or somewhere in it."

"All right," Sidney said. "At the risk of a jail term, you drove up Friday, the day before your brother was due. But you didn't go straight home. Now, from other evidence, I hope to show that, as Martha says, you sneaked home and took the dog for a long walk. Then I will show that during the following week you made two visits to the animal clinic. I can't prove that you stole the counter journal, but I can strongly suggest it. I *can* prove that you went to Bala to talk to the two girls who were on weekend duty at the clinic when the dog was admitted. You probably wore sunglasses and hoped to remain anonymous, which is a good way of making yourself conspicuous.

"But the other question I will have to ask you is: Have you ever been convicted of an offense? You will have to say yes, of course."

"You won't mind hitting below the belt, will you?" Gerald said.

"No, not a bit," Sidney said. "I will have to show that you did six months in Guelph..."

"On a traffic charge," Gerald put in.

"Yes, on a traffic charge, but it gave you the chance to meet the rising young generation of criminals who were in for other things. Now then, that will be all I'll need. When I talk to the jury I will point out that Easting's alleged confession is palpable balderdash and unworthy of any credence. I will then outline a hypothesis. Gerald Thurston was broke and desperate. His mother had refused all help. Her refusal destroyed the last shred of his filial sentiment. When he heard that, for one night, the watchdog would be away, he got in touch with old underworld acquaintances. He bird-dogged them onto a rich store of furs. He told them that they would find the house empty, the family away. He had an accomplice—his mother's nurse, with whom he had been having an affair—"

"God damn you and god damn that sister of mine," Gerald said. "Does poor Edna have to be dragged into the mud..."

"Yes," Sidney said. He was warming up to his work. "This accomplice saw that everyone in the house had a heavy dose of sedative. Gerald, desperately trying to straighten his affairs, stayed in Sarnia until the last minute. Perhaps he meant to stay all night, who knows? But his accomplice phoned him in Sarnia with bad news: Mrs. Thurston refused to let the dog out of the house. Or perhaps, after Gerald arrived in Toronto, he phoned his accomplice and she told him then. He had been drinking and wasn't thinking too straight. The only thing he could think of was to rush home and take the dog for a walk. His sister, in spite of her sedative, woke up and heard him.

"That cleared the way for the burglars. Very cleverly the burglars had been directed to the wrong bedroom—an empty bedroom. The nurse put the furs and jewels there, and got into the bed. As soon as her ears told her that the burglar had pocketed the jewels, she reached out and seized him. He pushed her and ran. She remained quiet. It was dark; the burglar was young and confused, and he thought he might actually have strangled a woman. But the woman had already been strangled, by somebody else. Which explained Gerald's guilty conduct in the days that followed."

During his recital Sidney had got up and walked about, dramatizing the whole scene, and Gerald had sat back turning paler and paler, and beginning to tremble a little.

"And there, My Lord, is our case," Sidney said.

"Jesus H. Christ," Gerald said. "You son of a bitch, Sid. Oh you son of a bitch. You bastard, you'll ruin me. Everyone will believe it. June, take that bloody tea tray to hell out of here and bring me a whiskey. God almighty, Sidney, you've got me by the short and curly hairs, and no bloody mistake. Now listen, just tell me one thing, Sid. Do you believe this stuff yourself?"

Sidney sat down and grinned. "I respectfully decline to answer," he said, "on the grounds that my answer might tend to incriminate you. Now, old man, the next move is up to you."

June arrived with a tray of Scotch, ice and glasses to replace the tea tray.

Ten

DRINKS WERE POURED. Gerald Thurston wandered about the room cursing, while Sidney sat in a yoga crouch in his chair.

"Okay, okay, I get the message," Gerald said. "The game is up. What do you want?"

"Well, what I would like best would be for you to punch me on the nose and dash madly off screaming, 'Foiled! Curses!'" Sidney said. "And then I would like to hear that you've been recognized on the beach at Rio de Janeiro. Failing that, I'd like to hear the truth about all this."

"The truth?"

"Yes. And in leveling with you, I'm giving up a trump card that I intended to play for my client. And I'm doing it on a hunch. Now how about it?"

"All right," Gerald said. "You've got me. I know when I'm licked. We cooked the business of the dog's absence, and I tried to cover up. And I'll tell you why."

"Good. Tell ahead," Sidney said.

"Pretty well everything you said was true," Gerald said. "I *was* broke. I was strapped for even pocket money. I was scared to borrow bus fare, for fear of causing more rumors about me. I had lunch on Friday in Port Huron, Michigan, with a lumber tycoon. I hoped he was going to tide me over. He ate a thirty-dollar lunch and laughed at me. I wanted to get out of Sarnia, because people were coming around asking me questions. The only credit card I had that was any good was my gasoline card. I wheeled out my old Buick and headed for Toronto. I got there without incident. I heaved a mighty sigh of relief and shoved the car into the King Edward garage. But I couldn't face going home.

"You were quite right. I had bugged the old lady for months, but she wouldn't even listen. She'd say, 'Well you can't be a very good businessman, after all you could never even keep your room tidy, so I'm not going to throw good money after bad, and anyway I haven't got it.' I knew I'd lose my temper, so I went to the Armed Forces Club, the one spot I could drink on credit, and met a few comrades in arms who were summer bachelors. We tied one on, and then I staggered home. Someone drove me as far as the corner of Mount Pleasant and Elm, from which point I walked.

"But on Saturday morning, when I woke up, I couldn't even remember *that*. Did you ever have a mental blackout after a heavy evening?"

"Yes, I've had memory lapses," Sidney admitted.

"All right, you know then. I woke up at some ungodly hour with a splitting headache and a mouth like a hyena's armpit, and I couldn't remember a damn thing from the night before from about ten o'clock on. Not that I wanted to. I couldn't get back to sleep, because this blasted power mower was whining away outside, and a power mower is the most fiendish machine on earth to sleep against, because it pauses and the motor races and it turns and changes pitch, and finally you give up. So I crawled downstairs in my dressing gown and bumped into, of all people, my sister, Martha, also in dressing gown and also very palpably hung over. And we both bump into Edna the nurse, looking cool, crisp and efficient, and she turns on the sympathy and says, 'Let me make you coffee.' Martha says, 'Very good, Nurse,' in her snootiest manner. 'Bring it to the drawing room,' she says. Then she mutters 'That woman!' in a nasty way. Anyway, we got our coffee. While we were drinking it, around eleven maybe, the doorbell rings. I go. It's the cops. God, I nearly flipped! You see, I couldn't remember a damn thing about the night before. I wondered if I'd driven the car home and pranged it, or if I'd been in a brawl. The guy told me we'd had a burglary, and that, believe it or not, was a tremendous relief. They came in, and I had the impression of dozens of little detectives eighteen inches high scampering hither, thither and yon.

"So in the midst of this fog, I'm herded upstairs into Mother's bedroom, and there she is looking very, very dead indeed. Hellishly dead. Now I'll tell you frankly, the first awful thought that struck me was: Did I come home loaded, go to her room, get in an argument, blow my cork and throttle her? Now that's an awful thing to admit, but right then I—well, it crossed my mind.

"Look here. I was in a business war. I had big competitors that were trying to drive me to the wall. I was fighting back. Some contracts went bad. People let me down. I lived up to my contracts, and lost money. If I could have had sixty or seventy thousand dollars working capital, I could have won through. There was the old girl, absolutely loaded, but I couldn't get her to listen. She only wanted to tell me that Crawford and Gloria had given a dinner for Prince Whumpo or some damn thing. It was always this way. I win the middleweight boxing championship at school. 'Oh, very nice dear. Now what was I saying?' Crawford gets a B for his damn composition and she phones up all her friends and brags. My Oedipus complex was well under control before the age of puberty. So anyway, awful as it seems, when I saw my mother lying strangled, I wondered for a horrible moment if I'd done it!"

"It must have been a horrible moment," Sidney said.

"You're damn right it was. Look, you can't face financial disaster all summer, the way I did, and know that one life stands between you and rescue, and not have the odd terrible thought cross your mind. I just don't believe it's possible."

"I'm sure it's absolutely *im*possible," Sidney said.

"Okay, and so, when this happened, great goddam spasms of guilt swept over me. Were you ever in school when the teacher said, 'Some boy has stolen such and such,' and although you're innocent, you blush, and you figure guilt is writ large on your countenance?"

"I have had that unhappy experience," Sidney said.

"Well, okay, that was me. Guilt in my soul, guilt all over my face, and scared stiff the police would see it. So, still feeling terrible guilt qualms, I am down in the drawing room, nursing a much-needed brandy, and still trying to figure out what I'd been doing the night before, when a thought flits through my mind, and I say to sister Martha, 'But Chippy. What was Chippy doing when the burglars were here?' And you really need to know Martha to understand the rest of it.

"Look, to the pure all things are pure. Well, Martha is pure, oh, lily white, a lady of the highest principle, who can't stand deception, deceit, lies or anything second-rate. But goddam it, all things are not pure to Martha. She suspects. Awful things like sex and greed and self-will lurk everywhere. I, her brother, am constantly under suspicion. So Martha turns and looks at me with those accusing, angry eyes and, says, 'Gerald, you of all people ought to know!' I say, 'Me? How should I know?' And she starts in, 'Oh Gerald, you're not going to try to lie.' I get a little angry. I ask her what the hell she's driving at, and she tells me I took the dog for a walk. She heard me bringing him in. And then I turn sick. I very nearly tossed my cookies. Because *then* the whole lurid picture swam before my aching eyeballs."

He turned and extended his glass to June, who took it and recharged it.

"Yes, I saw it all," he continued. "Me. Monday morning. Phoning creditors, et cetera. Saying, it's okay, you'll get your dough in a day or so. Everything's fine. My mother's been murdered. And then they read in the paper that I conveniently took the dog for a walk. Hell, there was gossip as it was. Pretty lucky for old Thurston that someone bumped his mother at the right moment. Damn it, guilt, fear and hangover possessed my soul. I had the wind up the whole way. And like a fool I pleaded with Martha. She was stern, pure and obdurate. I tackled Viola Lang, who had taken the dog in early that morning. She was much more sympathetic, but against Martha's stony purity I could get nowhere.

"And the guilt was getting worse, because the first flashback had just whickered through my brain. I could dimly remember Chippy barking in the hall, and me telling him to shut up, and taking him to the fridge and feeding him. Oh God! All was lost. I argued and pleaded with Martha, and then, by God, I threatened her! But all I got was this: as you know, I wanted her to tell the police the dog had been away all night. Well, after I blackmailed her, she changed from 'I wouldn't dream of deceiving the police' to 'But they'd be bound to check up and find out.' Big step, all same. Then the cop came in with Chippy's bed, and I gather you know what happened. He got the thing twisted, and Martha allowed it to ride. Then I realized that my action might look guilty—hell, I still *felt* guilty—and I did these damn fool things to cover up. And that, sir, is the way it happened. Yes, please, Juney, another large one."

Sidney also passed his glass.

There was a long silence.

"Interesting," Sidney said, breaking it, "that you were able to blackmail your sister."

"Yes, isn't it?" Gerald said. "But ah! We all have our little weak spots, and I happened to have found hers, and I used it with complete unscrupulousness, because, you see, I was scared of being put in a false position. I mean, I still couldn't remember what I'd done the night before. Now don't start asking me what it was I used against Martha. It had nothing to do with the business at all, so it shall remain buried. Hah! Martha the pure didn't mind telling you about me having a little cuddle with Edna, but that doesn't mean I have to drag out all *her* guilty secrets into the light."

Naturally, at that moment, Sidney wanted above all things to know what Martha's guilty secret was, but he decided not to ask at the very moment when Gerald was congratulating himself on the superiority of his principles over those of Martha.

So he said nothing, and Gerald paced about the room for a minute. When he sat down again, he changed the subject completely.

"You know, it's funny," he said. "This sister of mine talks about facing the music and 'fessing up like a little man. Well damn it, *I* once had the choice of facing the music or running out. I chose to face the music. The truth shall make you free, they say. Well it bloody well put me behind bars for six months. No, it didn't. *I* told the truth, but other witnesses choosing to lie, I went into stir, and not a damn soul will believe me to this day."

"You weren't guilty?" Sidney said.

"No! Look, you be the judge. I'd had traffic trouble. Speeding, et cetera, and a couple of impaired charges. I had had a license suspension, so I wasn't on very good ground when this thing happened. My record was agin me. So here it is. I am driving east on No. 7 Highway, and a car is approaching me, swerving from side to side, and refuses to dim his lights. I started to brake, and this oncomer swerved at me so violently that I had to pull to the right. I got around him all right and straightened out, but I felt a very slight bump as I went by. Now take note, I was going under sixty, and I hadn't had a drink all day. I kept on going, but I was worried about that bump.

"Better go back and see. So a mile or so up the road I pulled up, turned and came back. There was a small knot of people collected around something. So I found out I had hit an elderly man, stone deaf, wearing a black suit and walking on the right-hand side of the road. The old boy hadn't given me a chance, and he was instantly killed. I spoke right up and said my piece. Well, someone had sent for a doctor. He arrived, took one look at the body, then turned to me and said, "Here, you need a drink, old man." And I, like a fool, took it. Naturally the doctor was sort of dutifully trying to give me an alibi, and I didn't need one. So the police smelled liquor on my breath, all nicely explained by the doctor, of course, but nobody would believe it was my first drink that day. And because I *demanded* a blood test, the police didn't get round to it until it couldn't prove a thing. Then they tried to suggest that I'd left the scene of an accident, gone up the road a couple of miles to throw away an open bottle, and had then come back. So to put the lid on it, a couple of peasants out smooching claimed they'd seen the accident—but they hadn't seen the oncoming car that made me swerve. So they threw the book at me in the country court, and everybody said old Gerry Thurston got off lightly, it should have been murder."

"Did your lawyer really have a go at this courting couple?" Sidney asked. "Did he find out exactly where they were and what they were doing, with diagrams? Did he test them? Did he visit the scene?"

"No," Gerald said. "He said they were sticking right to their story and it was better not to make too much of a thing about it. I wish, old man, that *you* had been around at the time. Actually, my lawyer didn't believe me. He was..."

"Don't tell me who he was," Sidney said. "I'd rather not know."

June glanced at her husband sharply. The name of the lawyer in question was in the file marked "Gerald," which both of them had read carefully half a dozen times.

"Martha, by the way," Sidney said, "told me you went up to visit the nurse after you got the dog quieted down. Is that true?"

"Damn that Martha!" Gerald said. "She accused me of immoral prowlings on the Saturday morning. She said she'd heard me go up, and she'd heard Edna helping me down, and do you know I couldn't remember a thing about it. Also, it seemed highly unlikely to me at the time, I mean because of my condition. Well, you know how it is..."

"Quite," Sidney said.

"Well, that little incident didn't flash back to me until midafternoon. You know how your memory starts coming back in dribs and drabs? Well, at first I just didn't believe it, then it came through dimly. I *did* go up, but 'twas not tender passion that guided my feet. Not by no means, nohow. Hell, I've told you everything else, I suppose I might as well spill it, but it really sounds like hell."

"Go ahead," Sidney said. "June, how about throwing together some supper for the three of us?"

"And miss the sexy part?" June said. "Only if the entire meeting adjourns to the kitchen."

Sidney frowned his disapproval, but the remark did not appear to have fazed Gerald, and the three of them took their drinks to the kitchen, where June set about preparing a meal.

"So go ahead and tell us about Edna," June said.

"Ah! Edna!" Gerald said. "A delightful little woman. I met her at my mother's bedside. Mother was working hard to make me feel miserable. In that high, disagreeable voice she was cataloging all my faults. And this demure creature, who really *had* something, was gliding about with glasses and hypos and whatnot, and every now and then I would catch her eye and the exciting message it contained.

"Well, it so happened I bumped into her in the pantry downstairs, and there was a little desultory love-play. Ah, yes! You must remember I'm a two-time loser in the marriage league."

"Just say a two-timer," June suggested.

"Ah, Juney, how you misjudge me!" he said. "But anyway, one thing led, in a most delightful way, to another, and I received an invitation to prowl when the house was quiet. This happened on several subsequent visits. She's really quite long in the tooth, past forty, but young in looks and spirit. So what happens? With all this nice sympathy, I went a bit gaga over her for a while, and made that awful, awful mistake of writing letters, actually four in all. Why is it that when you're under the spell, you feel it's okay to pour forth your heart to some dame in a letter? And then, when your mind returns to a more practical plane, you begin to wonder.

"Holy cow! One night I woke up and started to think about the things I'd said, and how they might sound if read to or by the wrong person. You see, writing to her was quite an effort. I didn't dare send a letter postmarked Sarnia. But when I was in Windsor or Chatham I would write on hotel stationery, using my portable typewriter. Anyway, it came over me that I wanted to get those letters back, but I didn't want to make a thing of it by *asking* for them."

"They contained grave indiscretions?" Sidney said.

"Hah! Bloody awful, old man. In fact, I'll tell you how bad, in the light of later events. Like jesting suggestions about slipping the female parent an overdose of tablets. Yipe! Imagine the effect of that!

"But anyway, this night, after I got the dog quieted down, it came over me suddenly, the way a drunken mind will light on some compulsion, it came over me that I wanted those letters. And then it occurred to me that Edna, sly puss, it being Friday, might just have sneaked out when everyone was asleep to live it up a bit. She sometimes did. So I decided to chance it, once and for all. You see, that apartment on the top floor can be locked right off. There is a spring lock on the door at the top of the stairs, which just might have given Edna a false sense of security, supposing she attached any value to those letters. Because, you see, I've carried a key to that apartment these twenty-five years, since the time I used to live up there. So I got into my pyjamas, took the key and tiptoed up. I opened the door very quietly, tiptoed into the bedroom—and Edna was out!"

"She was out!" Sidney said.

"Yes," Gerald said, a little surprised at Sidney's vehemence. And then his face fell. "Oh hell," he said. "That ain't what the police were told. Sid, I ought to remember you're the enemy. Listen, Edna just didn't want her little nocturnal wanderings dragged into the light..."

"And so she agreed to silence for silence?" Sidney suggested. "She said she wouldn't torpedo your story about the dog if you wouldn't reveal that she'd been out."

Gerald looked thoroughly miserable.

"Sid, all I can say is please go easy! I've opened my big mouth too wide. But anyway, as I was saying, she was out, so I lurched silently about her room, searching. And I found them. She had them tucked away neatly in a blue leather writing case, all four of them. I took them out of their envelopes and made sure I had the lot, and I breathed a gigantic sigh of relief. Well, she had a little fireplace in the bedroom, which already had a lot of waste paper in it. So I laid these letters tenderly on top of the other junk, and set fire to it. I stood there until I saw that all four letters were burning well, then I went and sat on the bed and watched the flame...and watched...and watched. And next thing I knew Edna was bending over me, shaking me by the chin and saying, 'Wake up, you fool, you've got to get out of here.' So she helped me downstairs, and that was it."

"Evidently Martha didn't hear her come in," Sidney said.

"No. But Edna can move like a cat. I guess it was Edna helping me down the stairs that woke Martha. And this was what detonated Martha into upbraiding me, out of the corner of her mouth, while the police were running about the place."

June had quickly concocted supper out of scrambled eggs, crisp bacon and mushrooms. She put three plates on the kitchen table and distributed eating implements from a kitchen drawer. When they had commenced eating, she turned to Gerald and favored him with a look of ineffable tenderness.

"Gerry," she said, "you need a PR man. Everybody always misunderstood you. Outwardly you seem to be a rugged, hearty *homme moyen sensuel*. I don't think that people realize that you are inwardly sensitive and that you are a man of principles."

Gerald put down his fork and took his wallet from an inner pocket. He said, "Twenty bucks is the absolute limit, June. But carry on, I like this line."

She laughed wistfully, but kept her eyes on his. "I can remember when you went to jail," she said. "And some people treated it as a joke. I was only a little girl at the time, of course."

"That's right," Gerald said. "You were a little girl of nineteen or twenty. Now look, young June, cut it out. You're transparent. You want something. What is it?"

"Oh, I have no right to ask you," she said. "And if I do, you will simply swell with masculine pride and snub me. But I really *would* like to know about this affair of Martha's. Poor Martha, she always had such bad luck with men."

"Bad luck, my foot," Gerald said angrily. "Damn it all, she *asked* for it. I mean to say, these high standards of hers were the cause of all the trouble. Ugh! Men like me were anathema to her. Vile, coarse, sensual brutes, who only wanted Woman for One Thing. She insisted on finding a gentleman, a knight in shining armor, with high principles sprouting out all over him. I remember once she came home from a U.T.S. dance and cried and said she would never speak to that boy again, he'd tried to put his hand on her knee. Good God! So she gets just what you might expect: phonies."

"Poor Martha," June said.

"Oh yes, it was tough, even if it *was* her own fault. See, the trouble is, that house of ours had the smell of dough about it. So Martha always had lots of admirers who had an eye to the bucks. I once suggested that she should chase off any admirer who didn't try to assault her within two weeks, but oh, no! She liked the good, pious, high-sounding ones. With the result that she became engaged, just before the war, to this character that walked around wearing a Bible Class pin and looked like something peering from under a stone.

"When war was declared he went around saying it was the duty of every fit man to offer himself in the struggle against the evil of Hitler. No kidding, I've heard him say it. He offered himself, and got over with First Div, so he could find a cushy spot. When *I* went over, Martha told me to be sure to look up dear Lawrence. I did. The guy was tearing around with women in the West End of London, and also with the gals of the Aldershot area. He was killed by a bomb that hit the Café de Paris in London. Nothing wrong with that. Several Canadians killed by that bomb, and some really good guys, too. But the thing was, a few days later Martha gets a Dear John letter from him. He'd married a sweet little English rose, and he knew that she and Martha were going to be great buddies. And, funny thing, the new wife wasn't with him in the café when he was killed.

"The thing broke Martha up badly. See, this guy's mother didn't like Martha much. She cabled and pulled strings and arranged for this wife to be brought to Canada, because she wanted her little grandchild to be born a Canadian. Well it happened, and several months sooner than Granny had reckoned on it, and the gal came and called on Martha. Martha was spared nothing, but she learned nothing from the experience. So after that she became a WREN and made her way to Naval Headquarters in London. Well, since that time, Martha has had about eight unhappy romances, and all through the same cause. She helped some poor oaf put himself through divinity school, and then the guy was married, shotgun style, to some girl up on a mission field. There was a Hungarian colonel at the riding school, who turned out to have a wife and six kids.

"And every time the same story. Some fellow sees a rich-looking woman, he learns how to please her by saying nice things about humanity, and they get engaged. Then he either borrows money, like a playwright who got her to angel a play in a *barn*, believe it or not, or they find out that Martha hasn't got a nickel while her mother is alive, and they can't wait, or she discovers that they are secretly making time with some little babe with *low* principles."

"It's really pathetic," June, said. "And I suppose this last one was just the same as the others."

"*What* last one?" Gerald demanded.

"Well, you know, the one this year," June said lamely. "The one you threw up at her when the police were at the house."

"June Beattie," he said, "or Grant, if you prefer it, you are the most unscrupulous hussy I know. You just won't let that thing alone, *will* you? Your husband is a pretty average competent snooper, but you really take the bun. Now understand, once and for all, I don't propose to tell you about my sister's love affairs. There are limits."

"Well, you told me about Lawrence, and a colonel who turned out to be married, and a playwright and a parson, so what's the difference here?" June said. "Obviously it's that this time Martha was naughty and gave this gentleman woman's most precious gift, nicely matured. Is that it?"

Gerald Thurston got up from the table and stamped about the kitchen, emitting uncontrollable guffaws.

"Woman's most precious gift, nicely matured," he repeated. "Have you no reverence, June?"

"Gerald dear," she said, "you know that Martha is, as you might say, long in the tooth. Do you really need to maintain this mid-Victorian chaps' sisters attitude? Now you sit down while Juney goes to get the brandy and then you tell Juney all about it."

Gerald was beaten.

Eleven

THEY RETURNED TO THE living room to drink coffee and brandy, and June, playing Gerald like a rather large trout on a light line, kept him in the mood to tell all about Martha. As she said later to Sidney, Gerald could be talked into doing almost anything, provided he didn't think it involved Letting the Side Down.

She got him started with the help of Herr H. Upmann, of Hamburg and Havana, one of whose fine English Market Selection Panatelas was placed in his mouth.

He explained that in recent years Martha had become extremely sensitive about her unhappy loves. She was afraid that people were gossiping and laughing. So she became furtive and secretive, and her friends did not hear about the new admirer until close to the break-up of each romance. This tended to aggravate the problem, because she saw the man always alone and could not get the reaction of others to the charm that had captivated her.

Since early spring Martha had showed symptoms of being in love again, but Gerald had heard nothing official for some weeks. Then the name "George" had begun to crop up, and he caught echoes of quarrels between Martha and her mother about George.

According to Gerald, old Mrs. Thurston had a large share of responsibility for her daughter's unhappy love life. She herself had always behaved with a touch of coquetry. She had been fond of expensive dresses and jewels and furs (for which she had been duly punished), and she had been outrageous in her encouragement of male flattery. This had turned Martha a little sour on coquetry and flattery and the language of gallantry. The mother had goaded her and jibed at her for her lack of charm, but Martha's reaction had been towards tweeds and flat heels.

Through many of the unhappy romances Mrs. Thurston had carried on a campaign of raillery and derision, and had never failed to say "I told you so" when things turned out badly. Under it all, Gerald thought, there had been a desire on the part of the old lady to maintain her domination over the girl—and woman. It was a form of emotional slavery.

George, from the scraps that Gerald gleaned, was English, a retired colonel living on a small British Army pension, and writing an obscure volume of military history. He had a certain capital, but it was tied up in England, and it would take some time to get it free.

The question of marriage arose, which detonated a large-scale quarrel between mother and daughter. At that point Gerald became mildly involved. Gerald, at the time, was trying to persuade his mother to lend him money for his business battles. Martha, working at cross purposes, was trying to get some sort of allowance that would permit her to marry George and live in comfort. Martha had a job with a welfare agency connected with the church. The salary was adequate as pocket money, but even added to the alleged army pension it would scarcely have made a subsistence for a married couple.

But Mother was obdurate. George, she maintained, was after Martha only for her money. He had visited Mrs. Thurston several times in her sick room and had turned on his considerable charm like a tap. It was Mrs. Thurston's opinion that a man so charming could easily have found a girl with much more sex appeal than Martha. So Mother put her foot down. Under the terms of the trust fund, Martha had a right to lodging in the family home so long as she remained single. If she married, her mother decreed, she would have to go.

On the Sunday of the great quarrel, voices were raised.

"Why don't you put George to the test?" Mrs. Thurston almost screamed. "Tell him you have nothing but your little salary, and that you and he can't live here. Tell him you haven't got a cent and never will have. Tell him that I will leave everything to—to others—if you marry him. Unless, of course, you've been fool enough already to tell him about your expectation under the trust."

"Of course I haven't told him," Martha replied, and burst into tears. It would have been most unlike Martha to discuss finances and family business with an outsider, even a man she wanted to marry.

"Then put him to the test," her mother said. "See what he says when he knows he's marrying a penniless old maid. It will be just like that woman of Henry James's in *Washington Square*. He'll disappear."

Martha appealed to Gerald, but Gerald couldn't help feeling, even from second-hand accounts, that the colonel was a fraud. And then, by chance, he met him walking with Martha on Bloor Street. There were the usual mumbled introductions. Gerald didn't even get the last name. Something, he thought, like Partridge.

"And I'm telling you," Gerald said to June and Sidney, "the guy was as phony as the proverbial three-spot. Colonel! I sort of expected the old white-haired type, but this fellow was my age, or younger. Maybe fifty or a little less. Martha is fifty-three. I started asking questions, and he talked about the Indian Army and the Supplementary Reserve and the Western Desert. He's been on Wavell's intelligence staff, but it was vague, and I could tell that the guy was uncomfortable. He wanted to end the conversation and get away.

"I didn't tell the old lady what I thought, but I told Martha, and of course she burst into tears and said that was just like me. I hated any man who was decent and honorable. So there it was."

But then a strange thing happened. Gerald's theory was that Martha, knowing in her heart that Gerald was right, that Mother was right, couldn't face the test. Another dream of marriage and romance was about to shatter.

"And you know," he said, "I think that all along Martha had sort of wanted, without really knowing it, to, shall we say, pile into the sack. Underneath she had repressed sexual desires."

June suppressed a smile at Gerald's lapse into pseudo-Freudian language.

"So anyway," he said, "I figure she decided to be real gone wicked and have an affair before the thing broke up. Or maybe she had a pathetic idea that once this fellow and she had, so to speak, rolled in the *foine,* he would be hers for life. But anyway, I'm convinced that she gave herself to George before the break-up. Maybe she just felt that Mother wasn't going to rob her of *that* much. Now, what happened after that I can't even guess. Maybe Martha found that this thing wasn't up to expectations. Maybe it filled her with revulsion. Damned if I know. Maybe, after the little affair, she *did* put him to the test, and found that money meant more to him than—as June put it—woman's most precious gift, nicely matured. Anyway, shortly thereafter, there was no more George, and his name was anathema, and Martha, of all people, started hitting the bottle. And she really hit it. She went to her bedroom early in the evening and got sozzled drinking from her secret supply. Edna knew what was going on. She said the rate of consumption was about two bottles every three nights, which is a lot for a parvenu to the sauce like Mart."

"But you must have some concrete reason for thinking there was an affair," June said. "Not mere suspicion."

"Ah yes," Gerald said. "Her holidays were due to commence in mid-July, for three weeks. But before that time she ran out for four days. She said she was going away on business, to talk to some welfare people somewhere or other. That's the story I got from Mother, but she didn't specify *where* she was going. She got back on a Saturday morning, which in itself tells a story. Why not stay away for the weekend? Something had gone wrong. I saw her on the Sunday, and she looked like hell, eyes all red and ready to cry if you said boo. So I innocently asked her how she'd enjoyed her stay in Williamsburg, Virginia. God! She whirled round and flared up at me and demanded to know what *I* knew about Williamsburg, Virginia. It really shook her to the roots.

"So without thinking what I was doing, I said, 'Did you and George have a good time among all the antiques?' My God, you should have seen her! She went wild! She said that if it was any satisfaction to me, I was absolutely right about George, he was a frightful man and she never wanted to hear his name again, and if he should phone I was to say she was out and wouldn't be back. And then she gave the show away. She kept demanding to know how *I* knew she'd been to Williamsburg, and I kept kidding her along and being mysterious until she said—poor kid—'Did George tell you?' So there's your proof."

"And how *did* you know?" June asked.

"Aha!" he said. "Your husband is supposed to be a sort of lawyer-detective, but now he's met his match. I dedoosed it, kid, by very subtle cleverness. I don't think I should reveal my devilishly cunning methods."

"Oh you pig, Gerald!" June said.

He sat back and chuckled with a certain smugness.

"Ah well," he said at last, "you'd never sleep until I told you, so I will. You and I, dear girl, would never have heard of Ausable

Chasm, New York, if we hadn't seen cars running around with stickers on them saying they'd been there. It seems that in some of these tourist spots the Chamber of Commerce or somebody gives out stickers to parking lots, et cetera, where they stick them on visitors' cars. So when I saw a sticker on Martha's rear bumper saying 'Williamsburg, Va.,' I instantly deduced that she had been visiting the Old Dominion, and the city of Williamsburg. Now wasn't that pretty damn clever?"

"Fiendishly," June said.

"Well anyway, I let her off the hook. I told her how I'd guessed, and she went straight out and scraped the sticker off, and I never mentioned the business again—at least not until she backed me into the corner that Saturday morning."

"And you figure that fear of having this affair revealed caused her to play along with you on the dog question?" June said.

"No doubt about it," he said. "It knocked her for a loop. She would have done damn nearly anything to cover up that bit of scandal."

They sat in silence for several minutes, and Gerald began to look uncomfortable.

"I know it was damned unscrupulous of me," he said. "But you see, I had these awful guilt feelings, and my head was splitting. I didn't know what I had done the night before, and I could see all sorts of suspicions arising, simply because my mother's death was so opportune for me in the financial way."

"And so," Sidney said, shaking his head sadly, "that explains the mystery of the dog. Well, Gerald, old man, I think for your own sake you should go to the police at once and tell them what happened. Tell them about taking the dog for a walk, and—"

"But I didn't," Gerald said quietly.

Sidney stared at him incredulously. "What do you mean, you didn't?" he said. "This is hardly the time to change your story."

"I know it," Gerald said. "But the fact is that I did not take Chippy for a walk that night."

Sidney and June exchanged a long, searching look. "Then why were you so frightened of being accused of it?" Sidney asked.

"Because, of course," Gerald said, "I didn't know it at the time. On that Saturday morning I couldn't even have sworn that I hadn't, in a spasm of drunken rage, killed my own mother. At first I remembered nothing. Then, as I told you, I remembered being in the hall with the dog. And with Martha hurling accusing looks at me, I decided I must have been coming back from a walk with Chippy. It was nearly a week before I remembered exactly what had happened."

There was a long silence, broken when Sidney leapt up and said, "Great God! What *did* happen?"

"I'll tell you," Gerald said. "Suddenly one day I remembered drinking at the club with these chaps, and one of them driving a bunch of us home. We went up Jarvis and Mount Pleasant, and when we got to Elm Avenue I said he could let me out, I wanted to walk the rest of the way home. They kidded me and said I wanted to climb into the dormitories of Branksome Hall, the girls' school, but I pointed out that the girls were all away for their summer holidays. So we started to sing 'We are from Branksome' to the tune of 'Notre Dame,' and somebody said shut up, we didn't want to attract the police, and I got out and walked home. I let myself in and was just shutting the door when a thing hit me, and it was Chippy. All of a sudden he started to bark. He was pretty excited. I grabbed him and shushed him. I carried him into the kitchen and gave him some meatballs or something and had a glass of milk myself. Then I started to take him down cellar to put him in bed..."

"Down cellar?" Sidney said, repeating the quaint Toronto idiom. "Didn't he sleep in the room behind the kitchen?"

"No," Gerald said, somewhat surprised. "He always slept in the coal cellar. Well, we called it the coal cellar, although there hasn't been any coal in it since we got the oil furnace in 1928. But I took one look at the cellar stairs and immediately chickened out. I was in no condition for Alpine work. So I took him up to my room and he went to sleep on my bed, and then I remembered the letters and started my prowl."

Sidney looked at him closely.

"The dog was simply running loose in the house when you came in?" he said. Gerald nodded. "Then, when the burglars were there..." Sidney said, but checked himself.

"Nobody will ever believe me," Gerald said. "But that's the way it was."

Sidney walked about the room, thinking deeply.

"Gerald," he said at last. "My advice to you is to go to the police and tell them this whole story. Everything. That is your proper course."

"And what if I don't?" Gerald said.

"You will be acting the bad citizen," Sidney said. "But *I* won't complain. I've told you the proper thing to do. If you don't do it, I will have a chance to do some quiet investigating. I want to investigate the curious incident of the dog in the night."

"But the dog did nothing in the night," June said. She was a girl who knew her Sherlock Holmes.

Sidney grinned. "That was the curious incident," he quoted in rejoinder. "By the way, Gerald. Did this coal cellar of Chippy's have a window?"

"Yes, of course," Gerald said. "It opens onto the driveway, just in front of the porte cochère."

"Thank you," Sidney said. "Now we'll have one night cap. And I will promise to give you ample warning before I blow this thing up—just in case you decide not to talk to the police at once."

"Okay, okay," Gerald said. "I'm not as toffee-nosed as certain people when it comes to making a deal. I will wait to hear from *you*."

"Great," Sidney said.

Twelve

"WE HAD A BURGLARY and murder case," Sidney said. "Now we have a premeditated murder, and a damned ingenious one."

"How can you be sure?" June said.

They were sitting before the remains of a fire in the living room, drinking tea in their dressing gowns, having decided that sleep was impossible.

"Somebody moved the dog's bed," Sidney said. "Somebody decided to shift it away from the coal cellar."

"Why?"

"Because," Sidney said. "The coal cellar window was broken."

"Oh," June said. "They didn't want Chippy to catch cold."

"That is correct," Sidney said. "Say, that was some performance of Gerald's tonight. He may be weak on cost accounting or something, but he's a top-grade salesman. He has a natural grasp of sales psychology."

"Explain," June said, curling her feet up in her chair.

"Gerald came here tonight to sell something, to get the best deal he could. He started by offering me a fat bribe. He played that card first—not a very high card. He played it to lose, like sacrificing a queen to establish a lead in dummy. Gerald had figured out that the flimflam about the dog had been exploded. So he was retiring to a prepared position. All same what happened in Sarnia. His competitors were trying to drive him to the wall. He fought, he hung on. When he suddenly acquired the resources to survive, his competitors caved in, and Gerald made a deal. He sold out at a good profit and came away. And now, he couldn't make the dog swindle stick, so he comes out all frank and friendly. He wants to have a foot in our camp. Damn it, he reminds me of Long John Silver making a separate peace with Squire Trelawney. And he's a likable sort of oaf, too."

"But explain the bit about sales psychology," June said.

"All right. Gerald wants to tell us this: 'You are quite right, the dog went to the clinic on Saturday morning. But it so happens that I did not take him for a walk during the night.' Now, if he'd walked in here and made the bald statement, he would have been fighting an uphill battle to get us to believe him. Instead of that, he sat here and made himself pleasant and gained our confidence, and when he did tell us, he said he didn't expect us to believe him. It was damn clever. He got me to play my hand, then he played his."

"Do you think he's lying?" June said.

"No. I don't think he's clever enough to play an elaborate double bluff. Martha threw Gerald to the wolves; Gerald, without, I think, fully realizing it, has thrown Edna Foster to the wolves. Edna was *out* that night. Don't forget it. Did she take the dog with her? She agreed with Gerald not to torpedo the dog story; maybe she was laughing up her sleeve. Probably there was a silence-for-silence deal. Gerald says he won't reveal that Mrs. Foster went out, Mrs. Foster says she won't reveal that the dog was at home. There are vast permutations and combinations in this thing at the moment. Mrs. Foster had some compromising letters. She realized that the old lady's death would benefit Gerald. She arranged a burglary and murder, after which she could say to Gerald, 'Cough up or else.' Maybe she planned to trap him into marriage.

"And we now have to take a close look at Martha. Her emotions were in a turbulent state. Her mother had ruined her life and was destroying her last chance. Let's suppose she went away with George, as Gerald suggests, and in the midst of this little outing tells him she's penniless. So he walks out. She hates him, yet perhaps she wants him back. So she murders her mother. Or perhaps she levels with George. Tells him that only Mother stands between her and a fortune. They agree to come back and quarrel—but collaborate quietly on a murder scheme.

"Then there is the possibility that there was a Gerald-Martha axis, aided by the nurse. Or maybe the whole household, including old Viola, was in the deal, one vast murder conspiracy. All of these possibilities need to be considered and sorted out.

"First of all, look at Martha: she arranged for the dog to be away overnight. Her mother wouldn't allow it. She could easily have sneaked the dog out herself and brought him back. Perhaps she was standing in the dark with the dog when Gerald staggered in. That suggested to her the idea of convincing Gerald that *he* had been walking the dog.

"But all this gets crazier and crazier. We have to rationalize it. And the one man we know virtually nothing about is George Partridge, or some name like Partridge. Tomorrow I start looking for George."

"Darling," June said. "There's a little point that occurs to me that you may have missed. I seem to get the idea that Martha spoke venomously about the nurse."

"Yes. She did to me, as a matter of fact."

"Why would she hate the nurse with such venom?" June asked.

"Why? Because she was a prude and a Puritan," Sidney said. "She disapproved of her having an affair with her brother in the old family mansion."

"Uh-uh," June said. "If there is one thing a woman will be tolerant of, it's her brother's affairs. She might be a little disgusted, but not venomous. Did it occur to you that perhaps this nymph Edna might have drooped her pretty eyelids at George, and Martha found out?"

"Now what would make you suppose that?" Sidney said.

"I don't know. A kind of feeling," she said. "Martha might, of course, have felt that the nurse was exercising undue influence on her mother. But that touch of venom I detect suggests jealousy to me."

"My sweet hellcat," Sidney said. "It wouldn't have occurred to me for a minute. But now that you mention it, I write it down as a distinct possibility."

For an hour they continued to paw over the relationships in the Thurston house, and then Sidney put an end to it by saying, "But we have to look at the other end of this thing."

"What other end?" June said.

"The burglary end. You see, there was a burglary, and we don't know very much about it. We know that the fences, the Martin brothers, were alerted in advance to receive some stolen furs. Frank Young thinks they meant to process those furs and move them out of town over the weekend. They wouldn't have planned any such thing if they had thought the furs were going to be hot. That means that they believed the burglars were going to get into an empty house and bring the furs away clean—that the burglary wouldn't be detected for a day or so. They were taking a big gamble, because the minute that burglary was reported the police would start looking into the activities of possible fences.

"Now the Martins had the use of a loft that was ostensibly vacant. They didn't know the police knew about it. I suppose they thought they could hole up there with the coats from Saturday morning until night, maybe even until Sunday night, and let the police think they were at Wasaga Beach. But damn it, it's absolutely certain they didn't think the burglars were going to walk into a houseful of people. If they had, they'd have handled it a different way.

"Which brings us to the question: Who planned this thing, and who furnished the intelligence? There's a fellow called Webb who acts as a sort of go-between on these things. He has a sort of talent agency in his head. He hears of a chance to steal furs, money or what have you. He knows the right thieves to give the job to, the right fences to peddle the loot to. Young thinks that this Webb was on the outs with the Martins, which would explain all the bungling. There is a certain expertise in Webb's operations.

"All right. Let's suppose that *someone* at the Thurston place wants to organize a burglary to cover up a murder. That someone must somehow make connection with the underworld. Who? Hardly Martha, or Viola Lang. Possibly Gerald. More likely the nurse. We have a file on her, and she's had some trouble. She is really a trained nurse but has to call herself a practical nurse because of this trouble. Drugs missing from a hospital dispensary in Vancouver. Nothing proved, but Mrs. Foster was evidently pressured into resigning and giving up her qualification. Anyone involved in dope operations could establish underworld connections. Then there is the elusive George. Gerald says he's a phony. Perhaps *he* did it. But whoever it was certainly gave the criminals a bum steer. They *must* have been told the house was empty.

"The scheme could have been this: Burglars enter the house and take the furs. The inside plotter commits the murder. The burglars will be so frightened when they hear of it that they will bury the stuff and lie low. Unknown burglars will be blamed for the unsolved murder. So far so good. What ruins that picture is the jewelry. First of all, fur fences aren't interested in jewelry. Secondly, the burglars aren't likely to expect to find personal jewelry in an empty house. It won't fit. Thirdly, if someone in the house was collaborating in such a scheme, they would hardly direct a burglar to go into a room where someone was sleeping. They would most likely move the stuff downstairs, say to the hall clothes closet, and let the burglars believe that they *had* actually entered an empty house."

"Nothing fits," June said. "But you seem to be totally ignoring the fact that Stoopid Easting has confessed."

"No, I'm not," Sidney said. "But more and more I wish I could talk to Stoopid. He signed some sort of statement the night he was arrested, which was probably enough to have hanged him. He probably didn't know what he'd said or what he'd signed—Good God!"

"What?" June said.

"Suppose Easting *didn't* kill the old lady. Suppose he never went upstairs. Suppose he *did* find the coats in the hall closet. Suppose he tried to sell that one to the police. The police had already seen where the coats were kept. They wouldn't believe him. They kept confusing him until, in desperation, he said he went upstairs. He was in a state to sign anything. Later, Raines, the friend of humanity, wouldn't believe a word he said. He wasn't sufficiently interested to look into the state of the Thurston household. He conned Easting into making an elaborate statement, designed to be fully cooperative. Actually I'll bet that Easting knew *nothing* about the planning of the crime."

"Ah yes," June said. "But the jewels. You forget about the jewels."

"The hell I do. It now fits," Sidney said. "It all fits! The jewels were an absolutely necessary part of the scenario. And remember this. *Easting*, the stooge, kept the jewels. Why?"

"Why?" June said. "Suppose you tell me."

"I will!" Sidney said, "He kept them because—though I hate to say it—that boy is dishonest! He's a thief! His accomplices never even heard of the jewels. Also, I apologize to Miss Edith Moon, late of my staff. She has supplied the answer."

"Stop blithering, man, and say your piece," June said.

"Look. The murderer, the plotter, wanted to lay the burglar's trail right up to the bedside of Mrs. Thurston. The way to do it was to have the burglar take the jewels from the bedside table as well as the coats from the closet. So the plotters arranged, first, that Mrs. Thurston should have heavy sedation. Next, that the coats should be planted in the hall closet, and finally that the jewels should be shoved in the pocket of one of the coats! And that's where Easting found them! You see, his first crimes were pinching marbles out of pockets in the school cloakroom, as the good Miss Moon stated in her verbose report. His natural inclination in a cloakroom is to go through the pockets. He went through the pockets and found the jewels. So he pocketed them and kept them. He held out on his accomplices. And because even his own lawyer won't listen to him, the police have missed the whole significance of the jewels."

"Good lord, you might be right," June said.

"And there is another point," Sidney said. "The underworld characters, sometime on that Saturday, realized that they'd been given a bum steer. That the person who told them the house was empty was lying and had got Vince Lamberti mixed up in a murder charge. Underworld characters can be very resentful. Now, if the go-between was Martha's George, we may never see him alive. It is possible that he was rubbed out. He may, of course, have known the danger, so he may be in hiding a long way off. Tomorrow, my dear, my first concern will be to find George. But there's another point that will bear thinking about."

"No, not another," June said. "I've got enough now."

"But ponder this. Why is Vince Lamberti so completely silent, and why did Grandfather cough up ten thousand dollars for his defense?"

"Vince is silent on principle," she said, "and to protect the rest of the people in the game. And Grandfather didn't cough up the money. The Martins, or your Mr. Webb, or somebody in the underworld, in order to show Vince they love him for being silent, gave Grampa the money to give you."

"You may be right," Sidney said. "But Messrs. Dun and Bradstreet say that Grampa is quite capable of springing for the retainer out of his own pocket. This case is not simple. And by the way, Gerald said something else that was of interest."

"Yes?"

"He said he was awakened on that Saturday morning by the snarling of a power mower. It's a small point. It simply doesn't fit with the crime the way we've figured it. But we still have to bear it in mind."

"I don't get it," she said.

"Some burglars, the mere opportunists," he said, "break into empty houses in the summer, and the symptoms of empty houses are uncut grass, lights burning during the day (which are supposed to make the house look occupied by night) and handbills or milk bottles left on the porch. Easting, according to Raines, claimed he had first reported the Thurston house as empty, to Lamberti, because the grass was long. I don't believe Easting ever reconnoitered the house. But certainly the grass was cut between the time of the murder and the time the police arrived."

"Ug, ug, ug," June said. "I am now going to bed. It's all too much for me."

Thirteen

AT THE OUTSET IT appeared that the search for the mysterious George would be long, grueling and possibly hopeless. Sidney made a telephone call to Dr. Norris, but Dr. Norris said he could not possibly question Martha. She was in an extremely disturbed state. Dr. Dorothy Price? She might or might not have known something about George, but Sidney decided that it was best not to ask her. He and Georgie and Gibson, the new student, combed through directories and telephone books and made lists of Partridges, but sifting them all out was likely to take time.

In midmorning Miss Semple entered Sidney's private office unbidden and sat down to wait until he had finished reading a document.

"Yes?" he said.

"I have an idea about this man George," she said.

"Good. What is it?"

"I think he belongs to a very low order of the human race. I think he may be a professional victimizer of spinsters."

"You think so?"

"Yes," she said. "Spinsters who have saved a few shares of Bell Telephone are often vulnerable. At least the silly ones are. Not having acquired a husband and romance in the first bloom of youth, some of them go on believing that the knight in shining armor will arrive even when they're as wrinkled as old prunes. I find it disgusting. Oh, romances of a sort offer themselves. *I* had a proposal of marriage just before I joined your staff."

"And you refused it, praise be," Sidney said.

"Yes. It was my old boss. I did all his work for the last twenty years, so that he could give his mind to the top-level problems, like drinking three-hour lunches and curling all afternoon in winter and golfing all afternoon in summer. I kept everything straight for him."

"I'm sure you did," Sidney said uncomfortably.

"Oh *yes*. And he was going to miss me. So he proposed. I told him not to be a silly old goat. If he wanted a nurse, he should hire a nurse, and if he wanted a housekeeper, he should hire a housekeeper. And if he wanted...but he was close to eighty. Lots of men, widowers or old bachelors, want to marry late in life to get somebody to look after them—somebody old enough that she won't produce family problems."

"A wise precaution," Sidney said incautiously, and Miss Semple glanced at him sharply. "You think so?" she said.

But after a moment she resumed her dissertation. "I was expected to swoon with pleasure at this great honor," she said. "Damn it, men have some weird ideas. However, the men who merely want to marry aging spinsters to get their money and housekeeping services are relatively innocent. There are also men who try to sell phony stocks and muskrat farms and all sorts of things, and there are men who become engaged to women so they can get hold of their money and disappear. Now this George looks to me like a professional victimizer of women, the really cold, unscrupulous type. I wish *I* had met him."

"How would you have dealt with him?" Sidney asked.

"Ah!" she said with relish. "Once I stayed with a friend at Murray Bay. She was susceptible, poor dear. A charming, elderly, distinguished gentleman made our acquaintance. We played bridge with him. My friend—who was quite rich—fell. But I cut her out! I kept getting Mr. Smooth aside and asking his advice on my ten thousand shares of this and that, until I outshone poor Bertha. Mr. Smooth became sentimental. But he needed money to go to the Belgian Congo and sell out his diamond mines. He needed a couple of thousand. I kept asking was it enough, until he got really greedy and said he could buy out his partners for a mere thirty thousand and sell the whole lot in Brussels for a fantastic sum. So I gave him a check for thirty thousand."

"You did?"

"Oh yes, I pressed it on him and squeezed his hand, and begged him not to tell Bertha or the others. I wanted it to be our little secret. We never saw him again."

"But the check?"

"On a nonexistent account at a branch where I was unknown, and signed with an indecipherable scrawl. Poor Mr. Smooth may have died of a broken heart. That's the sort of treatment Martha's George needed. But Mr. Grant, I have a theory. It might or might not get us the man's name. I'm going out for half an hour to do a little checking."

"Do, by all means," Sidney said, and he sat pondering the fate of poor Mr. Smooth with his uncashable check.

Georgie Semple was back well within the half hour, and she laid before her employer the tracing of a signature and a deciphering of the signature in block letters.

"A. H. G. Attridge," she said. "Does that sound possible?"

"Highly possible," he said. "Where did you find it?"

She smiled enigmatically and said she normally didn't reveal her methods. However, she allowed herself to be persuaded, or coaxed. Miss Semple had a fine, legal filing-cabinet memory, and the name "Partridge" had caused a faint flicker in it. "Then I started thinking about victimizers," she said, "and I thought about how *I* would go about my research if I were a victimizer—and it came to me."

"How would you go about your research?" Sidney asked.

"Why, I'd see what I could dig out about an heiress from the Surrogate Court," she said. "And when that thought hit me, I remembered something. At the Surrogate Court you can get any will on record, as you know, of course, by paying a small fee and signing the card. Well, I remember that when I was looking up the will of the late Mr. Thurston, I noticed that someone else had been having a look at it this year. Well, today I went back. I didn't think it was likely that this George would sign the name he was operating under, but then again—anyway, it appears that he did! I don't suppose it ever occurred to him that anyone would try to trace him through that card. I make the signature Attridge or Attredge."

"So do I," Sidney said. "But my dear Georgie. What date was this, that he was looking up that will?"

"Last April," she said. "Late April. Hang on, I have a note…"

"Never mind," Sidney said. "Late April is near enough. Georgie, do you know what this means? It alters everything. Later on, old Mrs. Thurston was daring Martha to tempt George. To tell him she was penniless, but would marry him if he didn't mind being poor. Suppose she did try it?"

"Heavens!" Georgie said. "This George knew all along that only one life stood between Martha and a fortune."

"That is so right," Sidney said. "And what an opportunity for him to say, 'Ah, my dear, queen of my heart, what care I for money? Let us fly tonight and be united.' And that cad Gerald thought she had slipped away for an affair!"

"You may have noticed that Martha became a borrower from a small loan company," Georgie said. "This could have been for the financing of the honeymoon and all that."

"He would advise her to keep the thing secret from her mother—so that she could continue to live at home for a while," Sidney said. "And meanwhile he could think about ways of shortening the old lady's life. Georgie, I have a small check I want to make. Be back shortly."

He went out and caught a cab to the Armed Forces Club, where the records showed that guest privileges had been granted to Lt. Col. A. H. G. Attridge, D.S.O., who had shown a membership card in a London military club with which the Toronto club had a mutual-privileges arrangement. Sidney paid cash on the nail for a transatlantic telephone call to the London club to check on the colonel's *bona fides*, but it was useless to make the call until 2 P.M. owing to the time differential. Meanwhile, the guest book in the club's ladies' room clinched one thing once and for all: Col. Attridge had twice entertained, as a dinner guest, Miss Martha Thurston. Later in the day the club's secretary-manager reported that the colonel was a fake. His membership card from the London club was certainly spurious. "He behaved quite like an officer and a gentleman," the secretary-manager said in some embarrassment. "So of course we never bothered to check back."

But although he had the name, Sidney was still a long way from locating George. Directories proved useless. The only address left at the institute (and on the card at the Surrogate Court) was an apartment hotel where George Attridge had spent a few nights many months before. He had left no forwarding address at the hotel.

"It looks to me," he told Georgie Semple, "as if our man is dead. In order to cover up the murder of his new mother-in-law, he talked the underworld into laying on a burglary. He told them the house would be empty. When they found out the truth, they rubbed him out. But I want to find where he lived."

"Do you think he killed Mrs. Thurston?" Georgie said.

"Well, here's a theory for you. Under his hypnotic charm, Martha agreed to help kill her mother. She arranged for the dog to be away overnight. At the last minute Mother wouldn't hear of it, so Martha had to sneak out of bed and take the dog away while George's burglars did their work. She brought the dog back and was still downstairs when brother Gerald staggered drunkenly in. He interfered with Martha's extempore plan for getting rid of Chippy, but next morning she saw a chance to make Gerald the scapegoat. Pretty cunning. She had faked a fight with George to avert suspicion. After the murder she waited and waited and waited for George to get in touch with her. But he didn't, being dead. The loss shook her, caused guilt to flood in upon her and unhinged her mind. Any flaws?"

"Not really," she said. "Except that she doesn't seem like a person capable of premeditated murder. Impulse, possibly. But if they were married..."

"It's on record," he said. "Just have one more check at the Parliament buildings to be sure. If there's no dice, we'll send young Gibson to Williamsburg pronto. He can start by finding the hotel reservation and then check back to find where the marriage took place, whether it was in Virginia or Maryland. But meanwhile another thought swims uppermost in the mill-race of my mind. My wife."

"Yes, your wife?" she said.

"My wife deduces some relationship between George and Nurse Foster, purely from the venomous way Martha spoke about the nurse. I wonder if the nurse knew where Attridge's hangout was? And if she does, how can I worm it out of her?"

"Leave it to Georgie," Miss Semple said. "I'll have it in no time."

Sidney made a mental bet that she wouldn't, and he racked his brain to think of any possible way to approach the nurse and ask for the information without putting her back up. He was still thinking about it when Georgie re-entered, trying to appear calm and offhand, and laid an address before him.

"There it is," she said.

He looked at the address, and a strange excitement filled him. Attridge, it appeared, had lived just south of Bloor Street, in an area that had seen better days, but within easy walking distance of the Thurston house.

"Miss Semple," he said. "I advise against telling me you don't normally reveal your methods. Instantly tell me how you performed this miracle. Out with it!"

She smiled in a superior way and sat down. "Mrs. Foster," she said in the nasal voice used by the telephone pests. "This is the P. F. B. Collection Agency calling, we are seeking a postal address for a Mr. G-like-in-George Attridge who gave your name as a reference. Will you please give us the last postal address you had for Mr. Attridge? Oh, you never knew him? I'm sorry. Of course you are in no way liable, Mrs. Foster, all we want is the addray-us. Well, I'm sorry, in that case we will have to issue a subpoena and ask you to come into court and sway-urr that you never knew him. But if you could furnish an addray-us we would of course regard the entire matter as confidential, Mrs. Foster. One moment, what was the number again? Thank you so much Mrs. Foster, that will be all."

Sidney shook with laughter. It was a superb performance.

"Henceforward," he said, "this date shall be known in the office as Georgina E. Semple Day, to be celebrated by feasting and fireworks, for on this day and in this year Georgina E. Semple took the name George Partridge and from it conjured the full name and address of Lieutenant-Colonel A. H. G. Attridge, D.S.O., using no instruments except the compass and one edge of a ruler, for which exploit she is granted the privilege—"

"Never mind about privileges," Georgie said. "Just have a look at my wretched salary."

"That's the trouble with employees," Sidney said. "They have no sense of humor. It all comes round to money, money, money. Speaking of which, have we got enough to start Gibson on his way to Williamsburg?"

"Yes," she said. "Unless he finds anything at the Parliament buildings, which I don't suppose he will. He wants to ride down on his Vespa motor scooter."

"That's all right with me," Sidney said. "Provided we are absolved of all responsibility and we don't pay more than two cents a mile for his mileage. And now, Georgie, I am going to go and nose around this Attridge address, so expect me on the morrow."

But even before he could get away from the office, Gibson, the law student, returned empty-handed, and all excited about his motor scooter trip.

"Telephone, collect, the minute you find anything," Sidney called to him over his shoulder.

"Aye aye sir," Gibson shouted back.

❀❀❀

The colonel's address proved to be an apartment in a mews, one of the stables that in a bygone era had served the great brick houses of Jarvis and Sherbourne Streets. The ground floor of the building appeared to be a studio, and in it Sidney found a young woman in a smock, evidently making props for a play. She revealed that she was the owner of the entire building and landlady of the flats upstairs. Yes, she had known Colonel Attridge. Her own private name for him had been Lover Boy. Lover Boy had apparently exuded charm at every pore.

But Lover Boy had disappeared suddenly, and had never been seen since. Pinpointing the date of his disappearance was not difficult, and it proved to be the very weekend on which Mrs. Thurston had been murdered. The landlady had headed north on Friday to watch a dramatic production at Gravenhurst, but before leaving she had extracted a promise from Lover Boy that he would pay his August rent (eighty dollars) on the Monday, without fail.

But on the Monday he did not appear, and the landlady let herself into his apartment to find that he had flown the coop, bag and baggage. He had evidently packed hastily and vamoosed.

"Why hastily?" Sidney asked. "He had the whole weekend."

"Well, either he was hasty, or he was going into disguise. He forgot his shaving gear. It had fallen down behind the john. I'm saving it for him."

She went to a huge Welsh dresser and pulled a rectangular leather case from one of the drawers. It bore no initials. Sidney unzipped it part way and peeped in. He saw an array of chromium-plated tubes and boxes, so he shut it up again quickly.

"May I take this?" Sidney asked. "I'll look after it and return it..."

"Keep it," she said. "I've given up on Lover Boy. Aren't you the famous Gargoyle? Didn't you marry June Beattie?"

"Guilty on both counts," he said with a grin. "Would you mind calling me a cab?"

Ten minutes later, trembling with excitement, he bore the colonel's shaving case into the office of a fingerprint expert, a man whose services he had used before. The man was on the point of leaving for home. Sidney showed him the case.

"Chromium," the man said, peering into the interior. "It takes a swell print, and it holds it nicely, but it smears easily."

"Do you think you could pick out the prints of the man who owned it?" Sidney asked.

"If they're there, and if they're not smeared, I'll lift 'em somehow," the man said. "In fact, this bein' the wife's bridge evening, I'll stay down and do it right now."

"Wonderful," Sidney said. "And phone me at home as soon as you've got anything."

At home he wolfed his dinner, read the evening papers in such an explosive way that he hurled them across the room at intervals, attempted a game of solitaire, but cheated on such a massive scale that his wife confiscated the cards, and finally settled down to pacing like a caged beast. His wife threw things at him, tripped him, and set obstacles in the path of his pacing. Now and again they talked about the case, and the Gargoyle told June that she could go to the head of the class for her deduction of a Nurse Foster-George relationship.

At ten o'clock he ran out of cigarettes, and said bravely that he would do without until morning, but June, who knew about handling caged beasts, phoned for a couple of cartons to a late-delivering drugstore.

And at midnight the fingerprint expert arrived in person. He was a fattish man called Gord, with a matter-of-fact manner of speaking.

"Well, Gargoyle, old boy," he said. "This is on my way home to Willowdale, so I thought I'd drop the stuff off. Gee, this is a classy joint you got."

"We like it," Sidney said primly. "Have a drink—and what the hell result did you get?"

"I'll have rye, and ginger ale if you've got it," Gord said. "And talk about results, Gargoyle, you oughta be called 'Horseshoes.' Look, see this cylinder that holds the shaving soap stick? Old-fashioned cuss, this. Well, I got a complete right hand, thumb and four fingers off it, because of the way the guy held it when he screwed the top on. Hardly a smear. And I got most of the left hand off of the square soap box. One way and another, boy, I got all ten. I don't care where this guy is recorded or classified, you can get him from these. In fact, there's the classification—send that to the FBI and they'll pick him straight out if he's on their files, or the R.C.M.P. or Scotland Yard or the Sûreté or the Guardia Civil or the MVD. I got kind of fascinated so I stayed with it the whole evening. Will you give me an excuse to my missus if I need it?"

Sidney promised to represent Gord, free, in the Domestic Court, if necessary, and they sat and had a drink. Gord had brought a complete set of photographs of the prints and an identification chart. The elusive George was rapidly gaining in corporeality.

Though he was late getting to sleep, Sidney was up before six and downtown before seven, personally typing a letter to a firm of solicitors whose office lay near the Inns of Court in London, a sleepy, dusty firm with which Sidney had corresponded before, a firm that had handled business for Charles James Fox but could still move with reasonable speed.

With his letter, Sidney enclosed the fingerprint photographs and the classification chart. The letter simply requested that the London lawyers should somehow, fast, find out from Scotland Yard whether they knew the man who had called himself George Attridge, and if they did, to get as much of his criminal record as possible, also his marriage record. Sidney suggested that the nature of the man's record was probably such that Scotland Yard might well believe that the solicitors were enquiring on behalf of an injured client who wished to remain nameless. The envelope was sent off in an airmail packet by jet, early enough to arrive in London the same day.

By typing the letter himself, Sidney brought about a small crisis with Miss Semple, who was distinctly sniffy about it. She would have been pleased to have come in at any hour, she said, but she didn't like people doing her job.

Another crisis arose a few minutes later when Sidney summoned her and asked her to call the Wida-Wake Investigation Service and ask them to put a tail on Mrs. Foster, the nurse. Miss Semple said that the Wida-Wake people were completely incompetent.

"They only handle matrimonial stuff, and only collusive divorce cases," she said. "If you asked them to keep Mrs. Foster under surveillance they would probably send some three-hundred-pound plug-ugly in a derby hat with flat feet and a cheap cigar who would stand outside the house reading *Racing Form*. She'd spot him in no time. Let me call—"

"Are you quite sure the Wida-Wake people are like that?" Sidney asked.

"Absolutely," she said. "No reputable lawyer would *touch* them."

"Then call them at once," Sidney said. "They're the boys for us."

She stood and looked puzzled for a moment, and then the light dawned. "Oh, pardon *me*, Mr. Grant," she said. "I'd forgotten that employees are not supposed to think around here. I shall call them at once."

They were both under a strain, and for several days there was little to do but wait. The first break came when Gibson telephoned. He had found the registration for George and Martha as Mr. and Mrs. Attridge in a Williamsburg hotel. He had also found the registration of their marriage.

And so, the life and death of Mrs. Thurston had meant the difference, to George, between having a rich mother-in-law and having a rich wife. On Friday afternoon a letter arrived that put at rest any doubt there might have been about the character of George, and it gave Sidney much to think about over the weekend. Scotland Yard had proved to be the right place to apply.

Fourteen

HIS NAME WAS NOT George, and not Attridge. Nor was he English. By origin he was an Australian con-man, fair dinkum, and before narrowing into his specialty of victimizing women, he had tried all the rackets. It appeared from the record that George had tended to stray on occasion, to get mixed up in thefts and other types of crime instead of sticking to his own miserable, but fairly safe, vocation. These little forays had sometimes got him into trouble, which was the reason that Scotland Yard had a very good dossier on him. When convicted of other crimes, he had pleaded guilty to innumerable frauds on women, in order to clear the record.

His usual method was a blitz wooing at some seaside resort, followed either by the borrowing of a large sum to help settle his father's estate or to purchase a house and furniture for the prospective bride, or else an offer to look after the little woman's investment portfolio.

"The nurse knew his address," Sidney said to Miss Semple. "And George was a professional crook. Now, if we can discover that George was dickering for the sale of some furs, I think we have completed a very pretty chain."

"How could you hope to establish that?" she said.

"I don't need to prove it. I only want to be sure in my own mind."

"How," Georgie asked, "do out-of-town crooks get in touch with the local underworld?"

"If they are in the organized stuff like gambling or dope, they arrive with proper introductions," he said. "A small operator would simply find the right part of town and talk to a prostitute—ask her to put him in touch with the right people. Or sit around drinking in low joints and talk to the denizens. And that gives me an idea. I am going to go to a den of vice and see some denizens myself."

But first of all he wrote a letter to Dr. Norris and furnished him with the information that Martha had been married to George, although the marriage was very likely bigamous, and also gave him a run-down on George's criminal record.

After an early dinner that evening he left June to read an improving book and made his way south into a highly insalubrious quarter of the town, an area where prostitutes jostled with dope pushers on the sidewalks, and the sign "ROOMS" in huge letters meant "room by the hour." It was a quarter where pool halls and bowling alleys abounded, and low bars and taverns. The Gargoyle drew much of his clientele from the area, so he was inclined to be tolerant.

He found his destination without trouble. Its ghastly mauve and green neon sign was unmistakable. It was a hotel, with three entrances labeled, from left to right, "Men," "Hotel" and "Ladies and Escorts." Sidney entered the door marked "Men" and found himself in a vast room where men sat crowded around tables drinking beer and watching the television or carrying on shouted conversations. Waiters snake-hipped their precarious way among the tables carrying huge trays loaded with glasses of beer, which they whirled about with great expertise, never spilling a drop. Sidney fell in behind a waiter and wove his way through the room in the man's wake, until he came to the farthest corner, where the noise level was much lower. There, in the corner, was a round table where five men were sitting, idly watching a small-screen TV set on the side of a pillar. There were two vacant chairs at the table.

Sidney stood blinking to focus his eyes in the dim light, and looked at the five men, all roughly dressed, and one of them he recognized without difficulty as the notorious Spider Webb. This was Webb's headquarters, where he sat like King Arthur with his knights.

The strange thing about Webb was that his life was an open book. He spent his day wandering about the pool rooms and barbershops, chatting idly here and there, and in the evening he visited several bars, but seldom took a drink. His favorite spot, however, was the place where he was sitting at that moment.

There were many legends about Webb, who had fought his way up from being a newsboy. It was said that he made his fortune by handing out five-dollar bills and taking in tens. He never tried for big killings. He ran a sort of intelligence and talent agency. He knew everybody and everything, and he never talked, except to the right people. He was—it was said—not directly connected with any of the big organized rackets, like dope and bookmaking, but he knew all about them, and he often did little chores for the big boys—who respected him for his efficiency and integrity. Ordinary punks and strangers could not approach him. His table was sacred. If a young hoodlum had some information to sell, he passed the word indirectly, either by a waiter or by someone entitled to approach the big table.

Then—clients had told Sidney about it—the Spider might deign to send somebody over to talk to the kid at a faraway table and hear what he had to say. In due course the word would reach Webb. On one occasion a young hoodlum wanted to brag that he was making time with a girl who worked in a bank; eventually the Gargoyle had represented the girl when she went into court to plead guilty. Webb, it appeared, had weighed off the advantages of using the girl to stage an early-morning hold-up with inside help against the subtler forms of bank robbery, and on expert advice he had chosen to have the girl borrow the bank's certification stamp for twenty minutes. The flood of certified cheques that were passed next day brought in a rich return.

The men at the table became aware of Sidney's scrutiny and managed to convey their silent disapproval to him. Sidney, ignoring the coldness of the reception, stepped forward and took a vacant chair next to Webb.

"Good evening, Mr. Webb," he said politely as he sat down.

"Good evening, Mr. Grant," Webb said, with equal politeness. "Can I buy you a glass of beer? I'm sorry this isn't a liquor bar."

"You can get me a bottle of Molson's Ex," Sidney said.

Webb turned and looked for a waiter. "Hey, Joe," he barked, and a waiter pulled up in full flight. "Bring an Ex for Mr. Grant," Webb ordered, and the waiter turned and went out purposefully.

Quite suddenly conversation began to die out in the room, and Sidney heard the words "Gargoyle Grant" going from table to table. Gargoyle Grant, the mouthpiece, the guy that was defending Big Vince, Gargoyle was in visiting Webb, right at his table. Table after table went silent, and the men turned to stare. The waiter came hurrying back with the bottle of beer—it was the fastest service ever heard of in the hotel. Presently a curtain in the center wall was drawn aside, and bright eyes ringed with mascara peered through from the zenana quarter marked "Ladies and Escorts." A waiter had carried the news through to the other room, and some of the ladies had been unable to resist having a peek.

It was the law of Ontario that no man could enter the zenana section unless he were the escort of a lady, which meant that, officially, a lonely man had to remain in the Men's section all evening, and an unescorted lady had to remain unescorted.

However, the snake-hipped waiters were happy to act as Love's messengers, to dart back and forth like so many Cupids, if a Cupid can be imagined to have cauliflower ears and a broken nose. When a waiter spied a lonely man, he would creep toward him and whisper delicately in his ear, "You wanna dame, Jack?" If Jack wanted a dame, the waiter would find a lonely woman who would go to the lobby area and meet him, and incidentally, in accordance with a charming custom of the place, she would pay the waiter a small commission.

And so the Gargoyle's arrival at Webb's table became a sensation that spread through the entire drinking area. Webb appeared to ignore the silence and the curiosity, but somehow he conveyed an air of disapproval that spread out in waves. Heads turned away again, and conversation was resumed. Sidney sipped at his beer in silence. Nobody asked him what his errand was. It was made clear to him that he was expected to speak first.

"Mr. Webb," he said. "I came here to ask you a few questions." Tension showed in all five faces. After a long pause, a sallow man, seeming to speak at a signal from Webb, said, "We don't like guys comin' around here astin' questions, Mister."

"I'm sure you don't," Sidney said. "I get sick of surveys myself."

"What was the questions you wanted to ast?" Webb said, eyeing him shrewdly.

Sidney reached into his pocket and pulled out several pictures of Aubrey Miller, alias George Attridge, which had been enclosed with the letter from London. He laid them on the table in front of Webb.

"I want to know," he said, "if any of you people know this man. I want to know if this man ever came around trying to sell propositions in this area, and I want to know if he was favorably regarded by the citizens of these parts."

"Is that all you want to know?" Webb said.

"Yes. Oh—and I'd like to know what name you knew him by, if you knew him."

"That's everything, is it?" Webb said. "Supposin' somebody was to answer them questions, you wouldn't have six more things you wanted to know?"

"No, that's the lot," Sidney said.

Webb sat staring straight in front of him. Idly he took the pictures in his left hand and passed them to the man on his left, who glanced at them and passed them again, until eventually they reached Sidney and he put them back in his pocket. There was a long pause, and then the sallow man spoke, once more as if on a signal from Webb.

"Yeah, we've seen the guy," he said. "That's the Prof. He's been around here tryin' to peddle some deal, but the guys around here didn't think much of him."

"Got what you wanted?" Webb said. There was a note in his voice that suggested it was time to end the party.

"Yes, thank you very much," Sidney said. "You've been splendid. Can I buy a round of drinks? No? Well, thank you for your hospitality. I hate to rush away, but I have pressing engagements. Good-bye."

"Good-bye," Webb said.

Sidney departed, quickly.

❀❀❀

Fresh air smelled strange and exhilarating after the atmosphere of the beverage room, and Sidney was more than satisfied with the result of his enquiry. He had completed a chain from the bedside of Mrs. Thurston to the underworld. It appeared more than likely that George had tried to interest the "regulars" in a burglary and, having failed, had set something up with the Martins on his own account. His complete disappearance after the crime now looked even more sinister. It seemed eminently possible that a small delegation had gone to his flat, packed his belongings and taken him away to some deserted spot.

While Sidney stood thinking about it, a woman came close to him in the darkness. He turned and walked off rapidly, but she followed. She wore a fur coat, and she was heavily perfumed. She caught up to Sidney and took his arm.

"Go away," he said.

"No, listen, honest, I wanna talk to you," she said. "Make like I was a hustler pickin' you up."

"That would require very little imagination," Sidney said. "What are you?"

"I'm not a hustler," she said. "But like I sometimes go into that hotel for a few beers because I got old friends there. Like when my husband is away on a long haul. He's a transport driver. He runs to Texas. But listen, Mr. Grant, they said it was you in there, talkin' to Webb. I peeked through the curtain and seen you. Listen, Mr. Grant, I just gotta talk to you. I nearly come to your office a dozen times, but every time I chickened out."

"What did you want to see me about?" Sidney asked.

"About Big Vince," she said. "You're Vince's lawyer, and listen, I love that guy like no woman ever loved a man. Honest."

Sidney stopped and turned to her.

"I'll finish it," he said. "You are a married woman. On the night of the murder of Mrs. Thurston, your husband was in Texas with his truck. Vince Lamberti was with you. He spent the night with you. Afterwards, when he was arrested, you were frightened to come forward, because your husband would kill you. But your conscience has bothered you, and now you want to tell all and save Vince."

"Gee, but that's right!" she said. "How'd you know? Did the big guy tell you?"

"The big guy actually mentioned that he had been out tomcatting on the murder night," Sidney said. "But I didn't think I was expected to believe it. Now let me tell you something. The best thing you can do is go home and forget it. I wouldn't dare produce an alibi like this in court."

"Why not?" she said.

"Because, lacking any sort of corroboration, your story would do Vince more harm than good. No juror would believe it, and the jurors would all say, 'Well, if that's the best story he can cook up, he must be in a bad way.' And you've been a long time coming forward, if I may say so, ma'am."

"Long time? Lookit, right early on I got a note from Vince from the jail, a guard smuggled it out. It just said 'Clam up—don't say nothing.' Vince don't *want* me to speak up, see? But listen, if you want corroboration, like you said, I can give it to you, but good. Real good."

"You mean that one of your girl friends was with you or something?"

"No," she said. "Better'n that. Away better. But listen, we can't talk here. Take me to some bar where nobody knows us and we can talk."

His eyes had grown used to the darkness, and he could see that the girl was tall, slender—and built. She had a very pretty face, probably prettier in the half-light than in daylight. She reeked of perfume, and not too cheap a perfume, and she kept pressing herself against Sidney almost unconsciously as she talked so that Sidney determined to tell her to stop at the first reasonable opportunity, perhaps in ten minutes or so. He tried to think of some bar where he could take the girl, some spot where there was no possibility of bumping into an old classmate. But he could think of none. Suddenly he reached a decision, and he stepped out and hailed a cab. The driver pulled up and took a look at the girl. "Where to, Mac?" he said with a slight leer. Sidney gave his home address and sat back in the cushions. The girl turned and looked at him. "Mainly I go for big guys," she said ominously. Sidney edged farther over into his own corner.

The cab pulled up at the entrance of the apartment house just as June walked down the steps, pulling on her gloves.

"Hi!" she greeted as Sidney got out, and "Hi" again as the girl got out.

"Darling, I'd like you to meet Mrs—er—sorry, I didn't get your name," he said.

The girl surveyed June from head to foot, making a complete inventory of clothes and accessories, but as June was making a similar inventory it did not matter.

"Mrs. Borland," she said. "I'm very pleased to meetcha, Mrs. Grant."

"And I'm so pleased to meet *you*," June said. "Terribly sorry I can't stay. Sidney, Peggy phoned from the Wellesley. Friday night and she's lonely, absolutely everybody is at a party, and her husband's in New York so I said I'd go in for half an hour. You knew she had another girl?"

"No, I didn't," Sidney said. "But darling, I met Mrs. Borland down at Parliament and Dundas, and I wanted some place where we could talk…"

"Be my guest, Mrs. Borland," June said. "Sidney, you'll be quite cozy. There's a small fire going, and you'll find a tray of drinks all ready. I *do* hope you'll excuse me, Mrs. Borland."

Mrs. Borland was nonplussed, and didn't know whether to be frightened or angry, but she managed to remain bright and polite while June slipped away toward the Citroën, murmuring, "Sidney, you'll see that Mrs. Borland gets *everything* she wants, won't you?" Sidney managed a steps-of-the-gallows grin and went on up to the apartment with his guest, not without some trepidation.

But Mrs. Borland kept her distance and drank her drink with her little finger crooked and was in every way on her best behavior.

"Lookit, Mr. Grant," she said. "I want you to understand about me and Vince, see? I mean before he got sent down, I was his girl, see? But he got seven years, that's a long time in a girl's life, Mr. Grant. It seemed like forever. When he come out I was married to Slim. Listen, Slim is a great guy too, don't get me wrong, but see, Vince is sort of like the one and only. I mean, that *guy*! But Slim is so jealous it isn't even funny. I mean, he comes home off of a haul and the *questions* and where did I go and whom did I see and all that stuff, so of course I've gotta be real careful. Anyways, lately he's had these weekend layovers in

Houston, sometimes, so this Friday night I tell Vince it's for *us*. Well, he comes in before ten, and he was with me till six o'clock in the morning, which was getting a bit risky. But anyways, you was saying about corroboration."

"I was," Sidney said.

"Well okay, boy, we got it. See, sometime after eleven there's this knock on the apartment door, and Vince says never mind it. But I said maybe the neighbors would figure I was out if I don't answer it, so I go. And it's this freezer salesman."

"*Freezer* salesman!"

"Sure. He was selling deep freezes. Like you sign the contract and you get this freezer, and you buy so much meat and groceries for the next year and it saves you enough to pay for the freezer. Anyways, I told him it was a hell of a time to go around selling freezers, but he said lots of people liked to have him call after the news and before the late show.

"Well, I said anyways my husband wasn't home and he wouldn't let me sign no contracts when he wasn't there on account of some unlucky experiences, and he said well okay, let him leave his card and he'd come back sometime when my husband was home. And then he sort of pushed his way into the hall and put this card down on the hall table. Here it is."

She fished a large deckle-edged card from her handbag and handed it to Sidney. It said:

SUBARCTIC FASTFREEZE
Save on food costs, get the added quality
of fast-frozen meats, fruits, veges.

Your representative:
Alfred G. Lintott.

There were also various addresses and telephone numbers on the card.

"Well anyways," the woman continued, "this Lintott, see, he turns to me, and I'm wearing this long housecoat, and his eyes got that look and he said, 'The old man away? You must be kind of lonely, Baby.' I asked him whom he thought he was talking to, and he said, 'Don't get mad, Baby' and started to put his arms around my waist. Well I took both hands to shove him away—he was just a little guy, but sort of husky—and what do you think he does? He grabs my housecoat by the lapels and pulls it wide open, and me with...well, you should have seen me!"

"I'm sure I shouldn't have," Sidney said virtuously, trying to stop visualizing the scene.

"Anyways," she said. "I let out a yell and ran into the living room, and this fellow nearly pulled the housecoat right off, and he come in after me, and of course that's the moment that Vince comes bustin' out of the bedroom, and I wish you could have seen this Lintott! His eyes really bugged! Vince went for him, but he was so mad he kept swingin' and missin', which was probably a good thing, because finally he caught him one that didn't really connect right, but it laid this Lintott out cold. Well it took us nearly half an hour to bring the little guy around, and I was scared, but Vince said don't worry, he knew how to handle it, just see the guy's throat was clear and so on. Anyway, when he come round he was kind of dazed, but he got out of there real fast. So the guy got a good look at Vince, and he sure as hell won't forget it. How do you like that for corroboration?"

"You're telling the truth?" Sidney said.

"Honest. Hope to die," she said.

"And you would tell this story in court?"

"For Vince," she said throbbingly. "Yes, for Vince I would."

Sidney looked at her closely. He could see her enjoying the drama and notoriety of it.

"Very good," he said. "Now I don't somehow think we'll need you, but in case we do I'll take your address. However, in the meantime, will you keep this very quiet?"

"Will I ever!" she said. "Listen, I haven't told about this to a single soul, not to anybody, until I told you."

"Well keep it that way," he said. "Can I get you a cab? My wife has the car. Perhaps you'd like another drink before you go."

She elected for another drink and a cab.

June's first words when she got home were: "But Sidney, *where* did you get her? What a *dish*! I had no idea you had enough enterprise to go picking up women on Parliament Street."

"How little you really know me," he said. "At least you can say there's nothing queer about old Grant."

Then he told her the whole story, and June literally rolled on the floor. The picture of the freezer salesman was too much for her. "You have to add that your lover is in when you say your husband's out," she shrieked. "Oh God, Sidney! Can't you just see it?"

He had to restrain her physically from phoning Mr. Lintott at that very moment and asking him to come and explain his freezer service. "I'll wear my housecoat," she said, "and you hide in the bedroom."

"I ain't no Vince Lamberti," Sidney said.

But before the weekend was over, June had further cause for hilarity. She went with her husband to a cocktail party, where all the talk was about a car with two detectives in it that was watching and besetting a house in Forest Hill Village. It was such an obvious plant that every wife on the street had accused her husband of having her watched and vice versa, and much laughter was going about at cocktail parties as a result.

"Those apes," Sidney said. "They cost money too. It's eating its way into the retainer fee at a hell of a rate. I never should have sicked them onto Mrs. Foster." He was in half a mind to call them off then and there, but decided to try the effect of one more day on the nurse's nerves.

He had good reason to be glad of his decision. On Monday morning, when he was still pondering the weight of the alibi offered by Mrs. Borland, Miss Semple called to him to pick up line three and listen.

It was one of the private detectives on the line. He had to report that Mrs. Foster, the nurse, had run out. She had left the house where she was employed, carrying a small suitcase, and had roared away in a taxi. The detectives had followed, but had got hung up by a traffic light at St. Clair and Yonge. They had seen her jump from her cab and enter the St. Clair Avenue subway station. One man had dashed madly after her and had seen her enter a southbound train just as the doors shut. He had instantly dashed to the nearest pay phone to report.

"How long ago did the train leave?" Sidney asked.

"At ten thirty-six," the man said. "Just over three minutes ago."

"Good. Hang up and go home," Sidney said. He himself hung up and shouted for the entire office force to come at once.

Fifteen

THE OFFICE FORCE was not large. Sidney spoke rapidly.

"Money," he said, pulling out his wallet and throwing the bills from it on his desk. "Collect all the money we can. Now Georgie: you would recognize Foster, the nurse? Then hare down to the Union Station subway station and stand in the tunnel to intercept her. If she comes through, follow, buy a ticket on the same train, stay with her and phone collect when she reaches destination. Gibson—you'd know her? Same orders, only stand by the airport limousine and bus place. Go. Me, I'm heading for the Dundas Street bus terminal. Go go go!"

Georgie had emptied the petty cash on the desk, as well as her own funds. Each seized a handful of money and ran out. It was all that could be done to pick up the trail again. But it was in Mrs. Foster's power to leave the subway at any station she liked and go on by taxi.

Sidney ran to Yonge Street and flagged down a northbound cab. "Dundas!" he shouted as he jumped in. "And I'm in a hurry." The driver wanted to know whereabouts on Dundas. "Right at the corner of Yonge," Sidney said. The driver delivered the goods. He snaked through two lights just as they turned red and pulled up at Dundas before Sidney had recovered his breath. Sidney shoved a dollar in his hand and waited not for change.

And, as he stepped out, he saw that luck was with him. Mrs. Foster, in a light gray suit, was just emerging from the subway exit on the diagonally opposite corner. When she reached the surface, she walked over to a shop window, turned, and watched all the other passengers who had left her train as they came up the stairs. When the traffic trickled away, she began walking purposefully west on Dundas. A westbound streetcar was just pulling up. Sidney crossed and caught it. It passed Mrs. Foster halfway to Bay Street and allowed Sidney to enter the bus terminal ahead of his quarry. He was buying a magazine when she entered, and he watched her as she scanned the faces of the people following her. Evidently satisfied, she made for the wicket, and Sidney was able without effort to get directly behind her in the line-up. She bought a single ticket for Buffalo and was told that a bus would be leaving in twelve minutes. When she was out of earshot Sidney bought a return to Buffalo and asked which road the bus took. "Queen Elizabeth Highway, natch," he was told.

Mrs. Foster had found a seat on a bench. She was sitting up straight and alert, her legs crossed, and was smoking in short, nervous puffs. She was still watching the people who came in at the terminal entrance.

Without losing sight of her, Sidney went to a pay phone and called the office. He told the stenographer to go down to

Union Station and recall the forces deployed there. Then he called June.

"Operative X9 reporting," he said. "I'm on the trail of a sexy blonde. We are about to board a bus for Buffalo at the terminal."

"Grant, you're skirt-happy, that's all that's wrong with you," she said. "Bringing home sexy brunettes, chasing off to Niagara Falls with sexy blondes..."

"Buffalo," he said. "Look, I don't want to go the whole way with this woman..."

"You might just as well," she said. "It's really the thought that counts. I have been unfaithful to thee, Cynara, in—"

"Shut up," he said. "I mean I don't want to go to Buffalo. I'm going to get her off the bus before we reach Hamilton. Psychological warfare. Now how about you grabbing your ID *dix-neuf* and following the bus? It heads out along Lizzy Lane. I'll chalk J.G. on the back of it as a signal to you that this is the right bus."

"What will you use for chalk?" she said.

"There's a snag," he admitted, but after a moment's thought he said, "Lipstick. I'll buy a lipstick at the counter here and chalk your initials on the back of the bus, or rather lipstick them. Then you get in behind and pick us up when we bail out."

"Roger and out," she said.

Sidney left the telephone and went to the counter, where he paid eighty-nine cents for a large lipstick. The nurse was still puffing and looking about nervously. Within a minute or so the bus was called, and she went out to the platform. A line-up was forming.

Sidney stood back and waited until the nurse was in the bus, then he walked round to the rear of it and crayoned "J.G." in huge letters on the gray paint. He was pleased with the result. People were staring at him, but Sidney paid no attention. He kept his face drained of all expression, and when a man stared grinning right into his face, Sidney looked back blankly and the man turned away. A bus terminal employee who had seen what had happened shouted, "Hey you!" and started toward him, but

Sidney strolled away, around the wrong side of the bus, crossed the front end and joined the tail of the line-up.

As he made his way down the aisle, he noted that Mrs. Foster had taken an aisle seat and was blocking off the vacant window seat. She was trying to look as if she were saving the seat for a friend, but Sidney suspected that she merely wanted to be alone. He stopped beside her and said, "Is this seat taken?"

"No, go ahead," she said. With some irritation she shifted her knees out into the aisle to let him get through to the seat. She was busy scanning the faces of the people entering the bus, and Sidney's face had meant nothing to her. When the door finally slammed and the bus pulled away, she sat back and sighed audibly with relief.

Then she opened her handbag and began to fumble, obviously for cigarettes. Sidney, without haste, pulled his own out and lit one, and she still hadn't found her package when he had finished. Casually he extended his package to her. "You looking for a cigarette?" he said tonelessly.

Two emotions fought in the nurse's face. There was the natural desire to give the fresh stranger a quick brush-off. There was also the fear that she had left her package on the bench in the terminal, that she would find no cigarette in her bag and would either have to climb down or go smokeless. Sidney recognized in her the symptoms of tobaccoholism, since he was a tobaccoholic himself. She *had* to have a cigarette. So she allowed her features to thaw just a trifle and said, "Thank you, I don't mind if I do."

She took a cigarette, and Sidney lighted it. Then he passed her the package. "I've got another one," he said. "If you're out, you hang onto those. You'll need 'em before we hit Buffalo."

Once again there was a struggle. She glanced into her handbag, then looked at the nearly full package. Her fingers worked nervously. "It's very good of you," she said. "I guess you know what it's like when you *need* a smoke."

"Oh, you can say that again," Sidney said. "Like the last two weeks I been playin' the horses. There's a guy in the bar where I drink, he's had nine hot tips, see? Nine. And how many do you think come off? Seven. No kidding. Seven winners, one place, and one that's still running. Well you know something? I was luckier than a cut cat. I played them all both ways, see, *excepting* the one that lost. Now wasn't that a funny thing. Like a thought come over me, the hell with it, see? So I didn't bet it. I said the hell with it. Tony says to me, what do you want on this nag, and I said nuts, I said the hell with it. So wha'hoppen? The other guys drop a bundle on this cow, but not me, and I come out of this little spell absolutely loaded with dough, but loaded. And," he leaned over and spoke confidentially, "the nice thing is that the wife don't know nothin' about it. This is my own personal dough, see?"

"I see," she said chastely.

"Well where was I? Oh, like you were saying about needing a cigarette. Well, during this lucky streak my nerves were like a bunch of goddam banjo strings, no kidding. I mean, winning is harder on your nerves than losing. So finally I said the hell with it, I sent the wife off to visit her mother, and me, I headed out on business for Chicago. Believe it or not, I'm on a plane to Chicago right now."

"You're a very naughty man," she said approvingly. "I feel sorry for your poor wife."

"Huh!" he said. "Listen to me. If the wife was anything of a sport, she'd be with me right now on this trip. See, first I go to Buffalo, then to New York, and live it up. Well, I would have taken her along, but honest to God she'd frost the whole goddam deal. Talk about living it up! She'd want to spend half the day in Peck and Pecks or Bergdorf Goodmans and spend all our dough, and the rest of the time she'd go to this Museum of Modern Art or some goddam thing, and at night, when you like to find some joint with some music, she'd want to go and see some goddam play. And then"—he lowered his voice and leaned toward her again—"maybe I shouldn't say it, but you're over twenty-one"—she leaned closer to listen—"then we get home, and you know the old line. 'I'm exhausted. I'm too tired.' What kind of a holiday do you call that?"

"You men!" she said, with the mildest of disapproval.

"Now listen to me, Baby," he said, getting even more confidential. "And don't get mad, see? Because what I say, well, we're both grown-up. Okay, well, we come to the border. So we tell the U.S. Immigration we're man and wife, goin' for a little holiday to live it up in Buffalo. I got identification. So we go to Buffalo, maybe we stop over and go see the Widow McVan's Night Club. Tomorrow, we head for li'l old New York and live it up. So okay, we've only just met, but I can see you're a real sport, and I've got pull-enty of dough to give us a good time."

The hook was neatly baited. The chance of slipping over the border into the U.S.A. under a false name was too good to miss.

"You are a real shocker," she said, "and if I were your wife I think I'd..."

"Listen kid," he said huskily, "if you'd have been my wife, things would be different. How's about it, Baby?"

She sat up and smiled in a superior way. "I know what you'll think of me," she said. "You men! But it's a date." She seized his hand and squeezed it.

Sidney half rose and turned, so that he could look out the rear window. The bus was well out on the Queen Elizabeth Highway, and there, behind, was June's Citroën.

"What are you looking at?" the nurse asked.

"A little plant back there I've got an interest in," he said. He was grateful that June would never hear a tape recording of his recent conversation. Suddenly he began to feel qualms about his little game with the nurse. Psychological warfare can be cruel. Her nerves had reached a climax of tension, and he, Sidney Grant, had unscrupulously lulled all her fears and showed her a glimpse of hope. But he had gone too far to think of turning back. They chatted about this and that, and she began to be quite gay. She asked him about the requirements at the border, and he told her that Canadian citizens crossing for a weekend were hardly bothered at all. His driver's license would be sufficient identification, and if she could manage to look wifely she would probably not even be questioned.

"I just wondered," she said.

Sidney saw that it was time to unmask. They were approaching Burlington.

"Well, you can forget it," he said. "The police will have no way of tracing you to New York, Mrs. Foster. If you can get yourself a Social Security number some way, you'll have given the police the slip completely."

The face she turned to him was full of terror—and anger.

"You bastard!" she said. "Who are you?"

"Not the police," he said. "My name is Grant."

"Gargoyle Grant?"

"Sometimes so called."

"You bastard! What do you want?"

"I want to talk to you. But maybe you'd rather talk to the police."

She shuddered. Her head bowed over and she started to cry, but she quickly straightened up.

"They've been watching me," she said. "It got on my nerves. I'm...I'm in a hell of a spot."

"Well now," he said, "either you and George were conspiring and working together or you weren't. If you were, your best bet is to stab me with your nail scissors and run away. If you weren't, then you and I can get out of the bus right now and find some place to talk."

"Get out?" she said.

"Yes. Right here. If you'll answer some questions, I'll let you go. I'll give you a good head start. How about it?"

The anger had drained from her face, and there was only wild terror left. "I'll do anything you say," she said.

"Okay," he told her. "Let me through and follow me to the front of the bus." He worked his way into the aisle and took her suitcase off the shelf.

"Sorry, we don't stop here," the driver said. But when Sidney assured him that he was about to suffer in a sensational manner from motion sickness, the driver put the brake on, and a moment later Sidney was helping Mrs. Foster down to the grass verge. The bus door slammed, and the bus pulled away. It still bore the initials "J. G." in large red letters on its stern.

Immediately the Citroën pulled up and June called out, "Going my way?"

Sidney threw the nurse's case into the back seat and helped her into the front. "Drive like mad," he said, "to the Brant Inn, where we can get a good lunch. The place for me is redolent of Eartha Kitt, because that's where I first saw her."

"Aye aye sir," June said, and set the car in motion. The nurse, still terrified, appeared to be puzzled, but she said nothing until they reached the inn.

They pulled up in the car park beside a large, gay and glittering Chrysler New Yorker convertible, with the top down. It was the perfect car for a golden autumn day, and all three people looked at it with varying degrees of hunger as they headed for the restaurant.

❀❀❀

The dining room was almost empty. There was a sporty-looking gray-haired man eating by himself, and Sidney mentally identified him with the Chrysler, which had Wisconsin license plates. The Grants and their guest found a table and ordered martinis and lunch, but asked for lunch to be delayed for a reasonable time. The nurse sat forward, eyeing first one and then the other, and her lips worked in a way that suggested her mouth was dry.

"All right," she said suddenly. "What is it you want?"

"I want to know about you and George Attridge," Sidney said.

"Me?" she said. "What have *I* got to do with *him*? He was Martha's..." She paused.

"Martha's what?" Sidney asked.

"Her...her boyfriend," she said.

"You mean her husband," Sidney corrected.

"Really?" she said. "Well, I wouldn't know anything about that. That's none of my business."

"Isn't it? Do you mean to say you don't know why Martha broke up with George? Are you going to try to tell me that?"

"What did Martha say?" she demanded. "That stupid cow! Don't pay any attention to what she says."

"I went up and had a long talk with her in the rest home," Sidney said. He paused to let it sink in.

"Oh, and I suppose she gave you some jazz about me and George making time," she said. "Well, like I said, Martha is a stupid cow. She saw us and she jumped to conclusions and went all emotional, and she never gave him a chance to explain. Actually there wasn't anything in it at all. There was never any of that between me and George."

"Never?" Sidney said.

"No, never. The only reason I was out with him, having dinner, well, like he owed me this money. I had a right to try to get my money, didn't I? He promised he'd pay me after—"

"After he married Martha and was in the chips?"

"Yes, what's wrong with that? I mean, those people were loaded, they'd never miss it. He kept promising to pay me, and it was all hot air. He was *all* hot air."

"How did *he* come to owe you money?" Sidney asked.

"That would hardly classify as any of your business," she said. "But he did. Well, I might as well tell you. I met him last January, see? I was nursing this woman, and she belonged to the Art Gallery. There was her invitation to this Art Gallery opening night on the hall table. She couldn't use it, so I had nothing to do and I went down. It was all kind of dull, just a lot of snobs walking around looking at pictures, and I got into conversation with this fellow. I thought he was some rich character that belonged in that crowd, and how wrong I was! He picked me up very smoothly—a lot smoother than some crude characters"—she glanced meaningfully at Sidney—"but anyway, we had coffee and talked about these pictures, and I saw him a few times, and he borrowed eight hundred dollars from me. Eight hundred dollars is a lot of money."

"You can say that again," Sidney said.

"Damn it, I don't know why I was such a fool as to fall for this line, it was almost like I was hypnotized. And it was a long time before I could see he was just a cheap crook. But anyway, I kept after him, I wanted my money back. And then this lady I was nursing died, and I got the job nursing Mrs. Thurston, in April. And so George asked me all about the Thurstons, especially Martha, and he said, well he said if I would give him the right introduction to Martha, he thought he could get the money to pay me back."

Sidney hardly dared glance at June as this interesting new slant on the chronology came out.

"So it was *you* who introduced them?" Sidney said.

"Well, sort of, in a way. See, Martha asked me one day when I was going downtown if I would go to Moodey's and get her two tickets for the Royal Alex theater. I called George and he said, 'Splendid. Get three together and give *me* one.' Anyway I did, and Martha went with some old maid friend and of course they sat next to George and he got to shooting his well-known line and they talked during the intermissions, and of course I'd been able to tell him all the things she was interested in, so it was no trouble for him. He really wowed her. Well the thing went on and on, and then he told me he was going to marry her and after that he would really be in the chips. Well that was all right with me. All I wanted was my eight hundred dollars. I had a right to it, didn't I?"

"Certainly," Sidney lied. He did not really feel that anyone was entitled to be party to a fraud in order to recover a debt. "So then everything was ruined when Martha saw you with him in the restaurant?" he added.

"Yes! That cow! Listen, she came home from the honeymoon on Friday of all things. And why? Because every year since the year dot she's played this annual foursome with some of her old maid friends. They go out and play golf all day—that Price woman, the vet, is one of them—they play all day and the loser has to buy dinner, and they gush out all their girlish confidences and all that jazz, and she had to come home so she could keep this date with three *women*!"

"You're kidding!" June said.

"No, it's true. If you ask me, they're all a bunch of lezzes. Anyway, George called me and said he was off the leash and wanted to have dinner and tell me all about it. He said we'd be quite safe because Martha would be having dinner out at the golf club. What the bloody fool never thought about was that this Gaslight where we went, it was like *their* place, he'd proposed to her there, so of course she loses this golf game and says she wants to take the girls to dinner at the Gaslight, because, see, at dinner she was going to tell them her great big secret. George knew she was going to tell them, but he figured it would be at the golf club, only it turned out the golf club dining room was being redecorated. I heard that later.

"But anyway, George and I were having dinner upstairs, and I looked over and I saw her, behind the head waiter, with these women. I didn't let on I saw her, and she never let on she saw me. She just turned and disappeared downstairs. Well, you see, this fool George at that minute was lifting his glass and drinking a toast to me or something, and looking all romantic. That finished Martha. I guess she just went home and never told her girlfriends anything."

There was no trace of pity for Martha in her bearing. Only contempt.

"So you sat there with George in the Gaslight," Sidney said. "And he told you he had married the heiress. And he said there would now be lots of money and you would be paid with interest what you were owed. Isn't that right? And there was just one thing he wanted you to do. He wanted you to cooperate with him in killing Mrs. Thurston. Isn't that right? He knew that as soon as Mrs. Thurston was dead, Martha would be rich. Isn't it true that he asked you to kill Mrs. Thurston that night?"

She looked at him, but her eyes wavered. Her lips worked, and she drained her martini.

"He asked you to help him kill the old lady, didn't he?" Sidney repeated.

"Yes," she blurted out. "He did. I wanted no part of it. I told him he was a fool. He *was* a fool. He was always coming out with some idiotic scheme. Like he was always asking me couldn't we steal the furs or the silver or something. I mean, right after the first time he visited the house he was suggesting things to steal. He said the furs would fetch big money, because they were easy to fence. I know he went around investigating. He said he'd found fences that would buy those furs for cash. He wanted me to break the window catch and cut the screen and make it look like there'd been a burglary, and take the furs down to his place. I told him he was crazy."

"This was before the marriage?" Sidney said.

"Sure, long before. And get this, Mister. *He* wasn't the only one. Gerald Thurston had ideas too, and that's the truth. Oh, he always made like he was joking, but you know, if I'd taken him up it would have been different."

"Gerald had ideas?" Sidney said.

"Oh sure he did. He kiddingly suggested I should give his mother an overdose. You know, just playful. But you can bet he was glad when she really *was* dead. Ugh! And then he talked about what a fine old lady she was."

"He even wrote you a letter making that suggestion—the overdose—didn't he?" Sidney said.

"Yes," she spat. "He wrote me four letters. Love letters! See, when he's broke and can't go out, he finds little Edna very handy. Cheap, that's what I was, and he gets all sentimental and writes letters. But the minute he's in the chips, does he remember me? The hell he does. He's never even called."

"You saved these letters?" Sidney asked.

"You know goddam well what happened to those letters," she said. "He probably bragged about stealing them from me and burning them. They were all I had..."

"And they would have been worth plenty," Sidney said.

She glared at him. Lunch had been served, but she was past eating.

"You said Gerald was full of suggestions," Sidney said. "Was that the only one?"

"Oh no!" she said. "That boy had ideas. He kiddingly asked me to get his mother's keys. He suggested I should dope her and take the keys."

"What keys?"

"These keys. She kept them on a silver chain around her neck, under her nightie. I couldn't even take them off to bathe her. She went to sleep at night holding onto them, and she was even clutching them when she was dead. Gerald said one of them was a key to her safety deposit box. He said he thought she had a box full of...goodies, he used to call it. Meaning bonds and things. I said anyway even if he had the key he couldn't get into the safety deposit box, and he would say just get him the key and *he'd* figure something out. But then when I wouldn't play along, he'd make out that it was just a joke. Joke, my foot."

"What other keys did she have on the chain?" Sidney asked.

"Oh, a little key to a sort of jewel box, and the key to her desk that she had in her bedroom, a sort of escritoire that was always locked."

"You knew that this was the key to the desk?" Sidney said. She bit her lip. "You mean you got that key loose and went through the desk? What was in it?"

She floundered a moment. "All right. So what? I was curious," she said. "And there was nothing in there except papers. I didn't touch a thing, honestly."

"After this incident at the Gaslight, the marriage broke up? They didn't meet again?" Sidney said.

"No. I—I didn't tell George that she had seen us. He didn't know what happened. I just went on eating and never said a word. Well then she wouldn't talk to him on the phone or see him or let him come to the house, and she started drinking and crying in her room, and she wouldn't say a word to her mother or anyone. She never let on to me, I guess she was too damn proud. But what she did, she wrote to this brother, the ambassador, and I guess she told him the whole thing and asked him what she should do."

"She told you this?" Sidney asked.

"No, of course she didn't tell me. But you see, she got this letter from Europe, marked personal and confidential. Mostly his letters came to the old lady, so I wondered about this one, and it so happens she left it lying around and I found it."

"She left it lying around?"

"Yes, in this drawer in her room. I read it. Well all right, I wanted to know what gave. He said he had made investigations in the army list and at the War Office in London, and there was nobody of that name that had been a colonel. He had also looked up some people called Attridge, and they said they had been embarrassed by some crook who had used the name as an alias in England. He had also talked to the police—he'd been to London at this NATO meeting or some such—and they said they thought the man was probably a crook. So anyway, Crawford said the chances were the man was a bigamist, and the best way to get rid of him quietly was just tell him to go away and not bother her or she would hand him straight over to the police. Well she did. She told him, and he was fit to be tied. There was no way out of it. All that money. So he disappeared and—well, we never saw him again."

"Never?" Sidney said.

"No, never," she said quickly. "He just blew town."

"Mrs. Foster," he said. "You knew about his plans for stealing those furs."

"He talked about stealing them, yes," she said. Her mouth appeared to be dry again. She drank a tumbler of water, and then set about eating her veal cutlets with a wolfish appetite.

"On the night of the murder," Sidney said. "You left the house. You came back and found Gerald asleep on your bed. You found the dog, Chippy, asleep in Gerald's room. You let the police think you'd been home all night. You never said a word about the dog being at home. Why?"

But now, strangely, she was eating, gulping mouthfuls of home-fried potatoes and peas and veal, snatching at scraps of bread and butter. A food compulsion had seized her.

"Gerald. He asked me to shut up," she mumbled between bites.

"And you asked Gerald to shut up. Mrs. Foster, the police, very soon, are going to ask you where you went when you went out that night. What will you tell them?"

"I went visiting," she said. "I went to see a friend."

"And was the friend George? Did you find George at home? Did George perhaps borrow your latch key to go back and follow the burglars into the house? You knew, didn't you, that George was behind that burglary?"

"How could I know that?" she demanded.

The waiter appeared and cleared away their plates, setting down large slices of cherry pie and cups of coffee. Mrs. Foster at once began to attack her pie, as if to escape from the questions. Sidney reflected grimly that, if she had been his client, and the police had been questioning her in similar fashion, he would have advised her to answer no questions. He also reflected that he was lucky to have frightened a Crown witness into leaving town, so that he could have the field to himself for a while.

"You must have guessed it on Saturday morning at the latest," Sidney said. "But what about Friday night? The police will check your story right through, Mrs. Foster. If you went to George's flat that night, they'll find out. Did you take the dog there with you? Did you get home ahead of Gerald and hide in the dark while he took the dog upstairs? The police will want to know. They will want to know what you were up to, and what George was up to."

"I tell you I never saw George again, not after he disappeared that time. He knew it was no good killing the old lady, not once Martha was through with him. He went away, I tell you, and I never did get my eight hundred dollars."

"Not even when you went to his flat that night, the night he stole the furs? Did he ask you to dope the old lady well?"

"Look, you're crazy," she said. "Why don't you lay off me? Excuse me, I want to powder my nose." She gulped the last of her coffee and rose. She walked a few steps from the table, then came back and picked up her light suitcase. "I need my toilet case," she said. "I won't be a minute." June rose as if to follow her to the ladies' room, but Sidney motioned her back to her chair.

"Let's watch this," he said. The sporty-looking gentleman from Wisconsin had finished his lunch, and had wandered out toward the cigar counter. He and Mrs. Foster were out of sight. "The gal is a fast worker," Sidney added. "Let's see if she clicks." He ordered more coffee, and they waited.

Presently they heard the sound of a powerful engine starting. It raced for a few turns, then there was the crunch of wheels on gravel. Sidney walked to the front window, which looked out on the car park. The New Yorker was just pulling away, and there was a blonde head beside the gray one in the front seat. "She clicked fast," Sidney said. "She's on her way to Wisconsin. And if ever I'm sick, I don't want that little number to be giving me my needles."

"Not if you stand in the way of her getting her eight hundred clams," June said. "She really did want to get that money back."

Sixteen

"THE IMPORTANCE OF the alibi—Mrs. Borland's alibi," Sidney said, "is not so much that I can use it in court. Right now I don't think I dare use it in court, even with the freezer salesman to help. No, the importance of the thing is that I believe it myself. Which brings up one of the big mysteries: why is Vince Lamberti so silent? It's not to protect the honor of his little friend. She would love to be dragged into the limelight."

They were driving back along the Lakeshore Road after their luncheon party with Mrs. Foster.

"Wouldn't you love to examine the freezer salesman in court?" June said. "With his wife in the front row drinking it all in?"

"Don't be cruel," he said. "Another mystery. Did George believe that that house was empty when he arranged his burglary? Was he, in fact, reverting to his cheap crookhood, was he simply after what he could get from the furs? Did someone con him into thinking the house was empty? Did he walk around and see long grass and other symptoms? In other words, did he deliberately send Easting into an occupied house, or did he do it unwittingly?

"And again: did he have inside collaboration in the house, or did someone in the house know about his burglary and use it for his own purposes? For instance, did George tell the nurse what he was up to? And did the nurse tip off Gerald? Did Gerald see a chance to solve his financial problems?

"Another point: suppose there was an inside collaborator. What would happen if the collaborator simply handed the furs to young Easting and said, 'Don't tell anyone?' No, that sounds unlikely. Juney, dammit, I wish I could interview Chippy and ask him where he went that night. Did Gerald take him out after all? Or did the nurse take him down to George Attridge's flat and keep him there until it was all over? Damn it, I suddenly have a compulsive desire to go to the Thurston house and reconstruct the thing. To straighten it all out in my alleged mind. There are so many teasing points. Do you suppose Chippy is there?"

"No," she said. "Nobody is there. The place is more or less shut up. It's up for sale, but no ad in the paper and no sign on the lawn. They're asking sixty-nine five, which I think is away overpriced. Fifty-four thousand at the outside, I'd say. It's expensive to heat, and the taxes are immense, and it's sort of badly laid out, if you know what I mean..."

"Look, sweetie, never mind about the lecture on Rosedale real estate. We'll hear it all over and over again at the next six cocktail parties. You say it's up for sale?"

"Yes, but you see, they don't want to attract curiosity seekers, so they're not advertising. The house is privately listed. The furniture is being left there until the house is sold, and then the whole lot is to be packed off to Ward-Price's for auction. And darling, there's an old mahogany—"

"Never mind the old mahogany commodes," Sidney said. "Do you think we could disguise ourselves as non-curiosity seekers?"

"Ah, a superb idea," she said. "And I can show you this table—"

"Damn the table," he said. "I want to see the house. I want to get the atmosphere of it. I wish the dog were staying there till the auction. I'd like to test his powers. Did Gerald take him, do you know?"

"No," she said. "I understand he left Chippy with the Gilchrists. It might just be possible to borrow him. I'll try. Do you want to be dropped at your office?"

"Damn right," Sidney said. "My practice will go all to pot with these mad cap expeditions."

She asked him what he intended to do about Mrs. Foster, and he told her nothing at all. Mrs. Foster, he said, was probably more use to him as a fugitive than she would be in the flesh. As an absentee scapegoat, she could not possibly clear herself. June shook her head gravely at this unscrupulous attitude. She dropped him near his office and left him to spend the remainder of a golden afternoon doing paperwork.

❁❁❁

It was nearly seven when Sidney reached home, to be struck in the midriff by a guided terrier, an animal clever enough to deduce at once, by the smell, that Sidney lived in the apartment, and therefore abstained from biting.

"Chippy, old boy!" Sidney greeted him. "Welcome aboard. I've read your stuff in the papers and I think it's great."

Chippy wriggled with pleasure like any author whose work has won critical acclaim and followed Sidney to the kitchen, where he helped the Grants eat a hasty supper.

"The Gilchrists were glad to let us have Chippy," June said. "And darling, we're going house-hunting with a Mr. Reed, an agent. Our name, by the way, is Spencer—I changed the card in the mailbox downstairs."

"You think of everything," Sidney said.

"But Gargoyle darling, Mr. Reed is suspicious. He doesn't think we're serious buyers. He says the Thurston place is too rich for our blood. I said we wanted to make it into apartments, and he shook his head and talked about zoning restrictions. So lots of tact, eh?"

"Oh, plenty," Sidney promised.

They had scarcely finished their meal when Mr. Reed arrived. He was pale, he had a toothbrush mustache, and his black hair was thinning at the temples. He was dapper and earnest, and Sidney felt guilty to be using him in such a shameful manner.

"No youngsters yet," Mr. Reed said. "Honestly, I don't think this home is for you. I have some nice homes up by Bayview and Eglinton, really nice properties for young families."

"We might see them another evening, if we don't like this place," June said. "But I've always been terribly fond of the larger old houses."

Mr. Reed said it would be best if they rode with him in his car. He cast a baleful eye on Chippy, but June assured him that the dog was always well behaved. And so they arrived at the Thurston house, which looked extremely dark and deserted. Mr. Reed let them in by the door in the driveway, and they all stood in the large entrance hall with its parquet flooring and looked about.

"I'm mainly interested in bedrooms and cupboard space," June said. "Mr. Reed, you take me around upstairs, and my husband will look at furnaces and water pipes. That's *his* department."

Mr. Reed, whose nervousness was increasing, didn't seem to like the arrangement, but June had him by the arm and she managed to propel him upstairs. Sidney tried the big double doors to the dining room, but they were locked. He had to walk around through the kitchen in order to see the window by which Easting had entered. Then, still trailing Chippy behind him, he went back to the kitchen and found the cellar door. He unbolted it and descended. He found the old coal cellar and switched on the light in it. There, in the corner, lay a large wicker basket with a green velvet cushion in it. On top of the cushion lay a rubber bone.

"Lie down. Go to bed, Chippy," Sidney said. The dog whimpered slightly but went over to his basket. He picked up the rubber bone and dropped it petulantly on the floor, then sat on the cushion and looked pleadingly at Sidney. "Lie down, Chippy," Sidney said, and the dog, though looking heart-rendingly sad, obeyed. Sidney glanced up at the three-paned window and noted that the center pane was new. He switched out the light, shut the door, and went upstairs, leaving the dog in his basket. The animal had quite obviously had professional obedience training. Sidney went out, leaving the door ajar, and walked to the sidewalk. Then he walked back, noisily, and came in by the main entrance. There was no sound from the dog. He went out again, but this time he came up the driveway stealthily, and seized a down-pipe from the eavestroughs as if he were about to climb it.

Instantly the night was split by the voice of Chippy, raised in furious protest. Sidney hurried inside and stood in the hall. Chippy could be heard loud and clear. Sidney hurried down to the basement and reassured him. He told him everything was all right and ordered him back to his bed. Chippy dropped his head pleadingly, but once more obeyed. Sidney left the coal cellar, shut the door and listened. The dog remained silent. Then Sidney reopened the door, switched on the light and said, "All right, boy, come on." Chippy sprang up and approached, wriggling with pleasure from stem to stern. He curvetted in front of Sidney as they approached the stairs. He turned to lick his fingers, wagged some more and then ran ahead, but he did not let a single yelp out of him.

The front hall was dark when Sidney reached it, but he could make out the form of June standing there and looking at the front door. He approached, and emitted a low, ghostly moan. June screamed and seized his arm. "You fool," she said. "You've made my hair turn snow white. Now I'll have to have it dyed at Vince and Tony's, unless you like white hair."

"How come?" he asked.

"I've been standing alone in this dark hall," she said. "THINGS have crept past. A little luminous man crept out of the grandfather clock, peered about and disappeared into the drawing room. Then an old bearded monk in a cowl came and looked in the clock. He seemed puzzled, and vanished with a low moan. Then something—I didn't see it, but I could tell from the sound that it was dull white and had eight pairs of legs—went swooshing upstairs. I daren't look for fear it would turn me to stone. And then you come screaming Boo at me."

"Sorry," he said. "But where's Mr. Reed?"

"Upstairs, in a cupboard," she said. "Unless that thing ate him."

"In a cupboard? What the hell do you mean?"

"He's in Mrs. Thurston's clothes closet, where she kept her furs," June said. "He can't get out."

"How did he come to get locked in?" Sidney demanded.

"Well you see," she said patiently, "I ducked into this big room, while he was trying to show me a bathroom, and I found this clothes closet. Well, of all things, it has this fool spring lock on the outside, and no knob for opening it on the inside. But the key was in the lock. I opened it, and a light came on, so then I got an idea. I nipped in and unscrewed the bulb in the closet, and Mr. Reed called out where was I, so I said in the big bedroom. Well, when he came in, I said wasn't there a light in this cupboard, and he said yes, maybe the bulb was kaput. So he went in and screwed it up and it came on. So I said did it go out automatically when you shut the door, and he said of course it did, so I shut the door and he said yes, the light had gone out. So he said to open the door, and I told him it seemed to be locked. He said well the key was in it, but I told him truthfully it wasn't, because you see I'd taken it out and I had it in my hand. Well, honestly, Sidney, the man was positively rude."

"I don't blame him a bit," Sidney said. "He never really approved of us. Go and let him out at once."

"No hurry," she said. "I told him I'd phone his office. I thought it would give us a chance to look around without him yakking at us about tapestry wallpaper."

"Well, I've seen all I want to," Sidney said. "I've got the atmosphere. Look. Imagine drunken old Gerald waffling in at the front door. Back here, in the dark, his mother's murderer is standing, silent—with the dog. The whole plan is in danger. You see, the dog has just been brought back after the burglary and murder. The murderer doesn't intend to have the dog around in the morning as a witness. So, on the way in, the murderer kicked in the cellar window, and was just about to take Chippy down and feed him poisoned meat. The idea being that the burglar had thrown poisoned meat in, after breaking the window, to do away with the dog. But there was Gerald. The dog wriggled loose and rushed to greet him. The murderer stood back here in the dark, while Gerald had his milk and then took the dog upstairs. The dog's life was saved, because poisoning it would be useless after it had gone to bed in Gerald's room. So the murderer, seeing that the dog was going to pose a problem, went down cellar and fetched the basket upstairs to the back porch. Just so the juxtaposition of the broken window and the dog's bed wouldn't be immediately apparent to the police."

June shuddered. She tended to be sensitive to atmosphere. "Speaking of the dog, where did he go?" she said.

"Eh? Chippy, here boy," Sidney said. There was a sound of claws on the parquet floor, and Sidney realized that Chippy had been sitting silently behind him all the time. Now Chippy curvetted ahead, and in the dim light they could see him standing below a row of coat pegs on a board, wagging in silent ecstasy. "I bet they kept his leash there," Sidney said. "He wants to go walkies. Watch." He held up the leash, which was still in his hand, and placed it against one of the pegs. The dog wagged and snuffled Sidney's hand. "All right, boy," Sidney said, snapping the leash on the collar. I'll take you walkies. June, go up and let Mr. Reed out."

"Don't *use* that word 'walkies,'" she said, "and if you think I'm going up there alone in—"

But she did not finish her sentence, because, as she said later, a giant hand, reaching out of the dark, seized her husband and dragged him off into the blackness. He was simply jerked away into the back of the hall, and she heard his feet scrambling on the parquet floor as he struggled with his assailant and tried to regain his balance. Bravely, without a thought of personal danger, she rushed to the rescue and followed as Sidney, still trying to get his balance, was dragged through the dark kitchen.

"Darling," she said. "Where is it? What is it?"

"Don't talk like a blithering goddam fool," he said. "And turn the damn light on." His voice reassured her, and she walked about the center of the kitchen feeling in the air for the string that turned on the light. Her instinct was right. The main kitchen light was switched on by a cord hanging from the ceiling, which she found after a minute of futile waving. The light came on to reveal her husband standing by the back door, and Chippy prancing beside him.

"I thought the dog wanted to go out the *front* way," he said. "But the little beggar nearly pulled my arm out by the root, dragging me out the back way." He unbolted the door and opened it. Promptly Chippy dashed through, dragging Sidney after him into a room where empty bottles and old newspapers were stacked. It was obviously the room behind the kitchen where the detective had found Chippy's bed after the murder. Chippy charged through and stood wagging at the door leading to the backyard. Sidney unfastened a bolt and two locks and swung the door open. The dog instantly dashed out and yanked Sidney after him. June followed and pulled the door to.

"He wants to chase a cat," she said.

But Chippy set out as fast as he could go toward the far end of the garden, with June and Sidney following. At the end he shoved his nose under a loose fence board and wagged furiously. Sidney lifted the board, which was more or less hinged by the nails on the rail at the top, and Chippy dived through. Sidney followed, and found himself in a lane bordered by high fences and hedges of lilac. June joined him a moment later, and immediately Chippy began tugging at the leash, hauling Sidney along the lane.

"This is most curious," Sidney said. "We are seeing a well-conditioned reflex. Somebody was in the habit of taking Chippy for a walk through the back fence, probably in the evening. Going to sleep in his own bed after a month's absence has brought it all back to him."

"What do you suppose it means?" June asked. She and Sidney were half-trotting in the wake of the excited dog.

"Just that this is Chippy's favorite romp," he said. "He's done this walk often—and he's been trained to be silent too. That isn't easy with a high-spirited terrier."

They emerged on a curving street, and Chippy continued to drag them. There was no doubt in his attitude. He knew where he was going. He turned a couple of corners and brought them out to the old bridge over the ravine at the bottom of Glen Road. The bridge, no longer open for cars, led to a flight of steps that went up to the large artery of Bloor Street. It also led to a small tunnel for pedestrians that passed below Bloor Street, and it was for the tunnel that Chippy was making. Mr. Reed in his clothes closet was forgotten.

"Maybe he's taking us to Attridge's flat," June said. "This is the right direction, isn't it? He's trying to tell you where he went on the night of the murder."

"Maybe he is," Sidney said. "Only this reflex of his wasn't conditioned by one evening walk on the night of the murder. You are watching a well-developed habit." Nevertheless, Chippy led them on into Howard Street, and turned, and turned again. They were getting close to the mews where George Attridge had lived.

"Well I'm damned," Sidney said.

But a moment later Chippy turned again, into a little street filled with old red-brick houses built in terraces. Straining and panting, he dragged them to the end house in a terrace and turned up the walk to the front door. "God almighty," Sidney said. "Here is the answer, and it was staring me in the face all the time. Okay, I was stupid. Thanks, Chippy, old man, for putting me straight."

Chippy was clawing and whining at the front door of the little house. Sidney tried to drag him away, but after a moment the door opened and a woman looked out. She was a woman who could have been in her early sixties, but Sidney, from his records, knew that she was older.

"Good evening, Miss Lang," he said. "Chippy wanted to come and visit you."

"Chippy?" she said. "Who are you?" She looked at June. "You're June Beattie," she said. "Is this your husband?"

"Yes," June said. "Good evening, Miss Lang."

Suddenly Miss Lang looked apprehensive. "Won't you come in?" she said.

Seventeen

THERE WAS A LITTLE living room, with a little television, which was turned on, but with the sound turned down. Sidney felt sure that the living room had been called a parlor during its early years. It had a little fireplace in which a little fire of cannel coal was burning. There was a card table in the middle of the room, on which color transparencies were laid out. It appeared that Viola Lang had been cutting and mounting transparencies when she was interrupted by the arrival of visitors. June and Sidney sat down on the little sofa, while Chippy danced about and made a fuss of Miss Lang.

Miss Lang sat down at the card table and looked at her visitors with ill-concealed apprehension.

"Well, what can I do for you?" she said.

"We were making some investigations," Sidney said. "We'd like you to tell us what you know about Mrs. Foster and George Attridge."

"I really don't know very much about them," she said. There was a note of plaint in her voice.

"Cozy spot you have here," Sidney said. "Been here long?"

"No," she said. "After Jane's death, the children—Martha and Gerald and Crawford—very kindly agreed to give me a little income so I could be independent, and I took this place."

"You took it? Do you mean you bought it?" Sidney said.

She looked at him closely. "Yes, actually I bought it," she said. "I had saved a little money…"

"Very handy location," Sidney said. "And with your car you can get away quickly on the Don Valley Parkway, to go out photographing the autumn leaves."

"Yes I can," she said. "It's very handy."

"You have a little English car, don't you?" Sidney said. "Did I see it parked at the side? An Austin Cambridge?"

"That's right," she said, "I used to use Martha's car occasionally, her Pontiac, but when I came here I felt I needed a car of my own. It was very reasonable, it didn't have many miles on it. Gerald thinks it must have been a demonstrator."

"Does he really?" Sidney said. "Do you mind telling me exactly when you bought it?"

"Oh, I'm not sure," she said. "Two or three weeks ago."

"Now Miss Lang," Sidney said. "It is time to lay the cards on the table. According to my records, which I guess I didn't study closely enough, you bought that Austin Cambridge, brand new, last May. Furthermore, I know when you *bought* this house. That was a couple of weeks ago. I assumed you had received some sort of legacy. But it is obvious that you have been using the place for much, much longer. Chippy knew his way here in the dark. He found you. He must have known this place before the death of Mrs. Thurston. Now if you were renting this house, or part of it, before Mrs. Thurston's death, that fact will be easy to prove, so you may as well tell me frankly right now."

"Well, it's none of your business, but I was," she said. "I wanted a place of my own. I wanted a car of my own so I could go out and get photographs. I'd saved my money, so it was none of their business. I rented all of this house but one room. It was owned by a Pole whose wife had left him. I used to know an old lady who lived in this row when I was a small girl. I've always wanted a little house here. So I rented it, and it gave me a place to keep my car. What's wrong with that?"

"Nothing at all," Sidney said. "Provided it's true. But just consider this. Your sudden prosperity appeared after Mrs. Thurston became bedridden. Now the way I get it, you did most of the nursing between the time Mrs. Thurston returned from hospital and the time Mrs. Foster was hired."

"Yes, that's right," she said. "Whatever there was to do, I could do it. On the maid's day off, I was the maid, when we had a maid. So I did the nursing after the special nurses came off and before they found this practical nurse, but I didn't get paid what they paid her, let alone the specials." Her voice was growing more plaintive.

"Now Miss Lang, my files showed your burst of prosperity, I mean buying the car—for cash, all cash—but I didn't give it a serious thought. It never occurred to me that you could conceal it from the Thurstons. Now, however, the question arises, where did you suddenly get the money? Maybe you can show a bank book recording your steady savings. But I put it to you now: Mrs. Thurston kept the key to her safety deposit box around her neck. You gave her her sleeping mixture. You could have got that key. Is that the way you got the money—for the house and car?"

"You have nothing to base that on," she said. "You can't prove a thing. Anyway, you can't get into a deposit box with the key. You have to identify yourself and sign a card before the bank man will use *his* key. What about that?"

She was arguing rather than angrily denying, which, to a trained cross-examiner, told a story.

"How about it?" Sidney said. "If you chose the right day, when the regular was off, you might easily pose as Mrs. Thurston and sign her name. Perhaps you practiced. Miss Lang, very soon someone is going to examine the card that the owner signs when she wants to open that box. *If* there is a signature bearing a date after Mrs. Thurston became an invalid and before Mrs. Foster was hired, you are going to be on the hot spot. *You* know right now what the answer is."

"You mean you think I stole money from Jane?" she said. There was a quaver in her voice.

"Your behavior has been strange," he said. "I'm merely guessing at a possible explanation, but your manner tells me I am close to the mark. We will know a lot more about it tomorrow."

Her lip quivered. "I had a right to something," she said. "If it hadn't been for my birthday, I wouldn't have done it. Damn her, anyway."

"Your birthday?" he said.

"Yes, my birthday. I was an underpaid servant, I didn't get as much as a servant, and I was at the beck and call of everybody in the house. She treated me like dirt. Oh, when she was a girl *she* boarded with *us*! Her father was a clergyman away off in the wilds, where there were no proper schools. Her mother and mine were first cousins, so they sent her to board with us so she could go to a good girls' school as a day girl. At *our* house she was treated as a pet, all the fuss about her. And what's more she met Jack Thurston at our house, his father was a cousin of *my* father's. If Jack had lived she'd never have treated me the way she did."

"How did you come to live with them?" Sidney asked.

"Oh, my father left me a small income, and I tried to increase it by investing in stocks and so on, and anyway there was something about margins and I found I'd lost all my capital, and then I had gallbladder trouble, and Jack Thurston said I should go to their place to convalesce. Well, it was a long haul, and the Depression was on, so he said I should be a sort of social secretary and have a little salary or allowance, and he said, several times he said, in her hearing, 'Vi, you'll always have a home here.' I was a pet of his when he used to come to our house as a student. *He* would never have let her humiliate me, but he died, and she never quite dared turn me out, but oh, how often she rubbed my nose in the dirt. I mean, she'd say I would make the thirteenth at dinner, so would I mind having dinner in my room, and I knew very well there were sixteen guests. But I wasn't good enough. She never actually asked me to eat in the kitchen, but often I ate in my room when there were important guests."

"And then this birthday business arose?" Sidney said.

"Yes! Oh, I was looking forward to my birthday! I was seventy in March, and you know what *that* means. I would be getting fifty-five dollars a month from the federal old age pension, and I was planning to buy zoom lenses and a Zeiss Ikon Supercontiflex and a good projector and screen—I had everything planned out for months. Then she said there would be a surprise for my birthday. I knew she was going to Nassau right after that, and I suddenly thought she was going to take me to Nassau. I dreamed about it. But when the time came, the surprise was that she had a birthday *tea* party on Sunday afternoon, with some of my friends asked in. Nassau, indeed! That's not for the likes of me. But the real surprise came later. She was saving that."

"Yes?" Sidney said.

"Oh, but yes!" Viola Lang said. "She called me in to her room next day. I thought this would be the invitation to Nassau. But no. She spoke in this high, refined, arrogant way she had. She said she had been allowing me a hundred dollars a month—you can't get a maid for that—and she said I seemed to have been getting on very nicely with it. But now that I would have the old age pension, she felt sure I would understand if she cut my *allowance*—not my *salary*—to fifty dollars a month, because really costs of everything had gone up so much. And then she smiled and said I would be five dollars a month better off, and that would be *something*. And I knew very well what she would say if I protested. She would just be well-bred and say I was free to go anytime I chose. Oh, damn her! I went and cried all day, but she calmly ignored me—you could be dying and she wouldn't notice. Other people's troubles never even ruffled her. And she went off to Nassau and I just seethed and seethed, and then when she had her accident and was bedridden, I said it was time I got my own back, I felt I was entitled to have something of my own for once. And that's why I did it, why I took the bonds from her safety deposit box."

"Well well well," Sidney said. "Did you find it easy?"

"It wasn't too hard," she said. "I rented a box myself and got a key very much like hers. Then I doped her very heavily, until I could move her hand, and I switched the keys. I also took the key of her desk and opened it, and I got her list out. She kept a book in her desk listing all the securities in her safety deposit box. I copied out the whole book that night and then put it back. So I went to a broker and asked him which things were easiest to sell, the negotiable things they call them, and he was a big help. So then when the regular bank man was away, I went and posed as her, and it was no trouble. I had practiced her signature over and over again, for night after night, until I could do it perfectly. I'd watched the way she held her pen and all. I got twelve thousand dollars' worth of bonds out. There was a list in the box, a duplicate of the book she kept in her desk. I took it out and burned it when I took the bonds."

"Well, you've been very frank," Sidney said. "And what do you think will happen now?"

"Not one thing," she said smugly. "All right. You found out. But what can you do about it? Nothing at all."

"How about the family?" Sidney said. "The executors and heirs?"

"They wouldn't dare to touch me!" she said. "They wouldn't dare! I know too much. Why do you think they gave me such a good annuity? Do you think they cared a damn about me? No, they didn't care two hoots. But they wanted—well, never mind. I played along with them. But I knew about Gerald and the nurse. You should have seen the things he wrote to her! I steamed one of his letters open and read it before *she* died. And Martha with that colonel. And if they raised any fuss, you just watch me. Crawford thinks he's going to be prime minister some day—*he* wouldn't want a big fuss any more than the others. So just try and touch me, Mr. Grant, and see how far you get."

"Well, you've done a great job," Sidney said. "But unless I'm wrong, your chief weapon over the Thurstons is the matter of the dog."

"What do you mean?" she demanded. Her growing confidence was checked. She was on her guard.

"You took the dog to the vet's on the Saturday morning, *after* the murder," Sidney said. "Now Gerald and Martha decided they wanted to let the police think the dog had been away all night. *You*, better than anyone, knew it wasn't true. You could have exploded the whole thing. But you agreed to keep your mouth shut, and that, above all, is why you got such a generous settlement. You played that card well." He spoke with complete confidence. She looked at him and wavered.

"I've never told a single lie about it," she said. "I never said a word."

"No, you didn't have to," he said.

"Gerald took the dog for a walk. He felt silly about it," she said.

"Did he really? Miss Lang, the game is up. *You* knew that when Crawford came home he would go through his mother's affairs. Your theft would be discovered. You had acted rashly. You hadn't thought about that when you stole the bonds. Suddenly your whole position was threatened. You knew you'd be caught and ruined. Your only hope was to kill Jane Thurston. You'd heard a lot of argument about those furs—what a temptation they were for burglars. You'd probably talked about burglaries with George—wasn't he always fussing about and asking questions? So you kept putting the handyman off—we can check that point—so that the grass would be long. You left a hall light on all day. You let handbills lie on the porch. You wanted to attract burglars. But Chippy was a problem. You trained him and drilled him so that you could take him out quietly at night. You had this house, where you were hoarding the bits of furniture you liked, where you were making your darkroom for photography. After dark you brought him here, night after night, and fed him lots of hamburger to make him like it. He knew his way here perfectly.

"Finally the burglars came. That stupid boy never went near the bedroom. You put the furs on the stairs or somewhere so he wouldn't need to. You put the jewels in one of the pockets. When the burglars came, you killed Mrs. Thurston. And then, I'm prepared to bet, you opened her desk and destroyed the other list of securities. That's a point that can be checked. Then you came here and got Chippy. You took him home—via the lane and the back fence. But you went up the drive and kicked in the cellar window. You weren't going to be embarrassed by Chippy in the morning. You took him into the house, and you were just going to take him to the coal cellar and poison him when Gerald staggered in. For photography work you can easily obtain potassium cyanide. You had a ball of hamburger already filled with cyanide. You stood in the dark, struggling to get it out of your handbag and poison the dog there and then, but he was too excited. He wriggled loose and got to the door. You hid in the dark until Gerald took the dog upstairs, and then you were in a sweet pickle. The broken window in the cellar was a dead giveaway, or so it seemed. But Miss Lang, you were clever. You foresaw a morning of wild confusion. You quietly brought the dog's bed up to the back porch and said nothing. If the questions arose, you could perhaps claim that a boy had broken the window with a baseball. If you'd been one shade smarter, you'd have gone whole hog and cleaned up the broken glass and got rid of it that night. However, you carried on. You took the dog to the vet's in the morning. You kept mum. And then Gerald and Martha played right into your hands. *They*, for their own purposes, covered up the whereabouts of the dog, and you were able to sit back smugly and play along. You even got paid off handsomely for keeping your mouth shut.

"Now this is the truth, Miss Lang. You can't disprove it, and every scrap of investigation from here on in is going to tend to prove it. So the very best thing you can do is to come clean right now and get it over with."

At every word of his long dissertation she had looked more and more hopeless, and when he had finished she started to cry, almost like a little girl.

"Am I right?" Sidney said.

She looked up, with a certain resignation. "Yes, you're right," she said. "Please, I want a cup of tea. Would you like a cup of tea?"

"Yes," June said. "You sit still, Miss Lang. Let me get it."

"No, I'll get it," Miss Lang said. But Sidney ordered her to sit still. "Well, use the Crown Derby," she said. "It's in the glass china cabinet in the dining room, on the top shelf. I like the Crown Derby for visitors."

There was something pitiful about the little house, already, after a few months, filled with gewgaws. It was as if Miss Lang had taken to playing houses like a little girl, buying pretty things—some of them pretty frightful—at antique stores to fill her dream house. "Just plug in the electric kettle," Miss Lang called to June in the kitchen. "The tea is in a caddy by the stove, and you'll find a nice tray on the sideboard."

"But now, Miss Lang," Sidney said, "I'd be obliged if you'd clear up a mystery for me. How did you come to get George Attridge's help? How did you get him to organize the burglary for you?"

She sat up very straight and looked startled. She stared at him, and once again she looked to be on her guard.

"I didn't," she said. "George Attridge had nothing whatever to do with it. I did it all myself. Well, the only thing, Mr. Attridge once was looking around, and he said to me, 'Dear me, this dining room window is terribly dangerous. It would be extremely easy for a burglar to break in here—and with all those valuable furs in the house.' That made me think about the dining room. So I actually hung the fur coats there, from the light fixture. So the burglar would see them as soon as he came in."

"You did? How often did you do this?" Sidney asked.

"Oh, I don't know. Every night," she said. "I mean, after I had the idea. I mean, I had the idea, and then I read a piece in the paper warning people who were going away to keep their grass cut and all that, so that's when I started. As soon as Martha went away for her holidays. We knew then that Crawford was coming home, and I *had* to do something. Then Martha broke off her holiday and came home, and I thought all was lost, but she didn't seem to care about anything, and she was drinking, so it didn't matter."

"And you never discussed this plan with George?" he said.

"With George?" she said. "Of course not. Why would I discuss it with George?" She was genuinely puzzled, but even more on the defensive. Her eyes watched him anxiously, and Sidney felt little electric shocks running through him, as if he were on the edge of a great mystery. He recalled a vagrant thought that had flickered through his mind about George, and now it flickered through again, and he tried to seize it and make something of it. Something about shaving gear...

But June had arrived with the Crown Derby tea service on an Indian tray of beaten brass, and she set it on the card table in front of Miss Lang and said, "There, Miss Lang, you be mother."

Sidney kept one eye on Miss Lang as she began fussing with the tea things, while his brain chased after the vagrant thought about George's shaving gear. And then he had it. George hadn't packed his things and done a bunk, because, no matter how much of a hurry he was in, he would have taken his shaving things. He might have left something else, almost anything else. And if gangland had spirited him away to murder him, wasn't it likely that some thug would say, "Where's his electric razor? What did the guy shave with?" They might have overlooked the point, of course. But shaving is a prime consideration, and even a wife packing her husband's things isn't likely to forget the shaving gear… And then Sidney had hold of the silly thought that had flickered in his mind, which was that an old maid must have packed George's things. And he had fleetingly toyed with the idea that Martha, unused to the ways of men, had done away with her husband…

Now he took another look at Miss Lang, and his mind leaped madly over a great gulf. Miss Lang was handing June her tea and saying, "Just don't stir it, and you won't taste it." And now she was handing a cup to Sidney and saying, "You take sugar, I hope," and although he normally didn't, he wasn't fussy about it, so to be polite he said yes, he did.

Then he watched Miss Lang, and saw her eyes regarding June as June prepared to sip her tea, and there was a certain strange tension in the way she watched that caused all sorts of alarm bells to go off in his brain, though he didn't know what the alarm bells were trying to tell him, and wild panic swept over him. And then Miss Lang, sensing his scrutiny, turned to him and said, "Come, come, Mr. Grant, drink up your tea before it gets cold." But she was watching him in a funny way, and he looked down at the teacup and noted that his hand was on the spoon, and that he was stirring his tea, and then the barrier burst and he looked at June, whose cup was at her lips. He tried to speak, to shout, but no sound came, and he did the only thing he could. He hurled his cup and saucer at her and knocked the Crown Derby cup right out of her hand. Two fine cups and a saucer smashed on the floor, but Miss Lang made no protest. She simply seized the sugar spoon, plunged it into the Crown Derby sugar bowl—which was filled with granulated, not lump, sugar—and started to shovel a large spoonful toward her mouth.

Sidney was now in action, though he still couldn't speak. He reached forward and fetched the spoon a swipe, sending it flying, and then Chippy leapt at him and seized his arm. He wasn't going to allow anyone to strike Miss Lang.

The little room was in wild confusion. Sidney was determined to keep Miss Lang away from the sugar bowl, Chippy was determined to eat Sidney and June was just getting the Borgian drift of the action. Sidney detached Chippy with some difficulty and handed him to June. "Lock him in the dining room or something," he said. "He mustn't get at the spilled tea or sugar. Sit still, Miss Lang. You might as well tell me—was there cyanide in the sugar? We're going to know anyway."

"Yes," she said. She was broken. And Sidney marvelled at the funny way his head had observed and stored the data, almost like an electronic computer waiting for the order to compute. He had seen Miss Lang put sugar in June's cup and his own without asking if they took sugar—but not in her own. And then she had apologized to June and told her not to stir her tea, instead of pouring her a fresh cup. And then her tense watchfulness. He looked at June, and a vast wave of relief flooded over him. But then another horrible thought struck him, and he said, "Oh God! Mr. Reed."

Sidney ordered June—using the imperative in a way that few husbands ever get to use it—to remove the sugar bowl and get brooms and cloths to clean up the spillings. Then he got her to sit and watch Miss Lang while he telephoned Miss Semple at her apartment, and he told Miss Semple to phone Massingham, the Crown Attorney, wherever he was and tell him that Sidney was at Miss Lang's house and that Miss Lang had confessed to the murder of Mrs. Thurston.

"Gracious heavens!" Miss Semple said. "Mr. Grant—was there something fishy about her buying that Austin Cambridge last spring?"

"There sure as hell was," he said. "Nobody but us knew about it, and we only knew through the vehicle registration. If we'd asked one question about it, the whole case would have started to fall apart. Weren't we the mugs?"

He told her to get Massingham if she could and ask him to come at once, and if she couldn't to call the police. And he invited her to come herself, with a notebook and pencil, if she wished, which of course she did. And after that was done, he relieved June on guard and said, "Now go, fast, to the Thurston house and release Mr. Reed without delay from that clothes closet. Also, apologize to him as prettily as you can. Now go!"

"Yes sir," she said, and saluted. "I have the key here."

She went. Chippy was scratching and whining upstairs in the bedroom where June had incarcerated him, and Sidney was left in comparative silence with the strange murderess. She had caved in, but she was sullen.

"Now," he said, "to get back to George Attridge. Did you not know that he sent the burglars who took the furs?"

"George Attridge?" she said. "How could he?"

Sidney was puzzled. The coincidence was too huge.

"Did you never tell him anything at all about your plan?" he said. "Didn't you tell him what you were doing?"

"No, not a thing," she said.

She sat in silence, and her eyes flickered about the room. "George nearly wrecked my plan," she said. There was a sort of stupid cunning in the way she said it.

"Oh? How was that?" Sidney said.

"I met him on the street. Every night, when I was bringing the dog here, I used to be frightened of meeting people I knew. But most people were away at their cottages, so it was safe enough. Then I met George in the street. Right at the tunnel under Bloor Street. He was coming right toward me. I couldn't avoid him."

"And when was that?" Sidney asked.

"The night before," she said. "The Thursday, I guess. I was getting desperate. My plan hadn't worked. Crawford would be home in two days, and no burglar had come. And then I met Mr. Attridge that night, and he said he was just on his way up to call on Martha."

"Oh really?" Sidney said.

"Yes. I was terrified. If he rang the bell, someone would come down. They might have looked in the dining room and seen the coats hanging there. So I told him Martha wasn't at home. I said no one was at home. I said that they were all up at the cottage. He asked me if I were staying in the house all alone, and I said heavens no, I wouldn't dream of it, not with all those valuable furs and things there. I said Chippy and I were staying with a friend downtown. I said nobody would be home until after the weekend."

Light was, at last, breaking through.

Viola Lang said that Attridge, on hearing the news, turned back and walked with her through the tunnel, saying, "Alas, I must turn my footsteps to the south once more," and they walked together for some distance, until he turned into the old stable where he had his flat and wished her a good night.

"But I don't think he believed me," she said. "Because next morning he came snooping around the house. I looked out the window and saw him standing on the sidewalk with his cane, looking up at the windows, and then he walked up the drive to the door, and I thought he was going to ring. I was terrified. But he never rang. He walked right through to the backyard, and then he went away."

Sidney could scarcely keep from laughing, but he managed somehow.

"And it was a lucky thing," she said. "Because when he was going away, the nurse saw him from Jane's bedroom window, and she came rushing downstairs and said to me, "Was that Mr. Attridge? Did *he* come here?" I said I thought I saw him going along the street, but he hadn't rung the bell. She looked very anxious. If you ask me, she was having an affair with him. She was having an affair with Gerald. She was a terrible woman. And that night, after dark, before I'd set the coats out, she sneaked out of the house. She sometimes did. She used to frighten the life out of me, for fear she'd catch me on the stairs with the furs. Well, that night I began to be frightened that maybe she'd gone to see Mr. Attridge, and she'd tell him we were all at home. So when I brought Chippy here, I walked back past his flat. It was a very hot night, and the window was open and the curtains too, and I could see him standing there and

I could hear his voice, and I waited, and then he moved away from the window—and I saw her. At that moment I thought everything was lost."

Yet miraculously, in the morning, Gerald, Martha and the nurse had said nothing at all about the dog. The nurse had appeared to have no suspicion. Everything broke right, and by midafternoon, when the police interrogation was finished, Miss Lang appeared to be in the clear.

"Except," Sidney said, "that you had lied to George Attridge. You had told him the family were all away. Weren't you afraid he might come and tell Martha about it and start her thinking? Or that he might tell the nurse about it and start her thinking? When the news of the murder broke, he was bound to think it strange that you had said the family were away. Didn't that worry you at all?"

"Yes, it did," she said and looked down at her lap.

Sidney had come to the edge of the great gulf. He had already employed more guesswork and trial and error than his algebra teacher would have approved, yet nevertheless the little thought about the shaving gear drove him on. He lowered his voice and spoke very gently. "And is that why you went and killed George?" he said.

She looked at him and looked away. "Yes," she said, and started to cry.

Eighteen

PEOPLE BEGAN TO arrive. First Miss Semple, in her Valiant, who said that Massingham had said a bad word but would be arriving shortly. Then a police car, with the siren going, and then June, in a taxi. Sidney got June aside.

"Did you release Mr. Reed?" he demanded.

"Well yes," she said vaguely, "I fixed it."

"Don't equivocate, woman," he said. "Did you or did you not let him out?"

"Well, to tell you the truth," she said, "I simply couldn't face him, after the way I'd behaved. I chickened out, darling. So

I stopped a police cruiser and gave them the key and told them the address, and told them the back door would be open, and I gave them exact instructions where to find the closet."

"Didn't they want to know how he got in there?"

"Yes," she said. "I told them I locked him in."

Sidney shook his head. "Did you say why you locked him in?" he asked.

"No, I refused," she said. "I told them I didn't wish to discuss it. I said I wanted to forget the whole unsavory business."

"Great God!" Sidney said. "Do you know what you've done, woman?"

But Massingham's Buick was arriving, and there were other things to think of. Sidney took Massingham to the kitchen and gave him a fill-in. He suggested that the police should take the Crown Derby sugar bowl and have its contents analyzed. He told the Crown Attorney that the bowl of poisoned sugar, waiting in the china cabinet, was enough to prove the insane cunning of Miss Lang. He told him about the earlier confession, but suggested that, rather than ask Miss Lang to repeat it, they should question her gently about the killing of Mr., or Col., Attridge.

Massingham had never heard of Attridge in connection with the Thurstons, but he had drunk a whiskey with the man at the Armed Forces Club. "And I wondered about him," he said. "But you don't like to come out and challenge fellows with guest privileges from affiliated clubs."

And so, after Massingham had told Sidney what he thought of him in somewhat unflattering terms, they went into the little parlor quite amicably, and Sidney, speaking very gently, asked Viola if she wouldn't tell Mr. Massingham how she had dealt with George Attridge. She hung her head and looked about hopelessly.

"Oh, very well," she said, and after a short silence commenced her recital.

"I was frightened," she said. "I was beginning to realize what I'd done. I was afraid of getting caught. That's all I could think of. I thought Mr. Attridge would see through everything. I thought I had to get rid of him, so all day I was racking my brains for a plan. And then we were all released, and Martha was to go and get the dog at a certain time and Gerald was to pick up Crawford at Malton Airport, and the nurse went off to her sister's place, and I simply slipped away and agreed to meet Martha and Gerald and Crawford in the evening. They never asked where I was going. They weren't even interested in me. So I came here, you see, I had been renting this place, and I had all my photographic things here. So I came straight here and made some deviled ham sandwiches. I remembered how much Mr. Attridge like the deviled ham sandwiches when he came to tea at the house. I wrapped them in wax paper. I put cyanide in one, quite a lot of cyanide, but he would never taste it because the sandwiches were very spicy. Anyway, I specially marked the poisoned sandwich so I would know it, and I put some coffee in a thermos flask, and I threw a big coal shovel in the trunk of the car, and then I drove my little Austin Cambridge down to Mr. Attridge's flat."

She found George Attridge at home, in a considerable state of agitation. He asked her if everything was all right at home. She said she didn't know, because she hadn't been there. But she said Martha had called her and she desperately wanted to see George. George told her they had had a quarrel, and he asked if she thought Martha was ready to forgive him. She assured him that Martha wanted to see him and that she felt Martha had forgotten all about any quarrel. This appeared to please George, and then Miss Lang offered to drive him at once to see Martha who, she said, was staying with friends in the country. He thought about it for a moment and then gladly agreed to go with her. Miss Lang noted that his suitcases were in the middle of the room and he appeared to be packing.

But he went out with her and got into the Austin Cambridge, and she drove him, as slowly as she could, and by the worst possible routes, to the northeast approaches to the city. She was stalling for time. She wanted darkness, or at least dusk. He began to get impatient, and she was forced to head for her destination, which was the sand dunes. She obligingly produced color transparencies of the dunes and a small hand-viewer to look at them with.

Many years before, the trees had been cleared from a sandy section northeast of the city, and the topsoil had blown away. Sand dunes had emerged, and had been moved by the wind, engulfing farms and barns and houses. For a long time the dunes had moved unchecked, so that the soil erosion took in a large area and was giving conservationists a very hard time of it.

And it was to the edge of these dunes that Miss Lang conveyed George Attridge. It wasn't really dark enough for her purpose, but she was forced to act nevertheless, and George helped immensely by volunteering the information that he was absolutely famished with hunger.

So she produced her sandwiches, commencing to munch on a safe one herself and offering the loaded one to the unsuspecting George. He took it. He inserted a whole quarter in his mouth. He started to chew. He paused, stiffened, gave a sharp cry—and died.

Her plight was now desperate. She drove along to a suitable spot at the edge of the dunes, stopped, and hauled the body out into a shallow depression. She put the remains of the poisoned sandwich beside it. She got Attridge's keys from his pocket and put them in the glove compartment of the car.

Then she mounted to the top ridge of the dune with her big coal shovel and started a sandslide. She worked from the top, causing tons of sand to slide down nice and evenly, so that sand engulfed the body in a natural way. Then she got into her car, drove back to George's place, let herself in and finished his packing. She loaded the suitcases in the car, then shoved his apartment key in the landlady's mailbox. She knew which one it was because on the board it said: "Enquiries—Apartment One."

She drove the car back to her own little house and left it locked in the yard there, with the cases still in it, because already she was late for her rendezvous with the Thurstons. They did not even bother to ask her where she had been, and she was able to dispose of George's effects at her leisure. "I gave most of his things to the Salvation Army," she said, "and a few to Crippled Civilians."

It was an eminently sensible method of disposing of incriminating evidence, and Sidney, in spite of his mounting horror, was forced to admire it.

❁❁❁

It was decided, after consultation, to book Miss Lang on charge of theft and move her at once to the Psychiatric Hospital for observation. There was a general posting about and considerable excitement. A small but growing knot of people had formed outside on the street, attracted by the presence of the police car. When things began to settle, Massingham accepted an invitation to return to the Grants' apartment for a nightcap and further information. There was much that he wanted to know. Gerald Thurston was sent for, and he arrived white-faced and incredulous.

"God, that Viola," he said when he had been given an outline of the facts. "That woman is poison! She was a leech, a parasite. My old man was too damn weak-kneed to pitch her out. He let her get set in, and then she stayed. She never did anything bad enough for Mother to chuck her out, but she acted as if she had some sort of entitlement to live with us. She was sort of resentful whenever she was asked to do anything, and she expected to be in on all the parties, although she was the damnedest bore you ever saw. You know, I think she poisoned the whole atmosphere of the house. God, how we tripped over ourselves playing into her hands!"

But the matter that was agitating Massingham more than anything was Easting's confession.

"Why would the stupid idiot give such a full confession if he didn't do it?" he kept saying.

"Because he thought that it was the only way he could escape the gallows," Sidney explained patiently. "He had signed some sort of crude confession the night he was arrested, before he had even sobered up. I'm sure the police didn't like his statement. I'm sure your office didn't like it. They were charmed to get a fuller, more coherent statement, dictated by Lionel Raines, Q.C. And his face is going to be rosy red after this. John, do me one big favor. Get Easting to your office first thing in the morning and ask him about this. Get Raines there, to keep him from squawking. But let me be there too. You owe this much to Mr. Lamberti and me."

Massingham, under the pressure of good whiskey, followed by bacon, eggs and coffee, caved in and agreed.

As the guests were leaving, Gerald Thurston conveyed another piece of news. His sister Martha was making what the psychiatrists called a remarkable recovery, although he himself felt that she ought to be shut away permanently.

"She's supposed to be marrying some bloody clergyman she met in the loony bin," he said. "The woman is sex mad. Damn it, she's been engaged to some queer specimens before, but she never went to a loony bin to find them."

"That was probably her trouble," Sidney said. "Love is, after all, a sweet madness. I hope they will be very, very happy."

❀❀❀

The morning conference with Easting was short, but it gave Sidney Grant intense pleasure. Raines was there, and inclined to be sulky. He advised his client to answer no questions. He objected to the presence of Gargoyle Grant, who, he said, represented adverse interests. But Massingham was not in a mood for trifling.

"Mr. Raines," he said. "I want Easting to tell me the plain truth, quickly, and if he does, it may result in the withdrawal of the murder charge. Mind you, I'm promising nothing. I want him to tell me, straight, where he found the coats when he went into the Thurston house."

"Right in front of me when I got in the window," Easting said. "They was hangin' from this light fixture."

"And the jewels?" Massingham added.

"They was in the coat pocket," Easting said.

"So when you got outside," Massingham went on, "when you got into the Volkswagen with the stuff, you decided not to say anything to Lamberti about getting the jewels. You held out on him, and just kept them in your pocket?"

"I couldn't say nothin' to him, because he wasn't in the Volks when I come out," Easting said. "There wasn't nobody in the Volks."

"Then what *did* you do exactly?"

"Well, like I was told, I opened the trunk and put these furs in. I had them in one of these big plastic bags. I just stuffed them in and took my dough. My dough was sittin' there waitin' for me, in this envelope. I took my dough, fifty bucks, and walked back home, like the guy told me to."

"What guy? Do you mean Lamberti?" Massingham demanded.

"Yeah, I guess it must have been Lamberti," Easting said.

"What the hell do you mean, it must have been? Don't you know?"

"No. On account of I never seen him. But the police told me it was Lamberti. See, they ketched him, and they said he confessed."

Sidney managed, with difficulty, to control his features.

"But damn it, didn't he drive you up to the house in the Volks before the job?" Massingham said.

"Oh hell no. I hadda walk. He said I was to walk to the house—I knew the district good, because I useta deliver for a drugstore up there. He said to walk to the house and I'd see the Volks parked a couple doors down, see? Then I was to stop under a lamp and light a cigarette. If everything was okay the Volks would switch on its turning light for a right turn for five blips, see? As soon as I seen that I was to walk up the drive right into the backyard. He said there would be a stepladder leaning against the back of the garage, and I hadda bring it up by this window in the driveway. Well, it was there like he said. I got in easy, I never hadda go up and use this wrecking bar on the cupboard, like he said I'd hafta. I got the stuff, shoved it in the trunk and went home."

"Easting," Massingham said. "You keep saying 'he' told you this and that. Who was 'he'? Where did you talk to him?"

"On the phone," Easting said. "I never seen him. I was at the pool room, and a guy said, 'Hey Stoopid, you're wanted onna phone.' Some of these guys called me Stoopid, see? So I go to the phone, and there's this guy on the line. He says do I want to make fifty clams like duck soup. Sure I do. So he says okay, go straight out, walk to this house and look for this here signal from the Volks. He says look behind the phone book on the shelf in this phone booth and I'll find a paper bag, with a knife for cuttin' the screen and a thing to break the window catch and a small wrecking bar for the cupboard. He tells me all what I gotta do and makes me repeat it after him to make sure I got it. So I look on the shelf and sure enough this paper bag is hid behind the phone book. So you see, I never even seen the guy."

"And you have no idea who he was?"

"No," Easting said.

Later, when, on Massingham's insistence, Easting's original statement was found, it appeared that Easting had at first tried to give a true account, although he had claimed that he found the coats in a clothes closet in the front hall. This, he explained in a later interview with the Crown Attorney, was simply because he didn't think anyone would believe he found them in the dining room hanging from a light fixture. But at the moment Massingham could not concern himself with academic questions. He was facing an emergency. As a matter of courtesy, he called the provincial Attorney General to let him know what was going on. Raines and Sidney were asked to wait outside during the call, and Easting had been sent back to the cells.

The decision was inevitable. Just before noon the proceedings in the magistrate's court were interrupted, and Lamberti and Easting were marched into the dock. Sidney was in court, sitting with Lionel Raines.

"Mind if I offer a word of gratuitous advice?" Sidney said, knowing it was a mistake.

"Any advice from such a learned source will be welcomed hungrily and treated with the utmost consideration," Raines said.

"Then, when the murder count is withdrawn, you might consider having Easting plead guilty on the burglary count right away and have him whisked away to jail to avoid all the fuss."

"Your man, Lamberti, is pleading guilty, I take it?" Raines said.

"No, but he's in a somewhat different position."

"I'm sorry. I fail to see it," Raines said. "I shall certainly demand that Easting be released on bail."

At that moment a man from the Crown Attorney's office rose and said that the two men in the dock had been remanded in custody, charged with murder. The Crown now wished to withdraw the murder charge, but there were certain other charges against the men arising out of a burglary...

There was one reporter in court, representing a cooperative news bureau operated at City Hall by the city's three daily papers. His mouth fell open. Within a few moments both prisoners had been granted bail and were being led away to complete the necessary formalities. The lone reporter charged madly for a telephone.

Nineteen

AS A NEWS STORY, the Thurston murder had died away quietly with the hot weather. It had been done to death. Football, the approaching wind-up of the baseball season, space trials and international crises had squeezed it right out of the papers.

Now, suddenly, it came to life with a bang.

Even before the co-op reporter called the police desks, the papers had sensed that things were happening. The arrest of a Miss V. Lang, of an obscure address, charged with theft, had meant nothing. Yet the police desks, sensitive to events, were aware that things were happening at Police Headquarters, that general hell was being raised about something.

And then there was a mysterious digging expedition under police supervision out at the sand dunes, which reporters and photographers covered simply because the police refused to say what they were after.

And so, before Easting and Lamberti had been able to get clear of City Hall, the first platoons of press people were arriving in hot haste. The infallible Dulcie Dale and Stan paused to pick up Stoopid Easting's mother, so that they could photograph the tearful reunion on the City Hall steps. TV men with cameras, and radio newsmen with tape recorders, followed the first wave. Lionel Raines was photographed leaving the building, looking none too happy.

And then came Stoopid Easting, wearing a moronic grin. Shutters snapped, strobe lights flashed. In all the excitement Vince Lamberti got away almost unnoticed. It was Stoopid Easting's day.

Hour by hour new sensations flooded in to build the story. The body of George Attridge was found and identified. Miss Lang was formally charged with two murders. A Mr. Reed announced that he was filing suit against Mr. and Mrs. Sidney Grant because they had locked him in the Thurston house in line with some silly experiment. What was worse, Mrs. Grant had insinuated to police that he had made improper advances to her, if not an actual attempted assault. He had been released from a clothes closet by police, who took him to the station and questioned him rather roughly for an hour, demanding to know, again and again, what he had done to the lady. By four o'clock the front pages were all Thurston case. If John F. Kennedy and Nikita S. Khrushchev had been killed at that moment when their rival spacecraft collided in a race to see who would be the first chief of state to reach the moon, they could have made the front page but not the top banner line.

As for Stoopid Easting, he grew richer all day. Soon after his release, he was given one thousand dollars in cash to sign a contract for his exclusive first-person story of "How It Feels in Death Row," which was to appear in an evening paper. Not long afterward, the other evening paper paid him two thousand dollars for signing a similar exclusive contract. A magazine also bought his exclusive story, but for a much smaller price. However, he was also signed to appear as special guest on a TV panel show and to be interviewed on another TV show with a serious sociological purpose. The papers were full of pictures of him, kissing Mum, eating a hot dog, crossing a street and patting a dog.

Some of the kind ladies who had befriended him rallied round and managed to get him away to a good home, far from evil and temptation, to await his trial on the less serious counts remaining against him, and they drove him to the studios to meet his TV obligations and generally protected him from harm.

But poor Stoopid had huge wads of money burning holes in his pockets, and he had achieved a delicious celebrity. To see his own picture in the papers, to see himself on TV—these things were heady. And then there were his two exclusive stories, under his own byline, in the evening papers, one of which was certainly written by Dulcie Dale, though Marvin Easting almost believed he had written them himself.

So, after a couple of days in wholesome surroundings, Marvin Easting had had enough, and one night he went to bed at half past ten, then slid out of the window at eleven and returned to his old haunts. Already he had begun to fade as a public figure, but his image on the TV screen was still fresh in the minds of those who knew him. Furthermore, he was loaded with dough. He bought drinks and was surrounded with the friends who surround anyone who is buying drinks. His head swelled gently. He began to feel that he was a real celebrity. The money began to dwindle. He bought clothes the next day, the sharpest clothes that money could buy, and wherever he went he was accompanied by a little knot of hangers-on. But on his second night on the loose, he disappeared. No one ever discovered exactly what happened. He slipped away from a table in a barroom, ostensibly to go to the washroom, and he never came back. There were various theories of what happened. The most popular was that a girl had whispered to him that she wanted to take him to a swell joint and asked him to meet her in the lane where she had her car. According to the story, he went to the lane and indeed found a car, into which he climbed.

Anyhow, his body was found on the following morning in a lane far away, and to complete the squalor of his end, it had been partially concealed by someone tipping garbage cans over it. There was no money on him when he was found.

Sensation flared again. People asked if gangland vengeance had got to Easting. Had he been executed because he had talked? There were questions about Lamberti. Had he had a hand in it? But it became clear that the motive was simple robbery. A fool had been parted from his money—and his life—by young hoodlums who had grown up with him.

His funeral was immense. The church was crowded with morbid curiosity seekers, and his mum cried appropriately, though it was whispered that when they told her Marvin was dead, she said, "How much did he have left?" Dulcie Dale reached her greatest heights in her obituary of Marvin Easting. "They called him the kid that never had a chance," it began simply.

"And if the good Raines had listened to me, it would never have happened," Sidney said to June. "He'd have been safe in jail."

But the good Raines was no longer even tangentially interested in the Thurston case.

Sidney let things ride for a week or so, during which he spent pleasant evening hours walking in Craigleagh Gardens with Chippy, who was now a permanent resident of the Grants' flat—a present from Gerald Thurston. When he judged that the time was ripe, he elected trial for Vince Lamberti by a judge without a jury, and Massingham promptly threw his hand in.

"You are a damned clever scoundrel," he told Sidney. "Only a judge would see how weak the evidence is against Vince. We can't really prove that he ever had the furs in his possession."

It was all over, and even Mr. Reed, the real estate salesman, settled his claim for damages out of court, for an apology plus moderate legal costs and an informal promise that the Grants would call him when they went house-hunting in earnest.

It was all over. But Sidney leafed through the files on the Thurston case once more, and even read Miss Moon's treatise on the Lamberti-Ducatti tribe. And while he was reading he let out a terrible curse and called for Miss Semple.

"From start to finish of this idiotic case," he said, "my handling of affairs has been characterized by brute-like obtuseness and stupidity, mitigated by blind luck and fortunate guesswork. I have no cause for pride at all."

"All censure of a man's self is oblique praise," Miss Semple quoted. "What are you trying to tell me?"

"Look," he said. "The first, prime mystery was why old man Ducatti paid so handsomely for Vince's defense. Naturally, one connects this with Vince's determined silence. I racked my brains, and the best I could think of was that Vince was clamming up to save a brother or something—someone who meant more to old Ducatti, possibly, than Vince did. But I didn't pry into it. I didn't feel I needed to. However, I sluffed over this little bit. Miss Moon points out that old Ducatti was a bootlegger, and no particular angel, and that one of his sons was also at odds with the law. Then we descend to the next generation, which also produces one bad penny, but scads of fine, contributing citizens."

"Yes?" she said.

"This damn uncle—Ducatti's son, the one who went wrong. She doesn't give his age," Sidney said. "Damn it, he might be as young as Vince. Will you find his age, please, fast?"

Twenty

VINCE LAMBERTI, JUST as he had promised, turned up at Sidney's office at four o'clock in the afternoon. He was neatly dressed, and carried himself with superb poise and dignity.

"Nice to see you again, Mr. Grant. I never got to say thank you like I should of. But you done a real swell job for me, and if ever there's anything I can do for you, you only just have to ask."

"That's great," Sidney said. "Because there is something you can do for me. I'm curious. I've traced this damn mystery through layer after layer, but even now I don't know for sure what really happened."

"No?" Vince said. He was on guard.

"No," Sidney said. "Now you told me the strict truth. You said you spent the night with a married woman, and she came and told me all about it."

"That dumb cluck," Vince said. The expression sounded almost old world, it was so long since Sidney had heard it.

"Which brings up the question, how did you manage to get involved, why were you delivering the furs to the fence in the morning, and who were you protecting by shutting up? I have a theory about it. Your good Uncle Antonio—"

"I got no Uncle Antonio," Vince said.

"Tony?" Sidney said, and a light came on.

"Oh, Tony. Sure, I guess he's my uncle. He's my old lady's youngest brother, but he's about five years younger than me. What about Tony?" The long eyelashes flickered. Pay dirt, Sidney decided.

"Tony was in this thing with you, wasn't he?" he said. "But Tony got away to Montreal. Tony was the one that went to the house with Easting, wasn't he? You stayed in the background—you fixed yourself an alibi in case everything else failed. Tony is your grandfather's pet, isn't he? Isn't that why your grandfather paid for your defense, so you would keep quiet and thereby keep Tony's name out of it? I can't say I admire you. You were just as guilty lurking in the background as if you'd climbed in that window. If Easting—and Tony—had been guilty of murder, you'd have been just as guilty. In getting you off scot free, I was only doing my job. But I'm not happy that you evaded all responsibility for that burglary. And if ever you get into trouble again, please find yourself another lawyer."

"Now lookit, Mr. Grant," Vince said, and his eyes were smoldering. "I hope you're not going to get me too mad, on account of I can only take so much. But I want to tell you one thing. I didn't have anything to do with that fur job. I didn't send no punks into no houses, and I didn't fix no alibis for me or nobody else. I didn't have one goddam thing to do with it.

"Since I come out of Kingston Penitentiary, I been strictly legit. I got a legit job in this builder's supply yard, where they need a guy that can handle himself and sort out these truck drivers, see? It ain't much dough, ninety a week, but an unmarried guy can make out good on that if he's careful. I don't drink nothing but beer, I stay away from dames except maybe the odd one like the gal you met, you know, old friends, and I do strictly no betting at all, except at the track. And if any guy come to me and asked me to work on a job, like a bank or anything, I'd punch him right in the nose. So kindly lay off of me, please."

"All right," Sidney said. "But my curiosity is aroused. I'm going to head for Montreal and look up your Uncle Tony, and I'm going to ask *him*."

"If I was you, Mr. Grant, I'd lay off of Tony," Vince said. "You done your job and you done it real good. Why not forget it?"

"Because," Sidney said, "I want to know what happened. Now, you can tell me if you like. If you don't like, there is something I can do very quickly. I can send pictures of Tony to the professor who sold his Volkswagen to the burglars. If the professor recognizes Tony as the man who bought the car, he may feel it's his duty—"

"Okay, I get it, Mr. Grant," Vince said. "You win. But if I tell you the whole story, you won't feel you got no duty to turn this kid in?"

"Well," Sidney said, conscience struggling with curiosity, not too successfully. "I imagine this fellow must have suffered a lot while you were taking the rap...he may have had sufficient scare that he'll stay out of trouble?"

"You're goddam right he will," Vince said. "He got the pants scared off of him. And what's more I told him I'd bust his goddam neck if he ever got into anything again. Anyway, you guessed most of it. This Tony, when I was in sport I was his big hero. He played junior hockey too, but he wasn't close to the big time like I was once. But when I got in with this mob, when I got caught and sent down, it kind of bust the kid up. He got surly, he done bad in school, he pinched cars, well, okay, he done time himself in Bordeaux jail. And Granpop blamed me. Maybe he was right. He wouldn't speak to me when I come out. Now between you and I, Granpop don't win no medals from the Pope when he's a kid. He's a hell of a fine one to talk, but maybe I'm the same now. Anyway, he loves this kid Tony, his youngest. He has him working in one of his restaurants. Big deal, see? But he's too damn strick. He don't let the kid out, don't let him have no fun. So the kid has a fight with him, and Granpop tans the hide off of Tony, old as he is. I'm tellin' you, the old guy is real tough, he could pretty near take *me*"—there was no immodesty in it—"so Tony slopes off and tells him what to do with his restaurants and all. He gets to gambling, he wins some dough at Blue Bonnets on the trots, he turns up in Toronto dressed like a hot shot with six-seven hundred clams on him, oh real smart. He comes to see me.

"Well, I tell him what a goddam fool he is. I tell him to go back and tell Granpop he's sorry. I tell him he's got something good, that Granpop will take him on again. Well, he figured he'd ruined his chances, see? That's what it was. It made him pig-headeder than he normally is, which is plenty pig-headed. He goes to the track here, he even wins a little more dough, then he gets hangin' around the wrong dives, and the next thing he tells me he's bought this Volks and hasn't sent in the registration. I asked him what he meant by that. He sits filing his nails and smirking till I could have busted him one, and he says he's teamed up with a pretty sharp operator that knows of some real good jobs. Duck soup, he says. Having this Volks registered in the Prof's name will be a big help maybe.

"So I let him have it. I told him how stupid he was, I told him what Kingston is like. He laughs, heh heh. He says a guy who's smart enough to play it right don't get caught and don't go to no Kingston. He says he's in with this Prof, who's a pretty smart cooky. He met him in a bar. This Prof knows a lot of society people, he knows all about the inside of their houses. He knows the fences, he can set things up good. I find that this Prof—not the prof that sold Tony the Volks, you know, but a guy called 'Prof'—this Prof had built Tony up, telling him how smart he is, and it nearly made me cry. Any guy tells me how smart or strong I am, I want to bust him one. Hell, I know what it means. Well, I was kind of worried."

He paused and looked around, almost furtively.

"You know all about Webb and that mob, I guess?" he said.

"I know a little about them," Sidney admitted.

"Okay. I went back to my old haunts. I hadn't been near them parts for years. I got hold of Webb and I asked him about this Prof. I asked him straight."

"You and me both," Sidney said.

"No kidding! Anyway, I said what about him. The guys told me this Prof is a cheap four-flusher. They don't like him. He's been around trying to sell the idea of stealing some furs from some joint. They check out the furs, and sure as hell there's furs in this outfit, and real valuable. It's the Prof that the boys don't like. But he keeps on smellin' around, and they get the wire he's tied in with these fences. You know, the Martins, that had tried to double-cross Webb. So of course they're on the outs. Anyway, the guys know there's a deal—that the Prof is waiting for a chance to get the stuff, on account of he's already sold it. And, this was the thing he was trying to get Tony into.

"Okay, I got hold of Tony. I told him to lay off this Prof. I told him to blow town and go back to Montreal. He laughed in my face. He said he was going to do a job that night, and he'd fixed it so there was no chance at all he could ever get caught. He kind of hinted that he was smarter than certain other guys. There was nothing more I could do, and I had a date that night. You heard all about it. You hear about the fight I had?"

"The freezer salesman?" Sidney said.

"Yeah. Him. Well, I'm tellin' you, in the morning I feel like I got rubber knees. I felt like I'd done fifteen rounds with Liston. I stagger away to look for breakfast, I need plenty of breakfast, and when I'm eating, who walks in but smart-ass Tony, feeling real proud of himself. He says he done the job and delivered the goods and there was no way he could ever be caught. I say yeah?

I wasn't too interested. But he wants to brag. He says he got all the dope from the Prof. Then he picked out a punk kid he'd been watchin' in a pool room. He had the tools he needed for the job. He hid 'em in a paper bag behind the phone book in the booth in this pool room. Then he goes to the booth across the room and calls the number of the other booth. He asks for this punk Easting—and he can watch him all the time he's talking to him. He fixes it so Easting don't ever know who he is. You've got to admit it was smart. He sends Easting up to get the furs, and follows him a piece, then passes him and parks near the house. As soon as Easting goes in the driveway, Tony gets out of the Volks and walks away. He waits down the street until he sees Easting shove the stuff in the car and go away. Then Tony gets in and drives off. He bundles the furs in a big brown paper parcel and delivers them after daylight to the fences.

"The Prof had told him he had to leave the parcel in a big garbage box with a certain mark in this lane. Naturally Tony had no idea who the fences were. So he took the furs and left them, and he felt real proud.

"So then I said, 'Tony, where's your dough?' And he said the Prof was going to pay him that night, after he'd collected from the fences. And I started to laugh and laugh and laugh. I said the fences might double-cross the Prof, or the Prof might double-cross Tony, or maybe the Prof would collect from the fences but tell Tony the fences had double-crossed him. But I said I would bet plenty the minute the Prof got his hooks on any dough, he'd blow town and Tony would never see him again. I laughed until Tony got mad. And then, Mr. Grant, I must have gone completely nuts. Honest to God, I deserved everything I got for the stupid thing I done. Maybe I was kind of weak after a hard night. Brains and dames don't go together. Anyway, I done the stupidest thing I ever done in my life."

"What *did* you do?" Sidney demanded.

"I said, 'Look, Tony. I talked to legit crooks about this Prof. He's a phony. He'll double-cross you sure as hell. Now,' I says, 'why don't you quit while you're winning?' I said he'd lumped out fifty bucks to pay this punk kid. The Prof was promising Tony guess what? Five gees! I pointed out that fences don't pay that kind of dough, that even this Prof wouldn't get half that. I kind of shook him, and then I said if Tony would go and catch the bus to Montreal and go back to Granpop, I said I would take the Volks and get those furs back out of the garbage bin. I would take them and hide them with the Volks in a garage I know about, and just leave them there. Then I would let the legit operators make a deal for them, and if it all worked I would sell the Volks later and send Tony

the dough. I told him also he would get any dough that was paid for the furs. So I put myself in the spot where I was going to handle hot goods and not a goddam thing in it for me. Tony is kind of changeable. All of a sudden he's almost cryin' and shakin' my hand and tellin' me I'm a great guy. He gives me the Volks keys but keeps the papers. I drive to this lane, and who the hell do I see but Young. I'd walked right into a goddam trap. And you know the rest."

"Yes," Sidney said. "I know most of the rest of the story."

"If it hadn't of been for me stickin' my nose in, Tony would have been right in the clear," Vince said. "So I figured I hadda clam up and keep him clear. But he told Granpop all about it. He wanted to come and confess, but old Granpop don't go off quite so fast. He told Tony to shut up. He said if Tony confessed, it wouldn't necessarily get me off the hook. He said people come to a lot less harm shutting up than they do talking. He come to see me in jail and told me about Tony. I said, 'Granddaddy, you old scoundrel, they'll open that goddam trap under my feet before I open mine.' No kiddin', the old guy nearly cried. He said, 'Vince, you're a no-good bum. I'll get you the best lawyer in Canada."

Sidney smiled and looked down modestly.

"But I said instead of getting the best, why not get some hungry young guy on his way up? So he got you."

"It was so good of him," Sidney said.

So Vince shook his lawyer's hand and went away, a free man, and Sidney went home to tell June the end of the mystery.

He had talked to the last witness. June listened raptly, but there was something strange in her manner. He wanted to take her out to dinner and a show, but she insisted on staying home. She did not want a final celebration.

"Why?" Sidney demanded. He knew June's manner when she was up to something.

"Well, I've invited a guest for later in the evening," she confessed.

"A guest? Who?" Sidney demanded.

She hung her head. "Darling, I couldn't resist it," she said. "A Mr. Lintott is coming. He wants to sell me a deep freeze that pays for itself in six months. Darling, I simply *had* to see Mr. Lintott."